SOME LIKE IT NOT

"Sit, Ms. Duncan," said Man in Black #1.

I pulled out a chair and did as he requested. After all, what choice did I have? "What's going on here?" I asked. "Did I do something wrong?" Even as I asked the question, I knew that couldn't be the case. After all, my current life consisted of reporting on new-and-improved microdermabrasion by day and watching *Sex and the City* reruns by night. Not exactly the stuff that trouble was made of.

Man in Black #2 shook his head. "No," he said. "On the contrary, we need your help."

I shot a skeptical look from one man to the next to the next. What on earth could they need my help with? And FYI, I'd retired from the helping business. I was a lowly features reporter now. I had no remaining FBI Helper Girl skills on reserve.

Man in Black #3 picked up a shiny silver remote control from the table and pressed a button. A slide projection illuminated on the far wall of the room. My eyes widened and I gasped as I recognized the image on the screen.

It was him. Nick. Nick the Prick. My ex.

Other *Love Spell* books by Marianne Mancusi:

A CONNECTICUT FASHIONISTA IN KING ARTHUR'S COURT

Writing as Mari Mancusi:

SK8ER BOY

PRAISE FOR MARIANNE MANCUSI AND *A CONNECTICUT FASHIONISTA IN KING ARTHUR'S COURT*!

"A sparkling debut...a nice twist on the modern girl's search for Prince Charming."
— *Publishers Weekly*

"Sassy...a cute hoot... Talented author Mancusi clearly knows her Arthurian lore."
— *RT BOOKclub*

"This is a wonderful book! The heroes (and heroines) are vivid and likeable, the romance is sizzling, and the villains are oh-so-bad! ...This is the perfect vacation novel—so don't forget to leave room for this fetching little Fashionista when you're packing for the beach."
—Roundtable Reviews

"This is not your mother's Camelot! Spicy romance, hilarious thrills, and a heroine who kicks butt in her stilettos—this book is a definite keeper."
—Alesia Holliday, author of *American Idle*

"Marianne Mancusi's debut is super-snappy, pure fun, fast-paced, and even educational—in more ways than one!"
—Melissa Senate, author of *See Jane Date*

"Marianne Mancusi rocks the Round Table with an equal mix of girl power, diva fashion sense, and some wicked, laugh-out-loud humor. Kat Jones is a heroine I'd have drinks with any day!"
—Cathy Yardley, author of *LA Woman* and *Couch Word*

"Fun, fashion, foul play, and fearless knights. Marianne Mancusi's fresh take on the Arthurian legend is a winner!"
—Michelle Cunnah, award-winning author of *32AA*

WHAT, NO ROSES?

MARIANNE MANCUSI

LOVE SPELL NEW YORK CITY

*To Hank—who started out
a mentor and became a friend.*

LOVE SPELL®

July 2006

Published by

Dorchester Publishing Co., Inc.
200 Madison Avenue
New York, NY 10016

ISBN 0-505-52675-1

Visit us on the web at www.dorchesterpub.com.

AUTHOR'S NOTE

Writing funny isn't always easy, especially when your house burns to the ground while you're at a writer's conference and you come back to find everything you own in the world reduced to a pile of black ashes. Photos, childhood scribblings, my great grandmother's diamond ring—you name it, I lost it last August. I was pretty sure at the time I'd never be able to write again—especially not a lighthearted comedy like this book.

But then something happened. The writing community rose up to help. I couldn't possibly name everyone who came forward during those black days because the list would go on for pages. Every day I would go to my P.O. box and find gift cards, checks, books, and presents to make me smile. From dear friends. From perfect strangers. From authors, editors, and agents. The love and support from the Romance Writers of America community and the publishing world was simply overwhelming and I'll never be able to express how much it meant to me at the time. How much it still means now.

So thank you all. I couldn't have done this without you.

—*Marianne*

PROLOGUE

Baghdad, Iraq
Valentine's Day, One Year Ago

I am perfectly safe. I am absolutely, perfectly safe.

I wondered how many times I'd have to silently repeat that mantra before I could convince my frantic brain that I was telling it the truth.

"Okay boys, lock and load. We're off like a dress on prom night."

Gulp. Probably more times than my ex-boyfriend Stuart Goldstein had tried to remove said prom dress back in high school—and that was saying something. How had I gotten myself into this mess? Or, perhaps more pressing question, how would I get out alive?

I followed as the camouflaged American platoon wove through the back alleyways of Baghdad, hidden camera securely placed inside the sleeve of my poncho. Sure, as a foreign correspondent working overseas for a television news network, I'd been in a few hairy situations, but nothing like this. This kind of action was more Nick's scene.

Damn you, Nick! Where are you? I thought, not for the first time. He was going to kill me when he found out I'd gone without him. But I couldn't just turn down an opportunity to nab the story of a lifetime just because he was running behind. He was always reminding me how important it was to get the story. Not that I needed reminding.

Colonel Devens and his band had developed quite the reputation in Baghdad for their unconventional methodology. They were rebels, though no one was quite sure their cause. They had flouted the local government's laws and restrictions several times, but had also produced results. The network had been begging for their story, salivating over the opportunity to have a member of the media along for one of their legendary raids. Nick had taken me to several of the repeated negotiations, hoping a woman's touch could sway the hard-nosed officer. And he'd been right. Problem was, Colonel Devens had decided to allow the media along on the one day Nick hadn't shown up on time. Today. Valentine's Day. And according to the Colonel, it was now or never.

"You want to go on a raid?" Devens had sneered a half hour before, over our coffee in the hotel bar. He reminded me of the guy in *Apocalypse Now*. The one who loved the smell of napalm in the morning. "Grab your gear, sweetheart. Now's your chance."

I'd tried to argue that he should wait for Nick to show up. That the experienced reporter was the one he wanted along for the ride, not me. But Nick was fifteen minutes late already and the Colonel ran a tight ship.

"I wait for no one, darling," he'd drawled. "You in or not?"

I was in. After all, I couldn't let the network lose the story, no matter how dangerous the situation was for me personally. I took my job way too seriously, even if no one else took me that way.

In that sense, this was pretty cool. A once-in-a-lifetime opportunity. If I got the story by myself, everyone would finally realize that I wasn't just some "Barbie in Baghdad" as the papers had dubbed me. They'd see that I was a real journalist. A valuable contributor to my station's success. Maybe they'd give me more undercover missions. More action. Maybe I could be more like Nick.

Nick had been doing this kind of thing for years. He lived for the danger. The intrigue. The *could-get-killed-at-any-moment* lifestyle. Not to mention the Nick Fitzgerald Internet fan sites of the desperate housewives back home. The women in America loved the sexy, suave thirty-six year old reporter, and he was definitely enjoying his fifteen minutes of fame.

Not that I minded their crushes. He'd had a storied career as a player, but all that was over. These days, no matter what happened, he always came home to me. Because you see, Nick was not only my mentor, he was also my boyfriend. The love of my life, if you wanted to be technical.

"And we're going in. Ready? On two . . . three . . ."

My heart pounded in my chest as the soldiers kicked down the door and ran into an Iraqi apartment building, yelling at the tops of their lungs. They'd got some intelligence that some Al Qaeda guy had been hiding out there, though this entire area was off-limits to American personnel. I wondered if I should fall in behind them or wait outside while they secured the premises. I hadn't been given any instructions by the Colonel except, "Don't get in the way, baby," and thus was completely winging this whole assignment. If Nick were here he'd know what to do.

I took a deep breath, then pulled the camera out from under my sleeve and switched it on. Just a few shots outside, maybe, then I'd go in. My hands shook as I raised the camera to my eye and I hoped all my shots wouldn't be too jittery.

"You, what are you doing?"

I froze in my tracks, instantly breaking out into a cold sweat. I slid the camera back into my sleeve as heavy footsteps pounded the stone street behind me. They echoed in a rapid, repeating, staccato beat. Getting closer. Louder. But I willed myself to stay put. To fight instinct and not turn around. *Turn around and they may shoot*, Colonel Devens had said, and I sure as hell didn't want that.

Of course they may shoot anyway, he had added with a chuckle. *Just don't get seen.*

I'd laughed along with him at the time. It didn't seem so funny now.

My heart pounded in my chest as I stood tall, silent. Waiting for the voice's owner to approach. I wondered if I should shout for help. Or would that just make the guy shoot me on the spot? I didn't want to take the chance.

"Who are you?" the man demanded, coming up behind me and circling around. "And where are you going?"

My brain, even in its panic, played observant reporter, cataloguing him. He was a fashionable gent, looked to be Iraqi regular army, with a black mustache, stylish combat fatigues, and most importantly, the very latest in semi-automatic machine guns strapped to his shoulder.

Aimed at my heart.

"Hi, um . . . my name's, like, Dora? And I think I'm, like, lost?" I said, giving him my best Valley Girl imitation. I didn't Netflix the entire first season of *The OC* for nothing. "Is this, um, the Red Cross place?" I lowered my head and batted my eyelashes for good measure, channeling the dumb American tree hugger who'd come to help the Iraqis in their time of need. That sometimes worked.

"No. This is not the Red Cross, *American*," the soldier said in broken, accented English. He spit out the word "American" like he was expelling poison, but lowered his gun a few precious inches. I allowed myself a quaky breath. Maybe this was going to work after all. "You must leave here now."

"Okay, no prob. I'm totally Audi 5000. Zoom, zoom, zoom," I assured him, backing away slowly. *Forget the story. Just get out alive.* That's what Nick would be telling me. *No assignment is worth dying for.*

I should have never left without him. Stupid, Dora. Really, really stupid.

As I backed up, my foot somehow got caught on the hem of my long skirt and I found myself flying backward, slamming my butt against the hard stone floor. But the initial shock and pain were nothing compared to the horror I felt as the tiny camera I'd hidden flew out from my sleeve. It bounced, once, twice, before landing right at the soldier's feet.

Uh-oh.

The guard stared at the camera for a minute, then released a stream of angry Arabic. I didn't understand exactly what he was saying, but the outrage in his voice told me all I needed to know. I swallowed hard as he reached down to pick up the camera, adrenaline surging through my veins, fight or flight mechanisms warring for dominance. Where was my platoon? Didn't they notice I was gone?

"You are . . . reporter?" he asked. His eyes flashed fire. Not such a big fan of the profession, it seemed. Not that I blamed the guy. At this very moment I would have preferred to be an accountant myself. Safe in some nondescript office. Crunching numbers before I went to munch on some overpriced sushi on the Upper West Side with my bland but safe Wall Street boyfriend.

A little dull, yeah, but it beat running for my life, which was, I assessed, what I was about to have to do.

He'd probably shoot me in the back, but I was willing to take the chance. It was better to die quickly than to be slowly tortured in some Iraqi prison. At least, that was the theory. In actuality, both options seemed pretty sucky. What was the penalty for being in a prohibited area?

Don't get seen, Colonel Devens had said.

I scrambled to my feet and began a dash down the alley, weaving from side to side, trying to make for a bad target. Too bad I lacked Keanu Reeves's bullet-dodging *Matrix* powers. They would have so come in handy right about now.

Behind, the man yelled for me to stop in a mixture of Arabic and English. To freeze. To surrender. To give up and come with him.

No dice. Well, not until I felt the exploding hot pain in the back of my thigh anyway; that was pretty much all the persuasion I needed to obey his "stop" command. In fact, the next thing I knew I was flying forward, my palms slamming and skidding against the pavement, followed by my body and my face. I landed with a sickening thump.

Damn it! I'd been shot. I'd been SHOT!

I reached down to grab my leg, almost crying. My face was bleeding. The pain flashed white-hot and my vision was fast turning spotty. Fear and agony fought for control of my brain as I watched the crimson stain on my skirt spread wider and wider.

I thought about trying to crawl away—a last desperate escape attempt. But the guard was already tramping over to check his marksmanship and I knew any more resistance, in this case, was most definitely futile. Looked like I'd be spending this Valentine's Day in an Iraqi prison, a venue I was pretty sure boycotted all forms of candy hearts and roses.

Thanks for standing me up, Nick, I thought wryly as I held up my hands in surrender. *I hope there was a damn good reason.*

CHAPTER ONE

San Diego
One Year Later

"I can't be the only one in the goddamned city who's too stressed for sex!"

I sucked down the remainder of my chocolate brownie frappuccino, struggling with a stubborn chunk caught in the straw. Finally I gave up on the last smidgen of chocolate (a total crime against humanity, I know!) and set the cup down, letting out my most frustrated sigh.

"I'm sure you're not," my photographer, Jenny, replied with a laugh. The pretty twenty-two-year-old brunette reached over and patted my hand. "But who wants to admit it on local TV news?"

"Right." I stared out into the crowd of people milling about the Fashion Valley mall. We'd scoured the area for hours that morning, asking the inane "Man on the

Street" question for my six P.M. news story—a fascinating feature on a new scientific study that found eighty percent of Americans feel uninterested in getting it on with their partners because of work pressures. Eighty percent claimed they were literally "too stressed for sex."

The problem was, zero percent wanted to go on camera and tell me about it.

"Besides, it's not that *you're* too stressed for sex," Jenny added with a twinkle in her sparkling blue eyes. "It's just that you only want to have it with a guy you refuse to talk to."

I groaned. Not this again. It constantly amazed me how even after nearly a year, Jenny still rooted for Nick the Prick and I to get back together. I should have never told her my "We'll always have Baghdad" romance story on that oh-so-boring eight hour stakeout we'd been on when I first came back to California. (No, not that kind of stakeout. No lurking criminals or bad guys. Angelina Jolie had been rumored to be staying at the Four Seasons, if you must know.) Ever since that day, Jenny had been like a pit bull with a bone, and no matter how much I protested that I would never, ever speak to that asshole again as long as we both shall live, my words fell on naively deaf ears. In her yet-to-be-scarred mind, our relationship was beautiful, broken, and just dying to be mended. With her help, evidently.

Sigh. She was as bad as Nick's geeky brother Tom. The dot-com billionaire whom *Forbes* claimed was busy revolutionizing interactive electronics seemed to have a lot of free time on his hands, trying everything under the sun to get Nick and me back together. He claimed his brother deserved a second chance, and nothing I said or did could dissuade him.

But hey, the two of them could hold out hope 'til Judgment Day for all I cared. After what Nick had done to me last Valentine's Day halfway around the world, I'd sooner run away and join the circus than speak to him again. And that was coming from someone with a major clown phobia.

Jenny grabbed her video camera as she stood up, and handed me the microphone. Time to get back to work. "You know, maybe you should call him sometime," she said, *oh-so-casually*. "See how he's doing up there in the City of Angels, all by his lonesome." She grinned. "Or maybe I should. I mean, he *is* really hot and all."

I rolled my eyes and play-swatted her with the mic. "Your pathetic attempts to stir me into a jealous rage are completely in vain," I informed her. "If I've told you once, I've told you a thousand times: Nick and I are through. Forever. *Finito*. End of story."

"Bah," Jenny scoffed, shaking her head. "Have it your way. It's none of my business anyway, right? I'll just shut up and take the pictures."

Grr. Great. Now she was going to go all sensitive on me. I drew in a breath and reached over to pat her on the shoulder.

"Look, Jen. I know you're trying to help. But you don't know the whole story. What Nick did to me on Valentine's Day last year—it was unforgivable. And not a day goes by when it doesn't hurt." I glanced down at the ugly scar on my forearm and thought about the one I couldn't see running down the side of my face. It was amazing the station had hired me to be on air—me channeling the Phantom of the Opera and all. Well, maybe Phantom of the Opera was overstating it a bit, but I knew as well as anyone how the tiniest mark could mean a pink slip in the pristine, porcelain-doll world of TV news.

Yup, I still hurt all right. Maybe not physically. But the mental pain. The fear. Stuff I knew would never completely go away.

Not that I wasn't trying to move on. After all, I'd left Iraq, quitting my high profile career as a foreign correspondent to take on the most innocuous, non-dangerous reporting job on the planet—albeit the cheesiest. I'd spent the last year healing. Living one day at a time. Erasing the past scandal and creating a life for myself, one without fear and danger and heartbreak at every turn. And I had to admit, I was pretty proud I'd gotten as far as I had. Not that I didn't have a long way to go.

Seeing Nick again would just hurl me backward. And I couldn't afford that. I just wasn't strong enough yet. I might never be.

"Okay, okay, I get ya," Jenny agreed, punching me lightly on the arm. Luckily she knew when to quit. "Let's go find some undersexed San Diegans."

I smiled, and together we walked down the open-air corridor of the Southern California mall where a good number of people were wandering about, carrying big bags of stuff they'd accumulated in their afternoon of shopping hedonism. Unfortunately, no one looked particularly interested in wasting five minutes of their life to get fifteen seconds of local news fame by exploiting the secrets of their sex lives. (Or in this case, lack of sex lives—which was technically worse.)

No one, that was, until an elderly woman with the stereotypical helmet of wispy blue hair hobbled over. "Can you interview me?" she asked, leaning on her knobby cane. "I want to be on television."

Hmm. I gave her the once-over. It was funny how some people were dying to be on air, while others avoided it like a Ben Affleck/J-Lo movie. (If I wasn't a reporter, I'd so be in the second category!) Of course, granny here wasn't our target demographic—at *News* 9 we only cared about the sex lives of twenty-five to forty-nine-year-old women with a lot of disposable income. But it was nearly three P.M., and I was getting desperate.

"Okay," I said, giving her my Big Reporter smile. I pointed the microphone at her. "Do you ever feel you're too stressed for sex?"

She stared at me a moment, her blue eyes wide, as if shocked at my brazen question. I felt my face heat. Of course. What was I thinking? Granny probably hadn't gotten it on in the last twenty years or so. Ever since her precious Wilbur died back when Reagan was president.

Sigh. Too bad my story wasn't "Too Senile for Sex."

"Too stressed for sex?" the old woman repeated, following the phrase with a tinkly laugh that sounded a little like Christmas bells. "My goodness, no. In fact, ever since I started using this female Viagra I got off the Internet, I've been having multiple orgasms at the drop of a hat. Henry loves it!" She beamed at me and then turned to look directly into the camera. "My sex life is great!" she informed the lens.

Hmph. Evidently these days even Granny was getting more action than me. I didn't know whether to laugh or cry.

"Okay," I said, lowering the microphone. She obviously wasn't going to help with my story. "I appreciate you taking the time to answer." *Not that you gave us anything we could use, my little senior sex kitten.*

The woman gave me a disapproving look over her bifocals. "You young people," she scolded. "You need to stop working so hard. Start enjoying life. When you're on your deathbed, you won't look back on your life and think, 'Why didn't I work more?' Trust me. But you might wonder why you didn't have more orgasms."

Ah. Even better. Not only was Granny boinking like a bunny, she was now offering up life lessons. Next thing you knew, Jenny was going to tell her the Nick story, and the two of them would be tag-teaming for a sex-filled reconciliation.

Can we say, no thank you?

"Thanks," I muttered, stepping backward to put as much distance as possible between me and the hot flash ho. "Now, if you'll excuse us . . ."

"Good luck, Sweetie," the woman said, then smiled patronizingly. "You'll find your Prince Charming eventually."

I swallowed hard and resisted the nearly overwhelming urge to tell her I'd already found him. And that when I'd kissed him, he'd turned into a total frog. I wanted to insist that relationships—while perhaps good for short-term, crazy, hot sex—always ended in pain. Leaving you vulnerable and wounded and crying in your tomato alphabet soup. Alone.

Instead, I channeled Self Protective Mode and turned to throw Jenny a smirk as Granny hobbled away. "Some people!"

My photographer shrugged. "She does have a point, Dora."

"Oh, don't start." I groaned. The last thing I needed was a lecture on relationships from an inexperienced twenty-two-year-old. The girl had been dating her boyfriend since the high school prom. She had no idea what was in store for her future love life.

Jenny opened her mouth to speak, then looked behind me and closed it again. I whirled around to see what had caught her attention and actually achieved the nearly impossible task of shutting her up, crossing my fingers it was a twenty-five to forty-nine-year-old woman who looked way too stressed to do the wild thing with her hubby. Instead, my eyes fell upon a very tall man, dressed entirely in black, standing before me, arms crossed against his broad chest. He had mirrored shades, slicked-back black hair, and a shiny Rolex that peeked out from under his suit coatsleeve. The whole look screamed *Men in Black*.

"Yes?" I asked, donning Indulgent Reporter Smile. He was probably from mall security and was about to ask us to leave the premises before he called the cops. Could this day get any worse?

"Dora Duncan?" he asked in a clipped accent I didn't recognize. "Are you Dora Duncan?"

I felt my face heat into a blush. Not a security guard. Maybe even a fan! A real, live fan!

I always got a kick out of people recognizing me on the street. Of course, back in the old days when Nick and I rocked Iraq, this was a more regular occurrence. We were network superstars then. A tag team everyone rooted for. Now, only a year after escaping the network to take this silly features reporter job in San Diego—where I was sure not to run face to face into a semiautomatic machine gun—nobody even knew my name.

Nick, on the other hand, was still *über*-famous. In fact, I didn't understand how any normal human being could manage to garner such a fan base without selling his soul to the devil. (Which, of course, I wouldn't put past him.) After leaving Baghdad and taking a job as a network news anchor in Los Angeles, he'd become more famous than ever. While I labored in local news obscurity, he walked the red carpet, schmoozing with starlets. While I covered craft fairs and dog shows, he interviewed senators and got laws changed. While I lived my life scarred and ugly because of *his* mistake, he made *People Magazine*'s "50 Most Beautiful People."

And Jenny wondered why I wouldn't take him back?

I realized the man in front of me had his hand outstretched and that I should be shaking it. Had to be gracious to the few fans I had left.

"Yes. Hi. How nice to meet you," I said with a smile. I wondered if my hair was covering my scar. I hated that I always wondered that while meeting someone new, but I couldn't help it.

"I'm Special Agent Fredricks," he said in response,

reaching into his back pocket and pulling out a badge encased in smooth black leather. He flashed it at me, and I raised an eyebrow. Not a fan. FBI. Figured. "We need your assistance, and I've been asked to have you come with me."

I furrowed my brows. The FBI needed my assistance? My assistance?

"What could you possibly need my assistance for?" I blurted, and then regretted it a moment later. After all, I didn't want to come off as rude and uncooperative to the FBI. But still . . .

"It's classified," Fredricks replied, tossing a glance at Jenny. "Now, if you could just come with me . . ."

I looked over at my photographer, then back to the special agent, trying to decide what I should do. I had a story to get on the air in a few hours, a story I wasn't exactly making much progress on. If I took time out to go with this man, I'd never make my slot. But, he was FBI. I couldn't say no to the FBI, could I? Plus, what if it was an important story he needed my assistance with? What if it were an inside scoop on a huge scandal? Even though I'd taken this job to get away from the danger I'd faced in Iraq, truth be told, lately I was getting a bit sick of covering sex and cellulite and celebrity C-sections for the evening news.

"Uh, let me call the desk. See if it's okay." The assignment desk was the Big Brother of the newsroom: always watching you. If I took off without checking in with them, I could be in big trouble.

I reached into my purse to dig out my phone. The agent placed a hand over mine. "No need, Ms. Duncan," he said. "We've already called your station. That's how we knew where you were."

"Oh." I looked over at Jenny. Should I believe this guy?

"We talked to a man named Mario. Your news director. He said he could move your story to the eleven P.M. news so you'd have time to finish it after we met with you."

I raised an eyebrow. Wow. Guess even my boss Mario was impressed that I'd been called upon by the FBI. Usually the guy wouldn't pull a story even as a personal favor to the pope. Go figure.

"It will only take a few minutes, Ms. Duncan," assured the agent. "Then we can return you here for your story."

"Go ahead, Dora," Jenny suggested. "I can hang here, go pick out a few thongs at Vicky Secrets. After all, Robbie's coming over tonight."

"Uh, great. A bit T.M.I, but great." I suppressed a shudder, then turned back to Special Agent Fredricks. "Fine, fine. Lead the way," I agreed.

I followed him out of the mall and into the parking lot, where a shiny black car with heavily tinted windows sat idling by the curb. A chauffeur type stepped up to open the back door and I ducked down to crawl inside. FBI Man entered after me, and soon we were speeding away from the mall.

"Where are we going?" I asked.

"Headquarters," Fredricks replied not-so-informatively.

"And what is it you need my help with again?"

"It will all be explained to you in due time, Ms. Duncan."

17

Of course it would be. I leaned back, settling into the plush leather seat. Might as well relax for a few moments. God knew I'd be scrambling the rest of the day to make my news slot after this inopportune field trip. Still, my pulse thrummed with anticipation. Relaxation was never my forté.

About ten minutes later, the car slowed to a stop and the chauffeur opened the door. I crawled out, looking around at my surroundings. We were in an underground parking garage. Agent Fredricks stepped out beside me and gestured for me to follow him.

Soon we were walking down a featureless corridor, flanked by even more featureless silver doors. It didn't look like anything I'd imagined FBI offices would look like. Not that my job had ever taken me anywhere higher up than the local police barracks.

Curiouser and curiouser, as Alice would say.

Of course, my brain decided to take that instant to re-mind me that I hadn't really checked this man's ID all that closely. What if he was lying about being part of the FBI? About speaking to Mario? What if he was really part of some secret underground Iraqi syndicate that had been looking for me this last year? What if I'd walked right into their trap?

I felt the all-too-familiar wave of panic rise like bile in my throat and attempted the breathing exercises the shrink had taught me to prevent yet another full-on panic attack.

Oh Dora, how do you get yourself into these messes?

I squeezed my hands into fists and struggled to regain

18

control of my rebellious, wildly beating heart. Being scared wouldn't help me escape if I needed to. Besides, I was being completely irrational. Why would some Iraqi group be looking for me? Ridiculous.

"Here we are," Fredricks announced, interrupting my racing thoughts. He slid a card key into a slot by one of the nondescript doors. It looked exactly like the other thirty some-odd doors we'd passed, and I wondered how he kept track.

A light above the slot turned green and the door slid open, revealing a circular, windowless conference room with a large mahogany table at its center. Sitting at the table were three men, also dressed in the uniform of black suit and mirrored shades. Which was odd, considering we were deep underground and the lighting didn't exactly lend itself to sunglasses.

This was beginning to get super freaky. If they started introducing me to any aliens like they did with Will Smith, I was so out of there.

"Sit, Ms. Duncan," said Man in Black #1.

I pulled out a chair and did as he requested. After all, what choice did I have? Sure, I knew Tae Kwon Do, but it didn't seem quite plausible that I'd be able to kick four men's asses all at once. Especially ones who appeared to be platinum members in good standing at their local gyms.

"What's going on here?" I asked. "Did I do something wrong?" Even as I asked the question, I knew that couldn't be the case. After all, my current life consisted of reporting on new-and-improved microdermabrasion by day and watching *Sex and the City* reruns by night. Not exactly the stuff of which trouble was made.

Unless they wanted to know more about my prison days in Iraq. I doubted that, though. I mean, I'd already been through the endless questioning a thousand times with a thousand different military men. The case had been closed—dismissed—long ago.

Man in Black #2 shook his head. "No," he said. "On the contrary, we need your help."

I shot a skeptical look from one to the next to the next. What on earth could they need my help with? And FYI, I'd retired from the helping business. I was a lowly features reporter now. I had no remaining FBI Helper Girl skills on reserve.

Man in Black #3 picked up a shiny silver remote control from the table and pressed a button. A slide projection illuminated the far wall of the room. My eyes widened and I gasped as I recognized the image on the screen.

Nick. Nick the Prick, to be exact.

"Do you know this man?" asked Agent Fredricks in a tone that told me he already knew the answer and wasn't going to allow me the luxury of lying.

Grr. I gritted my teeth. Why was it that everything in my life seemed to revolve around Nick? Why couldn't the world let me forget him and move on with my life? Allow me to meet a nice, normal investment banker who wanted nothing more than to transplant me to the suburbs and impregnate me with towheaded, blue-eyed suburban babies?

I stared at the picture. At Nick's bright green eyes. At

his endearingly cocky, Dennis Quaid-esque smirk. My heart squeezed and I reached up to brush the renegade tear from the corner of my eye. Damn it, why did it still have to hurt so much? Why did just looking at a picture of him serve to flood my heart with nearly unbearable pain? He'd moved on. He had a new life. Why couldn't I do the same?

Why was I still, deep down, so pathetically in love with this man? It didn't seem quite fair.

"Yeah, he's an anchor in LA," I muttered, turning my gaze back to the men. It was a bit unnerving to stare into four blank mirror-sunglassed faces, but I'd sooner stare longingly at the Crypt Keeper than look any more at that projected photo of Nick.

One of the men flipped through a legal pad filled with scrawled notes. "And your ex-boyfriend, right?" he asked.

I sighed. I'd been holding out the insane hope that they didn't know that little fact. But of course they did. They were the FBI. Also, there was that article in *Star*. . . .

"Yes. We . . . dated."

"And you broke up because of . . . ?"

I shifted in my seat. "These are awfully personal questions." The last thing I wanted to do was rehash what happened in Iraq. It was too horrible. And too humiliating.

Man in Black #2 nodded. "Our apologies if we're making you feel uncomfortable, Ms. Duncan. Maybe we should explain."

I nodded. "Good idea."

My eyes involuntarily wandered back to the projection, wishing the lump that had formed in my throat would go away. I stared at the photo and it seemed to stare back at me.

What on earth kind of trouble have you gotten yourself into this time, Nick?

"We have reason to believe that Nick Fitzgerald has joined an underground fringe group known as 'The Time Warriors,'" said Man in Black #1.

I raised an eyebrow. *Uh, what? The Time Warriors? What kind of group was that? And what's with the tacky name?* I couldn't imagine even Nick being *that* cheesy.

"The faction formed a few years ago," Man in Black #2 explained. "A group of rich white men, sick of the golf circuit, with nothing better to do. They bought a . . . machine of sorts off of the KGB back at the end of the Cold War."

"A machine?" I asked. He'd better not be talking about some nuclear bomb type thing. I mean, I knew Nick was a little wild, but I couldn't see him going all terrorist on me.

"An XR-2300, to be exact."

Oh, right. An XR-2300. Of course. That cleared everything up.

I cocked my head in question. "An XR—"

Man in Black #3 cleared his throat. "In layman's terms, Ms. Duncan, a time machine."

A what? A time machine? A freaking time machine?

I stared at him. I think my mouth even dropped open

for a moment. Was he for real? This had to be some joke, right? I glanced around the room, looking for peepholes. One-way glass. Where was the candid camera? Ashton Kutcher, telling me I'd been Punk'd? Then again, Ashton only Punk'd celebrities, and I wasn't a celebrity anymore. Not by any stretch of the imagination.

But still. A time machine? Give me a break!

Annoyance gnawed at my insides. "Gentlemen, I don't know what little game you're playing here," I started, trying to keep my voice even. "But I don't appreciate being dicked around. I've got a story to get on the air and—"

"You're not being . . . dicked around," Man in Black #2 interjected, rising from his seat. "The XR-2300 facilitates energy modulation through experimental quantum physics technology."

"What, do you think I just fell off the turnip truck?" I demanded, suddenly realizing my hands were shaking. I shoved them behind my back. "There's no such thing as a time machine."

Or was there? I mean, how did I really know there wasn't? Just because they didn't have TimeTravel.com kiosks at the local 7-Eleven didn't mean the government hadn't secretly developed the technology. After all, they'd been hiding aliens in Area 51 for fifty years. I was sure they had tons of crazy stuff we average citizens knew nothing about.

But still. A time machine? I had a hard time wrapping my head around that one.

"Look, ma'am, I know this is hard to grasp, but if you

23

can just accept the fact that this technology exists, we can move on to briefing you for your mission." Man in Black #1 looked at his watch. "We're almost out of time."

"Uh, right. Well, then why don't you cook up some new time then? If you've got a time machine and all."

Man in Black #2 sighed deeply, my sarcasm evidently making him extremely weary. "It doesn't work like that, Ms. Duncan. The XR-2300 burns a complex plutonium blend. One trip back in time costs more than Bill Gates's monthly income."

"Wow. I guess time really is money," I quipped, unable to resist. I looked from man to man. None even cracked a smile at what I considered a pretty clever joke. Tough room.

"Um, fine then. Go on. Don't let me hold you back," I said with a wave of my hand. After all, the sooner they got through their spiel, the sooner I could be on my way.

"As we were saying, the Time Warriors got their machine through the black market. And they've been using it as an expensive toy. Going back in time to experience different historic events through the eyes of those who lived them."

"Uh, like that guy in *Quantum Leap?*" I asked, raising a skeptical eyebrow.

"Something like that. Except they can return to their twenty-first century bodies anytime they choose."

Well, that was convenient, now wasn't it? "What kind of events?" I queried, all Question Girl as usual. Not that I believed these morons for one minute. But I figured I could play along.

24

"Battles, mostly. They seem to really enjoy those. And we do know one of them went back as Joe DiMaggio. To play baseball and sleep with Marilyn Monroe."

Ah, right. Sex and violence and sports. All the important stuff to the male gender.

"And by doing this they messed up history?" I asked.

"We believe so, though of course it's hard to tell, since we're living the current version. But we suspect they may be to blame for Furbies, New Coke, even the Macarena."

I shuddered. "So, um, what does this all have to do with me?" That was, of course, the sixty-four thousand dollar question. I doubted they wanted me to expose this group on local TV news, so there had to be some other purpose for dragging me in here and revealing this earth-shattering secret.

If, of course, this wasn't just one big reality show setup. And I wasn't at all convinced it wasn't. Though, if it was, they were totally wasting their time. I was so not about to sign a waiver.

"We've been after this group for years," Man in Black #3 explained. "But it's difficult. We usually don't know where they're going—what time period they're jumping into and whose body they're invading—until it's all over." He cleared his throat. "But this time we've got a tip."

Man in Black #1 glanced at the projection of Nick and then back at me. "We have intelligence that says your ex-boyfriend, Nick Fitzgerald, has traveled back in time to 1929—to witness the St. Valentine's Day Massacre."

A bitter chuckle escaped my lips. How ironic. Nick taking part in yet another Valentine's Day massacre. After what happened last year, it seemed all too appropriate.

"Do you find this humorous, Ms. Duncan?"

I cleared my throat and threw on what I hoped appeared an abashed face. "Um, no. Sorry. Go on."

"I'm not sure how familiar you are with the event. Basically, it's believed that Jack 'Machine Gun' McGurn, a known mobster of the time, ordered the murder of rival North End gangster Bugs Moran on Valentine's Day, 1929."

"On V-Day, huh? What a Hallmark moment that must have been."

"Yes, evidently McGurn cared enough to send the very best . . . assassins," Man in Black #2 quipped back wryly. The other two men turned to stare at him, evidently unappreciative of his attempt at humor. "Uh, anyway, Bugs and his men were supposed to meet a truck on Clark Street, to obtain a shipment of bootleg whiskey from Canada. McGurn's men dressed as police, made like it was a bust, then killed seven men. But Bugs overslept and so they missed their real target."

"Before this, the Time Warriors have simply been time tourists," Man in Black #3 spoke up. "Sure, they interfered in a few things here and there, but they never changed big historical events." He cleared his throat. "This time is different.

"This time we believe Nick Fitzgerald is planning on waking Bugs up on time so that he'll get whacked as well.

26

And since something like that could completely wreak havoc on history, we need someone to stop him."

"Right. And you think that 'someone' should be me," I concluded.

The four men nodded in perfect unison.

"No." I shook my head.

"No?"

"Is that word not part of your FBI vocabulary?" I asked. "First of all, even if what you're saying is true and I'm not in some weirdo reality show, I am way too busy to go back in time. I've got a story on the air tonight and I haven't found anyone to interview for it. The rest of my week"— I fished in my purse for my DayTimer and flipped through the pages—"is completely booked. As is the rest of my month. So I have absolutely no time to play your little reindeer time travel games." I stuffed the DayTimer back in my purse. "Secondly, what makes you think I could stop Nick Fitzgerald from doing this, anyway? Even when we were dating, he'd never ever listen to a word I said. The pig-headed prick. It's safe to assume he's not going to start now."

"Ms. Duncan—"

I rose from my seat, nodding to each man in turn. "Thank you for inviting me and telling me about your little time machine. It's fascinating stuff, really, and when you're ready to release it to the media, definitely fax me a press release. But for now, I must be on my way. Unless . . . ," I smiled sweetly, "any of you would like to tell me how you're too stressed for sex?"

Two of the men shot each other uncomfortable looks,

leading me to believe that perhaps I wasn't too far off the mark with my question. But neither seemed too interested in confessing, which was really fine, considering I didn't have a camera with me to record it all, anyway.

"Ms. Duncan," Man in Black #1 said, "we understand your busy schedule and that this request might be seen as a bit inconvenient. But I don't think you grasp the severe implications of this scenario."

Against my better judgment, I paused at the door.

"If Nick Fitzgerald is not stopped, he will alter history forever. The world as we know it will cease to exist and we will spiral off into some parallel universe. Quite simply, the future of the world rests in your hands."

My shoulders slumped. *Sheesh*, talk about laying on the guilt! These guys were better than my Catholic grandmother. And she was the master. "I'm sorry. I'm not really the 'save the world' type," I argued, my defenses already crumbling. "Not anymore."

"Look, Ms. Duncan, we know what Nick did to you back in Iraq. And we understand why your facing him would be a somewhat . . . undesirable situation. But think about the damage he could do. Not just to you this time, but to the entire world."

I turned around slowly. What else could I do? Even though this whole thing seemed so ridiculous, I couldn't exactly refuse to save the world—could I? Especially from Nick the Prick.

I drew in a breath. "Fine. What is it you need me to do?"

"Sit down, Ms. Duncan," Man in Black #2 said with a

wide smile, looking far too smug for my liking. "We'll brief you on your mission."

They blabbed on forever, but here's the gist: they could send me back in time, but not as myself. Not as Dora. No, instead I had to basically body snatch someone who already existed in 1929. For this mission, they had chosen Louise Rolfe, girlfriend of the infamous Jack "Machine Gun" McGurn, the gangster who'd ordered the hit on Bugs Moran. They felt that by me being on the inside, I'd be better able to figure out Nick's whereabouts and stop him from his future-altering plan.

I asked them what made them think I wouldn't inadvertently screw things up on my own (that was my specialty, after all) and accidentally change history myself. But they evidently had a contingency plan in place. I'd be meeting up with a contact who would help me learn the lay of the land and let me in on just how things should play out, historically speaking. Besides, they said, if small things changed because of my actions, it wouldn't be a big deal—might lead to a sequel to *Showgirls* or something. It was the big historical events they were most concerned with.

And why me? Why not someone trained for this kind of thing? Well, mainly because there was one big snag in their otherwise oh-so-perfect plan. None of them had any idea whose body Nick had jumped into. Not one clue. He could be absolutely anyone. And so these rocket scientists figured with my "extensive" knowledge of his personality, I could figure out who he was in time to stop him.

So, basically I had to go find a lazy, arrogant jerk who still had the ability to make my toes curl and was looking to change the world.

Oh yeah. Piece of cake.

CHAPTER TWO

Chicago
February 11, 1929

"Hiya, doll, wanna dance?"

My eyes fluttered open at the sudden sound of a male voice addressing me.

Was I here?

I looked around the room. No more titanium walls. No more Men in Black. Instead, I stood in a swanky, old-fashioned-club-looking place with dark mahogany furniture and ornate chandeliers. And the people! The men were dressed to the nines in smart tuxes, and the women wore loose-fitting fringed dresses with long, dangly pearls and beaded headbands. Flapper gear.

I swallowed hard. Ohmigod, it worked. It actually worked. I'd had my doubts, believe me, as they strapped me down to the chair and put that ugly cap of weird blue gel over my head. I mean, even up to the last second, the moment of truth, when they'd pricked me with a sedative and I'd blacked out into oblivion, I'd still figured it all had to be some big game or trick. Some weird form of hypnosis or something. The concept of going back in time was way too far-fetched to be believable.

But now, as I glanced around the room with my own eyes (or technically the eyes of the girl I'd body snatched) I realized they must have been telling the truth. This looked too real to be in my head. To be a trick. There were sights, sounds, smells—I grabbed a canapé off a waiter's tray and popped it into my mouth. Yup, even tastes.

They'd actually done it. Actually sent me back in time to the 1920s.

Holy time travel, Batman.

"What do you think, you're too good for me or somethin'?"

I whirled back around, realizing that in my shock and awe of being transported through time seventy-some-odd years in what felt like no time at all, I hadn't answered the man's request for a dance. I drew in a breath.

Act normal, Dora. Stop shaking. They think you belong here. They think you're Louise Rolfe, that mobster's girlfriend. Stay in character. Just think, what would Louise do?

What *would* Louise do? How the hell should I know what Louise would do? I didn't know anything about the chick except her name and the fact she dated a mobster named Machine Gun. Was she flirtatious? Shy? Silly? Serious? Would she dance with a stranger? *Was* this guy a stranger? Maybe he was her best friend.

Ohmigod. I was so in over my head.

I took a deep breath. I could do this. I was smart and savvy. Not like one of those stupid back-in-time heroines you always see in the movies or read about in books. The ones who can't adjust. Who can't play along. Who stupidly spout off pop culture references and twenty-first century-isms to anyone who will listen. Who get accused of being witches and sentenced to burn at the stake. (Of course, those heroines always ended up getting rescued by some shiny highland hero before they burned. I'd probably be stuck with someone like Nick in the hero's role, who wouldn't show up 'til I was nice and crispy.)

"Sure, I'll dance," I agreed cautiously.

The guy grinned, and I noticed he was missing a couple teeth. Attractive. Very pre-Angelina Jolie Billy Bob Thornton. However, I realized, this was not the time to be picky. After all, he could prove useful. I had three days to find out all I could about this place. To discover Nick the Prick's 1920s identity and save the world. And that would require mucho mingling to find the 411. And Billy Bob here had just inadvertently volunteered to be my first victim.

Before I could start my interrogation, the guy grabbed my hand and led me toward the dance floor. I took a moment as we walked by an ornate gold mirror to take stock of myself. Or of Louise Rolfe, technically speaking.

I nearly fainted at my reflection. Oh. My. God. I was a blonde. A beautiful, bobbed blonde. I'd always wanted to be blonde, and now here I had finally gotten my wish. I wondered if I'd start having more fun immediately or if there was a break-in period. I fingered my hair, rejoicing in the silky strands. If only there was a way I could keep these locks when I went back to 2006. . . .

I had wide blue eyes, pencil-thin eyebrows, and a red pouty mouth. I was slim and wore a black fringed dress and knee-high stockings (held up by garters—no spandex cling here!). And best of all, no ugly facial scar! I was a porcelain doll of perfection. Rock on. At least the FBI hadn't sent me back as some ugly chick.

I flexed my arm for a moment, fascinated by the idea of controlling someone else's body. Was Louise inside here at all, trapped in the very recesses of the brain I was borrowing? I tried to search my mind for a foreign presence, but felt nothing. Nobody home. Which was probably for the best.

"Gonna check out your reflection all day, sweetheart?" the man beside me asked, looking impatient. I guess I would be too if I wanted to dance and my partner suddenly developed a fascination with his own reflection. But still! I could stare for hours. This was just too weird. Too surreal.

"Um, sorry," I muttered, feeling my/Louise's face heat. "Let's go dance."

The five-piece band at the end of the room picked that moment to strike up a slow waltz, and my partner took me in his arms. Luckily, I'd watched *Dirty Dancing* about a hundred times too many in my Swayze-crazed youth, so I could keep up with the steps.

I swiveled my head to glance around the room in awe. So this was what 1929 looked like. Besides having watched a few movies like *The Untouchables* and *Thor-*

oughly Modern Millie, I really didn't have a good background on the decade. Was this what you called a speakeasy? It looked classier than I had imagined it would. The floors were shiny and there were chandeliers hanging from the high ceiling, and ornate gold mirrors adorned almost every wall. I guess I had thought these places would be more like dark and dirty underground dive bars.

"So, um, come here often?" I asked my dance partner, a lame attempt to start up conversation. It was a dumb line, to be sure, but I figured perhaps eighty or so years back it hadn't been made cliché yet. You never know.

"Every night," he replied, flashing his gap-toothed grin. Now that I was up close and personal I could smell the booze and cigarettes on his breath and the sweat under his arms. Lovely. But at least I could cross him off as a possible Nick. There was no way my metrosexual ex would walk around with nasty BO. "But you should already know that, Louisey Peasey."

Ugh. I'd almost forgotten. I wasn't some stranger here. I was the gangster boss's girlfriend. Even though I didn't have a clue as to who they were, everyone here knew me. D'oh.

I laughed nervously. "Oh, yeah. Right. Of course."

"Yer lookin' very pretty tonight," the man added.

"Thanks," I replied, hoping he didn't expect any compliments in return, as I'd be hard pressed to come up with one. *Lovely tobacco stainage on your remaining three and a half teeth? I was always a sucker for pockmarks? Let me run my fingers through your greasy hair?*

He staggered backward for a second before righting

himself, and I realized he not only smelled like booze, he was lit up like a Christmas tree. Hopefully, his inebriation didn't preclude him from acting like a gentleman or, assignment or not, I'd *so* have to kick his ass.

Hmm. How to start questioning him? Since I had no idea which body Nick had jumped into, I couldn't exactly describe the guy and ask my drunken dance partner if he'd seen him hanging around. So, how was I supposed to proceed? Ask if they'd noticed anyone acting weird? Like they'd been—oh, let's just say for kicks—body snatched?

Um, right.

"Yer lookin' very, *very* pretty, Louisey," the man slurred for a second time. I felt his fingers travel oh-so-slightly down my back. I sighed. This loser obviously wasn't going to be a wealth of information no matter what questions I came up with—at least not without me getting felt up in the process, which I was not about to submit to, even if it was for a good cause. Oh well, I couldn't really expect to waltz (literally!) up to the first guy I met in the 1920s and expect him to spill the beans.

"Thanks. I think we've established that," I replied, gently pushing him away. "Not that I don't appreciate the sentiment, of course." After all, I had to take my compliments where they came. God knew I didn't get very many these days when I was in my own skin.

The man stared at me a moment, and I could see the unmasked, drunken lust darkening his eyes. Yipes. Luckily I managed to turn my head just as he leaned in for the kill. Or for the kiss, in this case. He ended up connecting with my ear instead, which would have been fine, except I wasn't entirely convinced he realized he'd missed his mark. Yup. Out came a slimy tongue, lapping away.

"Ew!" I cried, attempting to leap back in disgust. But the man had a kung fu grip on me, latching on to fistfuls of dress, not ready to relinquish his hold. Excellent. Now I'd have to give him the Dora Duncan special. Two seconds in the 1920s and I was already going to cause a stir. But it couldn't be helped. No man groped me. My three times a week at Tae Kwon Do would see to that. I readied my knee for some intimate groin contact.

"Is this man bothering you?" a deep, baritone voice cut through the ear-slobbering. I lowered my knee. Maybe I wouldn't have to go all *Charlie's Angels* after all.

Sure enough, the ear-licking coward let go immediately, backing away in the most apologetic manner.

"Sorry mister, sorry," he muttered. "I didn't mean nuthin' by it. Honest. I's just . . . drunk. Don't tell Machine Gun, please." Still mumbling his apologies, along with other less intelligible ramblings about semiautomatic weapons, he fled and disappeared into the crowd. Phew.

I turned to face my hero and offer my sincerest thanks. My eyes widened as they fell upon his face.

Wow. Talk about being saved by the hottie.

The guy who'd interrupted my dance partner's advances had to be the most de-lish guy I'd ever laid eyes on. About six foot, with a lanky build and dirty blond hair that he had slicked back with gel. He had a solid face with a square jaw and cheekbones that looked as if they had been chiseled by Michelangelo himself. Top that with a strong Roman nose and the most amazing, piercing blue eyes known to mankind. Think Ewan McGregor and Jude Law rolled into one and you had your man.

Yummy.

He was dressed in a sexy, well-fitted tux that accented his lean body and prompted me to fight a nearly overwhelming urge to run my fingers down his chest to see if he had the six-pack abs my sex-starved brain imagined on him. But I restrained myself. After all, he'd just saved me from a groper. Hardly appropriate to start pawing him in return.

"Thanks," I said, suddenly realizing I'd been staring and not appropriately conveying my deepest gratitude for his just-in-time rescue. Still, with a face like his he must be used to women drooling over him, unable to form complete sentences.

"Not a problem," he replied lazily. He dragged his piercing gaze down my body and I resisted the urge to shiver at his unabashed examination of my/Louise's frame. "Always got to look out for the boss's girl."

My heart sank. Damn. I'd forgot about that tiny little detail. I couldn't be checking out hot guys while I was hanging out in Louise's body. She already had a boyfriend—and he happened to be the big mob boss. No guy in his right mind would dare touch me. There would be no "flapper" action in this story. I was as doomed to celibacy here as I was in the next millennium.

Um, not that I'd been hoping to hook up, mind you.

After all, I had a mission. A job. I didn't have time to be hitting on Ewan McGregor look-alikes anyway. Nope. No time at all.

"What's your name again?" I asked, hoping Louise wasn't bosom buddies with this guy.

"Sam," he answered, disappointment washing over his handsome face. "You don't remember me? From the other night? Wow." He shook his head. "Guess I don't make much of an impression."

I opened my mouth to say something—anything—to avoid hurting his feelings. To tell him I had a terrible memory or that I was just kidding. Something. But at that moment, loud sirens started wailing, drowning out the opportunity to apologize. Sam glanced at the club's front doors and cursed under his breath.

"What's going on?" I asked, my gaze darting around the room. Utter chaos. People were running in every direction, screaming. Knocking over tables. Drinks flew. Glass shattered.

"Come on," Sam said, grabbing me by the hand. "We've got to get you out of here."

"Everyone stay where you are! Do not attempt to leave the building," a loud voice commanded from outside. Of course, no one paid any attention. Instead they ran around like kids at a busted keg party. And like those kids, it appeared many were too intoxicated to correctly determine the nearest exit.

Sam and I, hand in hand, ducked into a room at the back of the club that turned out to be the kitchen. The chefs had apparently exited stage left—no going down with the proverbial ship for them—leaving pots boiling over and thick slices of meat burning on the skillets. We ran down the center aisle (I was so wishing for my Reeboks instead of these ribbon-tied heels), out the end door, and into a long nondescript hallway.

"This way," my rescuer instructed, after looking left and right down the hall and seeing that the coast was clear. Thank goodness he knew where he was going, which also reassured me that my rescuer wasn't really Nick in disguise. This guy knew his way around; Nick would have been just as clueless as me in this foreign time period. Of course, he could have got there earlier, learned the lay of the land. But no, this guy was too smooth—too with-it—to simply be a tourist.

We ran down the hallway, our steps echoing loudly in the empty space. I sure hoped no one was too close behind us. The last thing I needed my first day of saving the 1920s world was to be locked up.

A few moments later the hallway ended at a massive iron door with a large lock. Sam stared at the door for a moment, as if trying to remember something. Then he reached into his pocket and pulled out a set of keys and started trying various ones. None seemed to fit.

"Hurry!" I whispered. I could hear the police shouting at one another, and they didn't sound that far away. Finally Sam found the right key and the lock clicked. He pushed on the door and it reluctantly creaked open, revealing a set of stone stairs descending into blackness.

"It may be a little dirty down here," Sam apologized with a rueful grin. "But it's better than the slammer."

Yup, dirty basements trumped slammers every day of

the week in my book. Still, it wasn't the dirt that bothered me. It was the lack of light. After spending all those weeks in that dark Iraqi prison, I'd developed a pretty severe aversion to darkness, to say the least. But this was no time to succumb to my fears. Not with the cops so close behind. So I took a tentative step and began my descent into the blackness, praying there were no rats this time around. Sam followed, pulling the door closed behind him.

Pitch black. Great. Just the thing to remind me of that no-electricity jail cell in Iraq. The nights had been so long. So dark. So scary . . .

I stopped midway down the staircase, frozen in panic. My heart thumped in my chest and my lungs squeezed, as if in a vise, making it almost impossible to suck in a breath.

"I-I can't see," I quavered, hating how squeaky and pathetic my voice sounded. After all, I was supposed to be a fearless, kick-ass, back-in-time secret agent girl, right? And here I was, *this*close to bawling like a baby. And not for some noble, understandable reason like being in a totally foreign time period or because there were angry cops hot on our tail. No, I was simply afraid of the dark. We could have been in the Tunnel of Love and I'd be freaking instead of making out.

The Men in Black were going to be extremely disappointed in me. I really hoped they weren't watching all of this through some time portal window or something. I didn't want them judging my performance before I even had time to rally.

"Hang on," Sam replied from the top of the stairs. In a

moment, I could feel him come up behind me, his hot breath suddenly singeing the back of my neck. It was a strange, almost erotic sensation, and, oddly enough, helped to get my mind off my fears.

"Give me your hand," he whispered in my ear. His mouth was so close it tickled the lobe.

I pawed through the darkness until my fingers contacted flesh. He wrapped his hand around mine and eased past me on the staircase, then led me downward, seeming to feel out each step carefully before pulling me along. At the bottom, he drew me down to a crouching position on the floor. The cement was cool and clammy against my already sweaty palms.

"I think we're safe," he informed me in a low voice. "They won't be able to break that lock, and the door's about a foot thick. We can hang here 'til they leave."

"Okay," I said, trying desperately to will my breathing back to normal. My heart banged against my ribcage. My hands trembled.

It's just darkness. Darkness can't hurt you.

You know, I used to be so cool. So in control in every situation. Even crazy ones like this. Too bad even in Louise's body I was still stuck with Dora's hang-ups.

A match scraped and a spark of light pierced the darkness. Using the glow of Sam's match, I rose to my feet and scanned the room. Spotting an old lamp in one corner, I ran over and switched it on. A dim orangey light bathed the room. Phew.

I leaned over, hands on my knees, and sucked in a deep breath in an attempt to control the impending panic attack. I ran through my shrink's suggested affirmations in rapid order.

I was fine. I was safe. No one could hurt me. I could get through this. It was all in my head.

So, why could I not stop trembling?

"Hey, hey, are you all right?" Sam asked, scrambling to his feet. He studied me with worried eyes, his face inches from mine. "You're shaking like crazy. What's got you so upset? Aren't you used to raids like this? It's not like the coppers don't show up here every time they're feeling poor and need a bribe."

I swallowed hard. Of course. My fear must look absolutely ridiculous to this guy. But what was I supposed to tell him? Certainly not the truth.

"Um, yes, sorry. I . . ." I babbled, my mouth choosing unintelligible stammering instead of clever explanations.

Luckily, he didn't insist on an explanation. "Come here," he said, holding out his arms. I stared at him for a minute, not sure what I should do. Then I gave in and leaned closer to him. I mean, what the hell, right? It was just a hug.

He pulled me into an embrace, his strong hands wrapping around me and his fingers stroking my back. "Shhh," he comforted. "We're safe. It's okay. You're okay."

Against my better judgment I cuddled a little closer. He felt so warm. So solid. I buried my face in his shoulder and he began to stroke my head, his nails lightly scraping my scalp. I hadn't been held in a long time. Hadn't wanted to be held by anyone but Nick, and I'd determined that that would never happen again. But this seemed okay, somehow. Even though the guy was a complete stranger. Weird.

I pulled my head away from his comforting shoulder to get a better look at him. He smiled back at me, still looking concerned. He really did have amazing eyes. Even in the dim light I could see their soft blue, with flecks of green and yellow all swirling into some kaleidoscope of color. A girl could lose herself in those eyes. Not that I was going to. After all, I had a mission to complete. An asshole ex-boyfriend to find. A . . . kiss from a stranger to contend with.

For a moment I wasn't sure what I should do as he leaned in, eyes closed, lips pressing against mine. His touch was far gentler than I'd anticipated. Light, soft lips, caressing mine. Like the wisp of a butterfly's wing. In an instant, tingles shot straight to my toes and other extremities.

Wow, didn't take much these days to get me completely turned on. How pathetic.

His tongue lightly darted at my lips. Gah. What should I do? Was this okay? I mean, I didn't want to go and be as bad as Nick—changing history and all with stranger make-out sessions—but at the same time, I hadn't been kissed in nearly a year. (Well, except that one time at Speed Dating where the man leaned across the table. Evidently he was a kiss-on-the-first-minute type of guy. Bleh.)

But this—I had to admit, it felt good. Really damn good. My insides warmed and my head went all gooey. Who knew I'd have to go back three-quarters of a century to find a man who made me want to purr like Nick used to.

Eh, screw it. History could take care of itself for five minutes.

I parted my lips slightly, allowing him to deepen his kiss. His tongue flicked at my mouth as if testing my taste, then delved in for deeper exploration. I kissed him back, rejoicing at the adrenaline rush shooting through my veins, the chills tripping down my spine.

First kisses, even in someone else's body, were always delicious.

As I submitted, the kiss hardened in intensity. Evidently no longer content to be gentle, his roving hands found my shoulders and pushed me against the basement wall, wrenching control from me and making me his willing prisoner. I allowed myself a moan of pleasure and in response his kissing grew lustier, more passionate. His hands wandered my body, fingertips exploring every inch of me, dragging up my thighs, tracing my hipbones, my waist, daring to cup my breasts and circle the tips until they rose into sharp peaks. With his hard body pressed against mine, I could feel how much he wanted me.

Or Louise, in any case.

Um, ew. Okay, that was a definite buzz-kill thought. How could I be enjoying this? He didn't want me. He didn't care about me. He only wanted the body of my alter ego. He wanted Louise. Beautiful, unscarred Louise. And for me to take willing advantage of this—well, that was just weird and dirty. Plus, I had a mission I was supposed to be accomplishing. There would be no time for sexual field trips, no matter how delicious the tour guide.

It took every once of willpower to push him away. "Stop," I commanded, my voice sounding a bit froggy.

To his credit, he did, though he didn't look too pleased about doing so. He raked a hand through his tousled hair. "What?" he asked.

"I can't do this," I replied, trying to catch my breath. Man, I was so turned on it wasn't funny. Sexually frustrated much, Dora? "I'm . . . I belong to my boyfriend. . . ." Dammit, what was the dude's name again? "Tommy Gun."

Yup, I can't justify making out with a total hottie, 'cause I've got some guy with a semiautomatic weapon as his first name. Classy, Louise. Real classy.

Sam cocked his head in confusion. "Tommy Gun?"

Shit. Classy, and one hundred percent wrong.

"Um, Machine? Gun?" I bit my lower lip in frustration. What was Louise's boyfriend's name again? The sexually charged air was screwing with my memory—and with my sentence-forming ability if we're being completely honest. "Tommy's just a . . . nickname I have for him."

"Oh." Sam took a deep breath and nodded. "Right. Okay. I understand. Sorry." He turned and started pacing to the other side of the room. "It won't happen again."

I had to bite down hard on my rebellious tongue to stop from telling Sam exactly how much I would *like* it to happen again. In fact, how much I wanted it to happen again right this very second. But no, that wasn't a wise thing to do. I had broken the kissing spell and it needed to stay broken. No matter how much I was dying to taste him again.

"What is this place, anyway?" I asked, scanning the

room, desperate for a subject change. It looked sort of like an ancient wine cellar, glass bottles of yellowish liquid stacked floor to ceiling.

"Looks like this is where Jack stores his gin," Sam said, appraising the area himself. "The secret room the coppers are dying to locate."

Ah, that made sense. Even I, with my perpetual C+ in history class (who had time to memorize all those dusty facts when there were hot boys to run after?) remembered the Roaring Twenties were the time of prohibition. Alcohol was illegal, so people made their own. From private home bathtub gin to big distilleries. And then there were those who carted the stuff in from other countries, like Canada. Bootlegging, they called it. And it was a very big, very black market business.

"Who's Jack?" I asked curiously.

Sam turned to stare at me, an "are you crazy?" look on his otherwise handsome face. Shit, Jack was evidently someone Louise knew. I quickly feigned a "just joking" smile and he laughed. "Funny," he said. "You almost had me for a moment."

Jack's your boyfriend, you moron! my brain reminded me suddenly. *Jack "Machine Gun" McGurn. Jeesh. You're not very good at this secret agent stuff, are you?*

"I'm a funny girl," I quipped, desperate to prove my brain wrong.

"Yes, you are." Sam said. His grin faded to a more serious expression as he reached out to trace the side of my cheek. *Oh no. Here we go again.* "Or maybe you just don't like to think about Jack when we're together," he murmured, his voice lowering to a husky whisper.

I stared at him, willing my mouth not to drop open like some cartoon character's. Now, wait just one time-traveling second. Was what we'd experienced a few minutes ago Sam and Louise's first kiss? Or had there been others? Were the two of them actually having an affair or something? 'Cause if they were, then I would technically be guiltier of changing history by *not* kissing him. I mean, I wouldn't want to break out of character by refusing his advances, right?

If Louise was getting it on the side from Adonis here, well, then I'd have to as well. It was only the right thing to do. After all, the FBI told me I was helping out my country. And that meant supreme sacrifices would have to be made.

Heh.

"What I meant to say, was, um . . ." I lowered my head and looked up demurely. I could totally do this. "When we're alone, all I can think of is you."

Sam raised an eyebrow, looking surprised. Hm. Had I misjudged the nature of their relationship after all? Or perhaps I was coming off too strong? After all, this was the twenties. Maybe women played harder to get.

Or maybe, my brain theorized wildly, he was simply a commitmentphobe who freaked out when women admitted their true feelings. A commitmentphobe like Nick the Prick used to be. Even in the twenties, show a guy you cared and he'd start running a marathon in the other direction—bad knees or no.

"I'm glad to hear that," Sam said, recovering quickly. Hm. Smooth. Very smooth. "I can't stop thinking of you, either." His fingers traveled from the side of my face to brush against my lips, then he lowered them to massage my neck. "You're a constant obsession, *ma cherie*."

Oh-kay then. I pressed my lips together in disapproval. That was just a tad bit too much like a line for my taste. I mean, what, did he think Louise would just melt at some slick words, forget her boyfriend, and be all over him?

Okay, fine. She might have been. She might have fallen hook, line, and sinker. Honestly I had no idea what the girl whose body I currently owned was like. She could have been a total slut for all I knew. But I did know that *I* sure as hell wouldn't fall. After all, I was a twenty-first century girl, able to dodge a cheesy pickup line in a single bound. Nick had been full of them, especially after he'd done something wrong. The guy could spout lines from freaking Shelley on the spot if he needed to derail my anger.

The worst part was, the tactic usually worked. I mean, how could one not swoon when said boyfriend quoted lines from the Romantics?

As for Louise, she needed to be careful not to get her heart broken by this guy. Like I had with Nick. And as current guardian of the organ in question, I wasn't going to let that happen.

"Oh please," I groaned, rolling my eyes to show him what I thought of his tactics. "I bet you say that to all the flappers."

His face fell, and for a moment I wasn't sure if I should feel bad for him. But no, that was just his good looks frazzling my brain. Stupid good-looking guys. If we girls were smart we'd grow up looking for geeks in shining armor who wanted nothing more in life than to play *Magic: The*

Gathering and worship us like the goddesses we are. Instead, we always go for the jerks whose butts looked good in Levi's. Or tuxes, in this particular case.

"You're one cruel dame, Louise," Sam muttered, turning away to study the bottles on the wall. Great. Now I'd pissed him off.

"So, um, Sam?" I ventured, wanting to change the subject again. We had to get back on target here. I had an ex-boyfriend to find and this melodramatic episode of *As the Twenties Turns* was not helping one bit. "Have you noticed anyone acting weird these days?"

He turned back to me, his head cocked in question. "Weird?" he repeated. "Like how?"

I shrugged. "I don't know, really. Just . . . weird. Like they're not themselves."

"Besides you, you mean?"

Touché. I felt my face heat into a blush. "Yes, besides me."

Sam shrugged. "Can't say that I have. Sorry, doll. Why?"

"Er, no reason. Never mind." I sighed. I really needed to work on my line of questioning. I was never going to locate Nick at this rate.

Sam glanced up the stairs to the locked door. "You know, it's probably safe to go back up," he suggested. "I'm sure the police are long gone."

I nodded, so ready to get out of the basement and the close proximity of Sam. I might have successfully dodged his verbal come-on, but the sight of him was still doing melty things to my insides.

We walked up the stairs and I wondered what I should

do next. Finding my home seemed like a logical move, but I had no idea where I lived. The FBI sure didn't give me a lot to go on. I was totally flying blind.

As we slowly made our way down the corridor, checking around each corner for any sign of police, I opened up my handbag and rummaged through, hoping for a clue. I had nothing.

"Looks like the coast is clear," Sam said as we exited the club. It was night and the streetlights cast a sickly yellow glow on the dreary landscape. "Want me to take you home?"

"Do you, uh, know where I live?" I asked hopefully.

"No, but you can surely tell me."

Darn. "Uh, no, that's okay. I'm good," I said, not wanting to raise his suspicions further by informing him I had no idea what building I called home.

Sam shook his head. "It's dangerous to walk out here at night. And I've got nothing else to do. So, um, tell me where you live and I'll take you in my car."

I laughed nervously. "No, really. It's fine. I can walk. Need the exercise, really. I mean, do you have any idea how many carbs are in your standard gin and tonic?"

Sam shot me a confused look. Duh. I'd inadvertently snuck a twenty-first centuryism into my vocabulary. He didn't know what carbs were. Heck, I wasn't even sure if the term "calorie" had been invented. I'd have to be more careful or they'd be carting me off to the insane asylum before V-Day.

"Er, never mind," I said with a wave of my hand. "Point is, I'll walk. It's not far."

At least I hoped it wasn't.

Sam opened his mouth, as if to say something, then shut it again and shrugged. "Have it your way, darlin'," he said. "Catch you later." And with a casual wave, he turned and walked over to a shiny new black Ford and jumped in.

I watched as he pulled away, driving off into the night, wondering what the heck I was supposed to do next. Go back inside? Ask someone how to get to my house? This time travel stuff was a lot harder than it first appeared.

"Dora?" A high-pitched, disembodied voice suddenly interrupted my reverie. I whirled around, searching the streetlamp-lit street for its owner.

"Who's there?" I asked.

No answer. Just a clattering in the darkness. I sucked in a breath, wishing I'd been allowed to time travel with my personal can of pepper spray.

"Dora Duncan?" There it was again. Still squeaky, but a little more impatient sounding.

I gulped, realization hitting me with the force of a ten ton truck. Oh my god. The voice was using my real name. Not Louise, my Roaring Twenties name. Not the name belonging to the body I was currently inhabiting. Whoever it was calling my name evidently knew my true identity.

Could it be Nick? Could he have found out what I was sent to do and which body I was sent to do it in?

And if so, what was he going to do to me now that he knew?

CHAPTER THREE

My heart pounded as I scanned the alleyway, searching for the identity of the voice. However, it still appeared completely vacant. So vacant, in fact, that you'd half expect some tumbleweed to float across like in a spaghetti western. So where the hell was the voice coming from?

Was it in my head? Could the Men in Black be trying to communicate with me in some telepathic way? Was that even possible?

I folded my arms across my chest, firming my resolve. There was no reason to freak out. Absolutely none. Even if I was, let's say, completely defenseless and alone nearly a hundred years in the past, trapped in someone else's body and hearing some invisible squeaky dude cry out my twenty-first century name.

Nope. Zero freak-out necessity.

I reached up to brush a lock of hair out of my eyes and realized my skin was damp with nervous perspiration. I remembered the old days in Iraq. How brave I used to be.

Perhaps foolishly so, but still . . . What would Nick's "Dora the Explorer" have done in a situation like this?

"Dora?" the voice repeated for a third time.

"That's my name. Don't wear it out," I called out into the darkness, hoping I sounded braver than I felt.

"Cute. Real cute," the voice replied, in actuality not sounding all that amused. "Now get over here. We need to talk."

I furrowed my brows. Yeah, right. If he thought I was going to step into the darkness so he could "talk," he had another think coming. I may not have been Dora the Explorer anymore, but I was still a few steps up from Dora the Dumb Ass, thank you very much.

"I'm, uh, all talked out, actually. Maybe in the A.M., you know?" I said, stepping backward in a hurried attempt to put more distance between myself and the invisible voice.

"Dora, don't be a dolt. Just get over here."

I pursed my lips. "No."

The voice let out an indignant squeak. "Fine. Fine. I'll come to you then."

I swallowed hard, wondering what I should do.

Are you going to just stand there? Let him come get you? Even in Iraq you made a run for it. At least you tried to escape. What the hell has happened to you? It's bad enough they broke your spirit. Don't let them subsequently cause your death as well.

Okay, maybe it wasn't as inspiring a pep talk as in *It's a Wonderful Life*, but it was rousing enough to jolt me into action—and that was all that mattered at the moment.

Without further contemplation, I turned and started running as fast as Louise's legs could carry me away.

I darted down the dimly lit road, past squat gray warehouses and other decrepit buildings, twisting and turning down various narrow streets lined with cars. I'd never figure out my way back to the club at this rate, but if I could lose the squeaky dude, it'd be worth it.

As I ran, I noticed that an oddly familiar feeling of excited adrenaline had started pumping through my veins. *Jam Juice*, Nick and I used to call it, since it nearly always started flowing the second you found yourself in an impossible jam. Near escapes had always been our favorite aphrodisiac back in the day. Exciting, death defying, and making for a great story down at the bar. (After the wild and crazy Jam Juice sex, that was! God, that had been good.)

Nope, I hadn't had this kind of rush since, well, you know. It felt . . . great, in a way.

I scrambled over a crumbling brick wall, around a growling dog chained to a tree, and dodged gravestones in a tiny weedy cemetery. Then I headed down a side alley and . . . found myself at a dead end, blocked by a chain-link fence, which was complemented with rusty barbed wire.

Hands on my knees, I sucked in a shaky breath. Louise evidently hadn't clocked as many hours at the local gym as I had, and she was hurting bad. From the way my lungs felt like they were collapsing in on me, I'd venture a guess that she was also quite the chain-smoker. Uh, not that I had the lung capacity of a killer whale myself lately. Ever since I signed up for Netflix I'd been skipping the gym in favor of the couch. After all, I had to make sure I got my money's worth each month, and all those movies sure didn't watch themselves.

I scanned the alley. Had I lost him? It was tough to know, as, of course, he'd been invisible. But I'd led him on quite a chase. I doubted anyone would be able to find me.

"You effing moron. Why the hell did you run?" asked an out-of-breath voice chittering closer down the alley-way.

Then again . . .

"Leave me alone!" I cried. "I've got a gun and I'm not afraid to use it."

"Oh, for Christ's sake," the voice growled. Well, it growled as much as a squeaky voice could manage. "I'm on your side, princess. I'm your contact. Didn't Fredricks and the gang tell you you'd be meeting a contact?"

A contact? I furrowed my brow, trying to think back. Had the Men in Black told me I was to meet a contact? And was it likely I'd forgotten about it if they had? I mean, I had a good memory and all, but the whole time travel thing in and of itself was a lot to take in and filter through. Some details definitely could have slipped through the cracks.

Then the lightbulb lit over my head like some idiot cartoon character's. I remembered what I'd been told.

"The Rat?" I asked. "Are you The Rat?"

"Yes." The voice sounded relieved. "Give the girl a gold frigging star."

I frowned. "So, how come I can't see you then? Are

you invisible?" Hm. An invisible contact might come in handy.

"No, but . . ." The Rat seemed to hesitate for a moment. "I wasn't sure if you were ready to see me. I look a little . . . different than I think you might assume."

"Different? How so?"

Was he scarred? Burned? Disfigured? I was the last person he should be worried about judging him on that. He could be the Elephant Man and I, for one, would feel his pain. I could see the beautiful soul lost behind the scarred face. He'd be tender. Sweet. And we'd fall in love—

"They call me The Rat, right?"

—and we'd live happily ever after until we got back to the present year, where we would both be able to see that awesome plastic surgeon I'd interviewed a few months ago about celebrity scarring and—

Oh. I should probably be paying attention.

"Right. The Rat. Who'd you rat out, anyway?" I asked. "And how do I know you won't rat me out next?"

The Rat gave a long wheezy sigh. "Not The Rat as in ratting someone out. The Rat because . . . well . . ."

Suddenly I felt something scamper across my feet. I leapt back, startled, managing to inadvertently slam my body into the chain-link fence. But the discomfort of wire gouging into my back was nothing compared to the shock of what I found at my feet.

A massive brown rat, complete with long bald tail, stood on his hindquarters and twitched his nose at me. But it wasn't the creature itself that threw me. I was never one of those silly girls who ran from rodents. It was the uncanny disapproving expression on his furry face that got me. Almost . . . human-like. Kind of channeling Nicodemus from *The Secret of NIMH*, except less friendly and more . . . annoyed.

"You're . . . ? You're . . . ? Oh my god! You're really . . . ?"

"Can you stop babbling for one second, please?"

I did. Mostly because I couldn't manage to form words after seeing what I just saw. It seemed impossible, but there was no denying it happened. The rat spoke. English words came out of his fuzzy little lips.

"Eesh. And you wonder why I didn't want to show myself. You women are all the same. What the hell is it about bald tails and beady eyes that cause you all to go wacko? I mean, you could easily crush me with your foot." He paused, then added, "Uh, not that I'm suggesting you do that."

I stopped screaming as the realization hit me. (Yes, I know, a little slow . . . it'd been a long day.) I swallowed hard. "You're . . . ?" I started, staring at the fuzzy creature as it stared back up at me. *"You're—?"*

"Wow. They sent an articulate one this time. Excellent."

My eyes widened in disbelief. His mouth had moved. He'd really talked. The creature before me was an actual, real live talking rat. How the hell . . . ? I so wished Jenny was here with her camera. Or any photographer, for that matter. We'd have the biggest exclusive story of the millennium.

Rats that rant, tonight at eleven.

"How can you talk?"

"How can I talk? I open my mouth and stuff comes out. I mean, I'm sure there's a scientific explanation as to how air is expelled through your vocal chords while your mouth and tongue shape the actual words, but you really don't need those kinds of details, do you?"

Wow. He not only talked, he'd mastered the art of sarcasm. Nice.

I crouched down onto the dirt-caked pavement to check him out more carefully. Getting up my nerve, I reached down to touch him. To see if he felt real.

"Hey! Watch the fur. Do you enjoy it when people start poking you?"

I pulled my hand away. "Um, sorry," I muttered. Touchy little fellow, wasn't he?

"So are you ready to listen now?" he asked impatiently.

"Uh, yeah. I guess?"

"Good. As I was saying just before you decided to take me on a marathoner's tour of Chicago, we need to talk."

"O-kay."

"As I mentioned before, I'm not just a rat. I'm *The* Rat. As in, your contact The Rat. Back in the Year of our Lord 2006, I'm Special Agent Rogers, and I'm six foot, two hundred pounds soaking wet, thank you very much. Pretty good-looking, too, in case you were wondering. The ladies love me."

"Uh . . . okay." I nodded, trying to accept it all. I mean, hey, why not? This morning I thought time travel was a ridiculous concept. So why not sarcastic talking rats who were really good-looking special agents in disguise? At the rate things were going, by the end of the day it was more than likely I'd be believing in the Tooth Fairy, the Easter Bunny, and maybe even jolly old St. Nick.

"Anyway, they sent me back here as a rodent to check out the scene, see what's going on. Figured a small creature like this could do better recon than a human. After all, I can slip into rooms and eavesdrop on private meetings without anyone knowing they're being watched."

"Very convenient."

"You'd think so, huh? But there are lots of on-the-job hazards. Cats, for one. You haven't lived 'til you've seen what a four-story Fluffy looks like when it's ready to go all postal on you. Scar-y. And then there's picking up chicks. There's a lotta lookers here in the twenties. Ain't even one of them interested in getting it on with a foot long rat. Go figure."

I shook my head. We were definitely verging on T.M.I. territory. I needed to reel the rodent in.

"So . . . what should I be doing? I'm a little lost here, to tell you the truth."

The Rat sighed a squeaky sigh—admittedly kind of cute, now that I'd gotten used to him—and gave me the once-over with his beady eyes. "Jeez Louise," he muttered. "They get dumber every time."

I frowned. "That seems a bit harsh coming from someone who has a fuzzy nose and whiskers."

"Fine. Make fun. I can take it. After all, I'm just some poor rat." He looked so miffed that I almost felt bad. Almost. At the same time, he was supposed to be my contact. Didn't the job description include some rudimentary tact?

Still, it was obvious that I needed The Rat more than The Rat needed me. And that meant I had to play nice. (*Or was that mice?*)

"Look, I'm sorry," I said in what I hoped sounded a somewhat apologetic voice. "We're on the same side here. Let's not fight. Let's plan." I leaned against the chain-link fence. "As you probably know, I need to find Nick Fitzgerald, member of the Time Warriors and all-around pain in my ass. He's evidently been sent back in time into someone else's body, and I need to figure out whose. Have you happened to see him in your travels?"

The Rat shrugged. Well, as much as something without any real shoulders could manage. "Nope."

I sighed. Oh well, that would have probably been too easy.

"So then, what's the plan?" Maybe he at least had some clever scheme to help me figure things out. After all, he was a pro at this kind of scenario, while I was simply stumbling my way through.

"Plan? You tell me. Jeesh, you're slow."

Grrr. Why had they even bothered sending me someone so useless and unpleasant? I gritted my teeth. "Why did they send you back here again?"

The Rat frowned. "To keep an eye on you, honey. To make sure you don't do anything stupid like change history yourself."

Oh. Nice. So he wasn't here to help me. He was here to babysit me. To make sure I didn't get into any trouble. So much for a super partner in saving the world. A Robin to my Batman. A Stimpy to my Ren. A Scrappy to my Scooby Doo.

"Fine. Then, if you're not going to help or be a productive member of my team, I suggest you go take a hike," I said, hands on my hips. "Raid the garbage. Find some cheese. Hook up with a sexy female rat and procreate. Whatever gets your rodental rocks off."

"You know, you're lucky I'm getting good overtime on this gig, princess," The Rat snarled back. "Because with an attitude like yours, I should just leave you to flounder out here in the streets and not tell you where you live or how to get there."

D'oh. Way to go, Dora.

"Uh, I'm sorry," I apologized quickly. "It's just been a . . . rough day. You know how it is."

The Rat twitched his nose at me but didn't respond. Great. Just great. I stifled a sigh.

"I would be eternally grateful if you were to show me where I lived," I tried.

Another twitch. More silence. Grrr.

"Uh, my, what a shiny fur coat you have?" I tried. "I've always dug a guy with white whiskers."

The Rat rolled his beady eyes and chuckled. "Nice to see how far you'll grovel for a warm bed." He laughed a laugh that I was pretty sure was at and not with me. "Fine. Let's go." He turned and scampered down the road. I followed him through the windy streets until we came to a somewhat dilapidated brick rooming house that rose up next to a weedy vacant lot.

"This is it," The Rat informed me. "Watch out for the landlady, though. She's a nosy one. Doesn't really care for rats either, I've found. Might be better off sticking me in your pocket until we get up to your room."

I squirmed a little at the idea of touching The Rat, never mind slipping him into a pocket of my dress and bringing him up to the area where I would sleep, but what could I do? I gingerly reached down and picked him up. His claws tickled my palms and I almost dropped him as I tried to tuck him into my dress pocket.

"Watch it!" he growled. "It's a long way to fall and there ain't any rat hospitals to set my leg if you break it."

"Sorry," I muttered.

"Louise! Who are you talking to?"

I looked up at the sound of a raspy smoker's voice from inside the building. A minute later, a heavyset, gray-haired woman came out the front door, wringing her hands in a dish towel. She wore a long colorless nightdress and her silver hair was pulled up into a Gibson Girl bun.

"Louise," she said, shaking her head disapprovingly. "You don't have a beau out here, do you? You know what I think of you girls bringing boys around. I run a proper house here. Respectable. And I plan to keep it that way."

"Her name is Mrs. Landers," The Rat squeaked in my pocket.

"No, Mrs. Landers," I said. "There are no boys here. I was just talking to myself. I, um, do that sometimes. I know, I know. My mom thinks it's odd, too."

Mrs. Landers narrowed her eyes and scanned the dark landscape beyond her front porch. Evidently Louise wasn't one to be taken on her word alone. But since the real guy I was talking to was a foot long and sitting nicely in my pocket, I felt I was pretty safe.

"I hope not, Ms. Rolfe," Mrs. Landers said at last, looking almost disappointed. "Because just a few minutes ago, a fella came by looking for you." I raised my eyebrows. Interesting. "Who was it?"

"Some *man*," Mrs. Landers said, spitting out the word. From the way she said it, I gathered Mr. Landers wasn't such a gem of a husband. "Said his name was Sam, and he wanted to make sure you got home alright."

A shiver of delight tickled down my spine. Sam had come here? To make sure I was okay? Wow, maybe he really did have a thing for me—er, Louise.

"Who the hell is Sam?" The Rat hissed from my pocket. I ignored him.

"Well, if he comes around again, you can tell him that I did," I said diplomatically, even though what I really wanted to say was that she could tell him to come up to my room and have his wicked way with me. Somehow I didn't think that would go over so well, however. With either Mrs. Landers or The Rat.

Stupid twenties chaperone types.

"Very well, Ms. Rolfe. Have a pleasant night." Mrs. Landers shot me one more suspicious glance from over her bifocals and disappeared into the house.

"So, which one's my room?" I whispered to The Rat as I made my way inside. The squeaky screen door slammed shut behind me, leading to a final rebuke from my dear landlady.

"Second floor. Third door on the left," The Rat hissed. "Now who the hell is Sam?"

"No one. Just some guy I met at the club."

"Does he already know Louise? You aren't going around changing history your first day out, are you?"

"Dude, will you relax? Take a cheese-flavored chill pill. I've got it all under control."

"Sure you do, princess. And you've got a bridge in Brooklyn you wanna sell me, too, right?"

I ignored him, climbing up the flight of stairs and heading down the hall. I fished through my purse for a key and found one. Sure enough, the rodent hadn't steered me wrong. The key worked and the door swung open.

I stepped inside and surveyed the place. Ugh. My room was just as lackluster as the rest of this 1929 world. Where was Pottery Barn when you needed it? Even an IKEA wouldn't go amiss here.

The walls were covered in a dark blue wallpaper that succeeded in sucking out all the light. The furniture was solid, but über plain. A kitchenette sat against one wall, a bed with gray sheets and blankets against the other. A couple of chairs, a coffee table covered with movie magazines, and a big-ass radio-like thing. That was it.

I stared at the radio in dismay. I had conveniently forgotten there was no TV in the twenties. Now I was going to miss who got kicked off *American Idol*. (Um, not that I watch that cheesy show. Really. What I was truly going to miss were the . . . documentaries on . . . important stuff. Yeah.)

You know, this wasn't at all what I'd expected as far as furnishings for a mob boss's girlfriend. I mean, where were the perks of sleeping with the head honcho? Look at Ray Liotta's chick in *Goodfellas*. He'd set her up with a really nice place. A little tacky, I suppose, but it was the seventies. Louise needed to start demanding her right to a good interior designer. I was thinking, until I get my matching sofa and love seat, Mr. McGurn ain't getting his jollies.

"Bleh," I remarked, as I pulled The Rat from my pocket and set him on the floor. "This place sure is dull."

"You were expecting The Four Seasons, perhaps?"

I shrugged. "At least something up to Motel Six standards."

"May I remind you that you're on a mission for the FBI, not a vacation to Club Med?"

"You can remind me all you want. Doesn't mean I'm going to suddenly enjoy sleeping on this lumpy bed." I sat down on the sleeper in question and bounced a few times. It creaked under my weight.

"Well, I'm sure it's more comfortable than the hard wood floor where I'll be sleeping,"

I looked down at The Rat. He looked up at me. I sighed.

"Fine," I relented. "You can sleep on the foot of the bed. But no squirming around at night. If your nasty bald tail brushes against my foot while I'm asleep, I can't be held responsible for what I'll do."

The Rat laughed and scrambled up onto the bed. I suppressed a shudder. I couldn't believe I was allowing a rat to share my sleeping accommodations. Even if he was a secret agent in real life.

I yawned. It wasn't that late, but I was exhausted. And since there was no sufficient entertainment in this bleak little room, I had nothing better to do than go to bed. I got up and searched through Louise's drawers and found a little silk negligee. Hm. I was normally more of a boxers and T-shirt kind of gal (much to my ex-boyfriend's dismay), but this would have to do.

After heading to the tiny ceramic tiled bathroom and donning the ensemble, I crawled into bed, careful not to touch The Rat, who was already sound asleep and sawing logs like a lumberjack. I felt more than a bit skeeved out from slipping into someone else's sheets—even if that someone else was technically me. But hey, I guess I wouldn't be giving myself any diseases. At least not ones I didn't already have.

I sank back down onto the pillows, staring up at the gray ceiling. Then I reached over and flipped off the light and released a slow sigh.

One night in the twenties and I'd already been chased, kissed, and rebuked by a talking rat. I wondered what tomorrow would bring.

CHAPTER FOUR

"Are you *ever* going to wake up?"

I groggily opened one eye, then the other, and stared at the owner of the now familiar squeaky voice tickling my ear.

"Ugh," I said, squeezing my eyes closed again. The sunlight streaming through the window felt like laser beams burning my corneas. I had never been a morning person, and waking up in some random chick's body who had lived and died years before I was even born made getting up all the less attractive.

"What, you think you're on some Caribbean vacation? That you can sleep in and then take out the catamarans when you finally wander out of bed at noon? You have a lot of work to do, princess. It's three days before Valentine's Day and I'm willing to bet you haven't a clue as to how to find this man of yours, never mind how to convince him not to change history. I mean, sure, maybe a complete change in history doesn't mean much to you, but think of the rest of the world, O Selfish One. There are a few of us out there that actually are pretty Zen with life, the universe and everything, and would appreciate keeping things as they are."

I groaned, pulling the covers over my head to drown out his nagging. "I'm tired. World-saving can wait five more minutes."

"Sure. Five minutes here. Five minutes there. Pretty soon you've slept away your entire trip to the twenties. You know, I'm supposed to be freaking nocturnal and I was up with the sun. What's your excuse?"

"Okay, okay. Jeesh." I tossed away the covers with an exaggerated flair. "I'm up. Happy?"

"I'm stuck in the twenties as a talking rat, having to keep an eye on a moron like you. Take a guess at the level of my delirious joy."

"About on par with mine at being stuck with a dirty rodent who thinks he's freaking Albert Brooks."

"Touché, princess," the Rat replied, but I could almost hear approval in his voice. "Now get the hell up."

I rolled my eyes and slipped out of bed, crossing the room to the bathroom. Why, oh why, couldn't my twenties contact have been some leather jacket wearing sexy biker boy with really good massage skills? I mean was that so much to ask?

Someone like Sam? my brain queried as I caught my reflection in the dingy bathroom mirror. My lips still appeared somewhat puffy and scraped—slightly bruised, as if I'd been kissed senseless by someone with a strong, aggressive mouth. Which, of course, I had, but I was surprised to see the evidence remaining on my face the next

day. Louise's face, technically speaking. Evidently she
didn't heal as quickly—probably due to a lack of avail-
ability of Prada Shielding Balm in Tint 02. Poor Louise.
So deprived.

I pressed a finger against my lower lip and then released it. Hopefully the guy Louise was supposed to be
dating—the one who saw nothing negative about being
called "Machine Gun" to his face—wouldn't notice her
"just been molested by an oh-so-sexy friend" glow. Ugh. I
was not being a good caretaker of my twenties body.
Good thing I hadn't put down a big deposit on her or I'd
so be forfeiting it by the end of my stay.

I rinsed my face and headed out of the bathroom. After shooing The Rat out of the room (rodent or no, he
wasn't about to see me/Louise naked) I approached the
chest of drawers to find something to wear. I rummaged
through lacy, belty undergarments and other frilly
unidentifiable things. Yuck. Why couldn't Nick have
chosen to hang with Charley Manson or something as
his crooked time travel mission? At least in the sixties
women could do the casual jeans/T-shirt thing. Not to
mention I could have been hanging out with movie stars
in oh-so-cool San Fran instead of gangsters in chilly,
gritty Chicago.

I glanced around the room. How the hell was I supposed to figure out what to wear? I had no idea what
made up an acceptable day outfit and what was only for
night. Stupid FBI, sending me back in time without letting me Google "twenties fashion" first. And I certainly
wasn't going to ask The Rat's advice. He'd get way too

much joy from the idea of teaching me Fashion 101, little fuzzy know-it-all that he was.

Then my eyes fell upon my salvation, lying innocently on the coffee table. A magazine. Rock on. I grabbed it and paged through, checking out the various outfits on the movie stars and models. Actually, twenties fashion was kind of cool in a weird way. I mean, it was so loose and flowy. You didn't have to worry about any tummy bulge or your thong hanging out the back of your low rise jeans. And I kind of dug the rebelliousness of it all. These girls didn't care about the conventions of their proper mothers, the modest long skirts and restricting corsets. And yet they weren't trying to be overly sexy, either. If anything, there was sort of a strange androgyny about the look. Potato sack dresses, unlaced brown floppy boots. Rolled up stockings. It was definitely the "I care enough to look like I don't care at all" kind of look. Sort of like the grungy Von Dutch-wearing, white trash-imitating rich kids in present day. They tried so hard to look like they had just rolled out of bed as they donned designer trucker hats and two hundred dollar wife beater T-shirts.

So I threw on a shapeless and sleeveless black dress and pulled on some silk stockings (my kingdom for Spandex blend!) and slipped into a pair of scuffed brown boots. Then I rummaged through Louise's jewelry box and selected a long string of pearls and a cute little felt hat to complete the outfit and alleviate the need to do something presentable with my hair. I glanced in the mirror and decided I/Louise looked pretty damned cute if

I did say so myself. I wondered if Sam would think so, too. Not that I cared, of course. In fact, I hoped I wouldn't run into him again. He was way too distracting. I had to concentrate on finding Nick. Find him and stop him. Somehow.

One last glance in the mirror and I headed out the door. *Watch out, Nick. Dora the Explorer is on the case.*

I walked out of the rooming house alone. The Rat told me he had some reconnaissance to take care of, which was fine by me. I decided my best bet was to head to the club where I'd first made my appearance the night before. Not a hard decision, seeing as: one, it was the only place in this foreign time period that The Rat agreed to give me directions to (he'd been worried I'd spend the whole day shopping if he pointed me downtown); and two, I had no wheels and the club happened to be down the street.

I also figured it was about time to meet my infamous mobster boyfriend Jack "Machine Gun" McGurn. My heart rate sped up just at the thought. Would I be able to play a convincing Louise in front of him? Would he be able to tell something was off? I mean, how close were they, really? Evidently not too close, maybe, if she was having an affair with Sam. But still, you'd think most boyfriends would be able to tell if their girlfriends had been body snatched. (Uh, except if it happened during football season—then it might take a few months for the realization to kick in.)

I squared my shoulders and exited the tenement house. Oh well, I'd just have to do my best. Jack "Machine Gun" McGurn was the one behind the St. Valentine's Day Massacre. Therefore, it only made sense that Nick would be hanging around him in some way. Who knew? Maybe Nick had body snatched McGurn himself. Then I'd be, in a weird *Twilight Zone* sense, actually dating him again. Ugh. I hoped that wasn't the case. Way too effed up.

I walked down the street 'til I came to the speakeasy. I studied the building with a critical eye. It sure looked different during the day. A grungy warehouse from the outside with no sign. In fact, I probably would have passed right by it if it wasn't for someone I recognized hanging out by the door.

"Sam!" I cried, actually somewhat happy to see a familiar face. Well, sort of familiar, anyway. Handsome at the very least—somehow managing to be rugged and smooth at the same time. "How are you?"

He smiled widely, flashing straight white teeth. Why did he have to be so sexy? Why did Louise have to be going out with Machine Gun instead of him? Was the girl blind? Could she not see the potential in the man right in front of her? I mean, I understood that all women had different tastes in men. Some liked Matthew McConaughey, some preferred Clive Owen. But then there were some men like Brad Pitt who had universal appeal. Sam was a Brad Pitt type without a doubt, and surely Louise must have realized this on some underlying timeless level.

"Hiya, Louise," Sam drawled, leaning casually against the wall. "Up before noon. I'm impressed."

I felt my face instantly heat into a blush, not quite

knowing why. "Yeah, yeah," I said, forcing myself to sound nonchalant. "Whatever." I almost made the W gesture with my fingers, but then realized that, since *Clueless* wouldn't hit theaters for about sixty something years, he wouldn't have any idea as to what I was doing.

"You here to see Jack?" he asked, his multicolored eyes twinkling. "Or maybe someone . . . else?" He raised his eyebrows suggestively, and I couldn't help but giggle.

"You think I got out of bed before noon to see *you*?" I teased, unable to resist a little flirtation. "As if."

Whoops, lapsed into *Clueless* land again. I was an incurable valley girl when I was flirting.

"Maybe someday you won't have to get out of bed at all." He smirked. "If you're lucky."

I laughed, despite myself. He certainly had that arrogant swagger about him. "Don't you mean if *you're* lucky?"

"I'm not lucky, baby. I'm worthy." He took off his hat and bowed mockingly in my direction. "I'm the only one worthy of a girl like you."

"I heard you stopped by my place last night. Thought you didn't know where I lived."

He grinned. "I asked around. I make it my business to map out all the pretty girls."

"Oh and here I thought I was special."

"Oh, you're special all right. 'Specially for me."

I rolled my eyes.

He laughed, effectively breaking the spell. His eyes lightened, telling me it had all been in jest. "Anyway . . . Go in and see your boyfriend, kiddo," he said. "It was nice seeing you again."

I nodded, noting an odd sense of disappointment rolling through my stomach. What had I wanted—him to beg me not to go see Machine Gun? To head to some sleazy hotel with him instead, maybe? Well, that was never going to happen. And besides, I needed to concentrate on my mission. I wasn't on vacation, as Ratty would say. Still, Sam's presence was doing bad things to my goals and motivation, and I wasn't sure I minded the conflict.

I pulled open the door to enter the club. The lights were low and several slightly grungy men were hanging by the bar, sipping their drinks. The place was a lot classier at night. But then, so were most twenty-first century bars.

I scanned the nearly vacant dance floor, wondering how I was going to find Machine Gun's office without looking like I wasn't in Kansas anymore. The Men in Black really should have sent me back with some high-tech GPS device, or at the very least, a low tech map.

"Hey, Louise," greeted a big-ass bald guy in a tux. A bouncer type, probably. A human GPS on steroids. And most likely the answer to my lost-in-a-speakeasy prayers. "You here to see Jack?"

"Yes, please," I said in the most demure voice I could muster, crossing my fingers that he'd take me to the man in question. "Will you be so kind as to escort me?" Hopefully Louise wasn't normally an "I don't need a man to show me around" type of girl.

The bouncer nodded and gestured for me to follow. *Yes.* I stepped in behind him, and together we headed to the back of the club. He slipped a silver key from his pocket into the lock of a wooden door. After unlocking and pulling the door open, he started up a narrow flight of stairs, and I followed. At the top, there was an ornate hallway, lined with over-the-top gaudy decorations, alabaster statues and gold-framed paintings. The place was so overdone Italian that it almost looked like a parody. He rapped on one of the three doors, and a voice instructed that we enter.

I swallowed hard. *Here we go.*

The room was luxurious and slightly less cheesy than the hallway outside. Machine Gun evidently spared no expense when it came to his private domain, which made me all the more furious at Louise's dump of an apartment. The walls were paneled with dark burnished wood, and overly large paintings with jewel tones further complemented their surroundings. The furniture was heavy and well built. Mahogany, perhaps, though I was no expert. At the far end of the room was an oversized desk, piled with papers. Behind the desk sat a stout, Italian-looking man, slightly balding. Machine Gun? He wasn't a bad-looking guy. Just . . . ordinary. Not sexy. Not handsome.

Not Sam.

Louise must have been one of those "go for the power" or "go for the cash" types, I guessed. 'Cause, seriously— there was no freaking way a girl who looked like her could really be head-over-heels for this tool when she had Über Hottie Sam waiting in the wings. But if you mixed in the probability that Über Hottie was probably Über Poor Church Mouse, then I could see some reason as to the appeal of having a rich mobster as your boyfriend.

Sure, it wasn't the way I ever selected my men, but hey, considering my track record maybe Louise was onto something. As my mom always said, you could fall in love with a rich man just as easily as you could fall in love with a poor man. (It was getting the rich man to love you back that I always found to be the tricky part.)

The bouncer patted me on the shoulder and exited the room, pulling the door closed behind him. I stood back, not sure whether it was the right opportunity to make my presence known. Louise's boyfriend was currently red-faced and yelling at a skinny, nervous-looking guy standing by his desk. The poor chap was wringing his hands and shaking like a leaf as Machine Gun berated him.

"I told you to fix that fight. You said it was a done deal!" McGurn shouted, shaking his diamond-bedecked hand. "In fact, I think your exact words were, 'Don't worry, Machine Gun. It's all set. It's a sure thing.' So I'm a fair guy. I says to myself, 'Johnny knows what he's talking about. He's an upstanding guy, that Johnny. I think of him as a brother, in fact. Like we have the same mother.' That's what I tell people, Johnny. That's how much I like yah. Trust yah. And so I says, 'If he says it's a sure thing, then it's a sure thing.' No question in my mind. So I go and place my bet. And then I go to bed. I wasn't feeling good, you know. Indigestion from my mother's cooking most like. She's a good woman, but cooking! Mary, Mother of God. Anyways, Johnny, so I goes to bed. And I have sweet dreams about how when I wake up I'm going to be a rich man. I think I'm going to be woken up with a suitcase of money from the bet I placed on the fight. This 'sure thing.' But you know what, Johnny? It doesn't happen like that. In fact, it doesn't happen like that at all. No."

"L-look boss," Johnny stammered. "None of this is my fault. The fight was fixed. I swear ta God and the angels. It was a done deal. Louis was supposed to go down in the third. Beano promised me he would. It's not my fault Louis decided he wanted to be a hero. What am I supposed to do? Jump into the ring? Stop the fight 'cause the idiot decided to do a double-cross?"

"It's your job to know these things. It's your job to make sure these things don't happen. Now I have to whack Louis. What a waste."

"You don't have to whack Louis. Let me talk to him first. Let me see what's going on. He can redeem himself. He's a good fighter. He deserves another chance."

"No. If I give him a chance, then I look weak. I look like I'm saying, 'Machine Gun's going soft. He lets guys like Louis walk all over him. When he gives an order you can choose to follow it, or you can choose to disrespect him.' And then where does that leave me, huh? No. I'm not going down that road, Johnny. Louis is dead to me. And you're the one who's going to kill him."

"Ah, boss, but he's my brother. My own flesh and blood," moaned the man.

"All the more reason the bullet should come from your gun."

I shifted from one foot to the other, feeling more than slightly uncomfortable. Sure, I knew the guy was a gangster, but knowing that and hearing him order a real life whacking were two different things entirely. What if he discovered the truth? That I wasn't really Louise? Would he order me to be whacked as well? And what would happen if he whacked Louise's body while I was still using it? Would I simply bounce back into my own body? Or would I die myself? And if I died in Louise's body, what would happen to my body back in the twenty-first century?

Also, for that matter, where was my body back in the twenty-first century, anyway? Was I still in the FBI headquarters? Strapped to a chair? Or was Louise possessing me? Was the flapper taking a road trip to Rodeo Drive and maxing out my MasterCard as we speak?

I should have asked a ton more questions before letting them put me under.

The two men suddenly noticed me hovering at the entrance of the room. Machine Gun smiled widely and Johnny looked at me like I was an angel from Heaven, come to save his soul.

"Johnny, as you can see, I have a visitor. Why don't we discuss this later?" Jack said, ushering him to the door. Johnny nodded, almost bowing in his relief. McGurn got up and walked him to the exit, pulling the heavy door shut behind him.

Now I was alone with Al Capone's right-hand man. Can we say, *gulp*?

Jack turned to me, his angry scowl replaced by a big goofy grin. He walked back to his desk, sat down in his chair, and patted his thighs.

"What you being shy for, doll face? Come sit on old Jackie's lap."

Ugh. Here we go. I swallowed hard, praying (without much optimism) that sitting on the guy's lap was all I'd be required to do in this scene. Approaching him, I climbed gingerly onto his wide lap, wrapping my arm around his shoulder. His skin was hot to the touch and his face dewy with sweat.

"How you been, Louise?" he asked, reaching up to stroke my hair with his pudgy fingers. When Sam did the same thing the night before, the gesture had sent tingles to my toes. Jack's touch only served to make me slightly nauseated. Or maybe that was his smell. Garlic and onions. Bleh.

"I was worried about you," he said. "I sent Tommy down to look for you when the coppers came and raided the place last night. He said he didn't see you anywhere." He shook his head in disapproval. "How come you didn't come up to my apartment?" He gestured to a suite of rooms just off the office. "You know that's the plan when we're raided."

I shrugged. As if I could be expected to know "the plan." I didn't even know where Louise kept her toothbrush. Still, what was I supposed to tell the guy? *Uh, yeah, instead of swinging by your office I hid in your gin cellar and got it on with an Adonis who works for you?*

Somehow I didn't think that would go over so well.

"It was . . . crazy," I explained, making it up as I went along. Luckily, as a reporter, I was used to ad-libbing. "Total chaos. There was no way I could make it to your apartment without the cops getting me. So I ended up taking off and going back to my place."

To my relief, Jack nodded his approval. "You're a smart girl," he said, ruffling my hair. "Don't want my baby here to get arrested. Especially not this week. As you know, we can't be drawin' a lot of attention to ourselves right now. Not with the plan all in place."

I raised my eyebrows. "Plan?" I said, hoping I didn't sound too eager. Was he talking about the St. Valentine's Day Massacre? Now we were getting somewhere.

"Louisey, what are you doing?" he asked suddenly, his face morphing into a frown. "You know what I like, baby. Don't hold out on me."

Uh . . .

"Why don't you tell me what you like, darling," I cooed. "I like to hear you say it." *Heh. Score one for Dora.*

Jack grinned a toothy grin. "Yeah?" he asked, looking eager as a puppy dog. I tried not to wince as I imagined all sorts of disgusting acts that could make up what he liked. "Well, um . . ." He blushed a deep crimson, making me worry all the more what he was about to ask me. "I'd . . . I'd like you to suck on my toes."

Okay. That would be score one for Jack. Or maybe ten. Hell, I think Jack just won the whole kitty.

I stared at him, wide-eyed and horrified. Oh God. Please, please, please let "suck on my toes" be a code phrase for something else entirely. Preferably something that had absolutely nothing to do with the process of me wrapping my mouth around his dirty little piggies.

81

But it seemed my luck wasn't being a freaking lady tonight. I watched in horror as Jack leaned over me to start taking off his shoes.

Ew. Ew. *Ew.*

Don't panic, Dora. You're in an office with a man who has no problem shooting people in the head. If the guy wants his toes sucked, you'd better get on your knees and start sucking.

"Uh," I tried to form words as I watched him peel off his socks, revealing filthy feet with yellowed (probably fungus-ridden) toenails. "Uh . . ." It wasn't my most articulate moment, but I doubted anyone would blame me. I had already felt a bit nauseated when I woke up this morning. Now my stomach started to churn.

He wiggled his disgusting feet in my direction. "Suck them, baby," he said, leaning back in his chair and closing his eyes.

"How about I . . . wash them first?" I suggested in sheer desperation. "I'll just go fill a bowl with warm water and soap. It'll feel really good, I promise."

Jack opened his eyes. "That sounds nice," he agreed. "You can get a bowl in the bathroom down the hall."

Breathing a sigh of extreme relief, I exited the office and found the bathroom. Hopefully he'd be satisfied with this amount of toe action, because there was no way I was sucking on those bad boys. I didn't care how much non-toe-suckage would change history. Even if that meant I'd never be born, like in the case of Marty McFly in *Back to the Future.* It'd almost be worth it just to avoid the dirty deed.

I reentered the office and walked over to Jack's desk. He was leaning back in his chair, eyes closed. Cursing the

Men in Black and Nick the Prick for putting me in this position, I got down on my knees and set the bowl by his feet. I picked up one foot, then the other, and placed them in the bowl. He moaned in pleasure as I started scrubbing.

I *so* wanted to puke.

"So, um, this plan you mentioned?" I began. If I was stuck washing his feet, I was damn sure going to get some useful information out of the sacrifice. "What's the deal with that?"

"You forget again?" Jack chided. "Not much goin' on in that pretty little head of yours, is there?"

I suppressed a grimace. Poor Louise.

"You know me," I said, with a forced airhead giggle.

"Yes, I do." He smiled and leaned down to kiss the top of my head. "Well, as you know, Al and I have been warring with Bugs Moran and his Northside boys for a while. Al thinks it's a good time to strike."

Al as in the infamous Al Capone? How fascinating! I was living history here. That almost made foot washing worthwhile. Almost.

"So we called up Moran's men. Told 'em we was a bootlegger from Canada with a big shipment, going cheap. They're gonna meet the men over on Clark Street, Valentine's Day morning. Then, our men are gonna dress up as cops and bust 'em. Except that, of course, what we're really gonna do is shoot them dead. When Bugs Moran takes his dying breath, he's gonna think he was shot by a copper. It's a beautiful thing, really."

"Right." I suppressed a grimace. I mean, I knew that

was the plan, but hearing it told with such zeal was a tad disturbing.

"Of course the Feds are gonna expect that Al and I are behind any kind of hit on Moran. They've already been poking their noses around too much lately as it is. That raid last night? I mean, what the hell was that? Half of Chicago's finest were in that joint already, having a gin. The other half comes to bust the joint? Doesn't make sense tah me." He shook his head. "Anyway, Al's already headed down to Florida so he won't be nearby. And you, my little turtledove, are going to be my alibi," he said, ruffling my hair again. It was going to look like I'd been through a wind tunnel by the time he was done with me.

"I am?"

"Yeah, three days from now we're going to check in to the Stevens Hotel. To celebrate Valentine's Day, you know? We'll dine out and go to the theater. We'll be seen everywhere except the scene of the crime. Then, if the Feds come askin' questions, I can just say I was with my best girl."

"Sounds like a good plan," I ventured cautiously. "Um, has anyone come to you suggesting you change it at all?" Maybe Nick was one of McGurn or Capone's hitmen and would suggest a change in plans in order to ensure Bugs Moran woke up in time to get killed with the rest of them.

Jack shook his head. "Ain't no one gonna change the plan, doll. It was set up by me and Al. And what's set up by me and Al, stays set up."

"Well, that's good then." At least it appeared Nick would have his work cut out for him.

"Look sweetheart, don't go worrying your pretty little head about all of these details," Jack said, reaching down to ruffle the hair on the head in question for a third time. God, that was getting annoying. Didn't he have any other gestures of endearment to spice things up? One that would allow me to keep my hair in a halfway presentable state? "It's all going to be fine. We'll whack Bugs and his Northsiders and be rewarded by Capone. You'll see. All you have to do is give me a weekend of your attention so I can wine and dine you like you deserve."

I smiled sweetly. "I'm looking forward to it, darling."

Jack grinned, evidently happy to have sated me. Then, to my utter horror, he once again wiggled his toes in my direction.

"My feet are clean, Louise. How about you suck on my toes now? You know I love when you do that, baby."

I stared at his toes. Damn it. The last thing in the known universe I wanted to do was put my mouth on those appendages. At the same time, it would be counterproductive to the mission to run out of the room screaming.

Nope. I'd have to do it. The future of the world as we knew it was depending on my ability to suck. But ew! There better be a damn good stipend waiting for me back in the twenty-first century for all these sacrifices I was making. Hopefully this got him off quick and wasn't an hour-long kink.

I pulled his foot onto my knee and leaned down to

take his toes into my mouth. But even after my extensive washing, they still reeked. My eyes watered and my stomach churned. Especially when, from my up close vantage point, I noticed black fungus growing under several nails.

Just do it, Dora. You have to do it.

I opened my mouth. Closed my eyes . . .

Oh God. My stomach gave out as my mouth came in contact with his big toe. I tried to pull away, but it was too late.

Yes, I, Dora Duncan, vomited on the mob boss's bare feet.

CHAPTER FIVE

Jack let out a roar of outrage as he yanked his foot away. He plunged it in the bowl of water, which had also, unfortunately, been the recipient of much of my puke and thus didn't have a lot in the way of cleaning potential.

"What the hell did you do that for, Louise?" the mobster cried, his face practically purple with rage. I jumped up and backed away, just in time to avoid being punched in the mouth. Yikes.

"Oh God, I'm sorry," I cried, my hands flying in front of my face to ward off any more attempted blows. As if they'd really provide any protection from an angry mobster covered in puke. "I didn't mean—my stomach . . . Oh!"

This was worse than that time in college when I drank a few too many frozen strawberry margaritas at a party and, on the way home, threw up in the lap of the guy I had a crush on. Ken, at least, saw humor in the admittedly unpleasant situation and still wanted to date me.

Jack looked like he'd sooner tear out my insides and feed them to hungry pigs than go for dinner and a movie any-time soon.

"I'll, um, get you something to clean that up," I stammered, backing away toward the door. *Way to fit in, Dora. Way not to cause a scene.*

"Don't fuckin' bother. Just get the hell out of here," the mobster growled. "And send Tommy in here to clean up this fucking mess."

"Um, okay. I'm really sorry," I said, making backward steps toward the door, hoping I didn't trip or do anything else that would prolong my hasty exodus. It was a hope that soon vanished, as I proceeded to accidentally back into a wall—right into a very expensive-looking painting. I whirled around, trying to save it, but the painting crashed to the ground. The sound of glass shattering drowned out my cry of surprise and dismay.

But not Jack's. Not by a long shot.

"Goddamn it, get out!" Jack bellowed. "Dumb Dora!"

Dumb Dora?

Dora?

I stopped dead in my tracks, fear dripping like melting icicles down my backside. Oh. My. God. He just called me by my twenty-first century name. Was my cover blown? Did he know who I really was? How could he? Unless . . .

Was Nick hiding out in this mobster's body all along? Telling me to suck his toes, just to see if I'd do it? Was he really clued in to me this whole time? Bastard!

"Nick?" I ventured softly, still staring at the smashed painting and not daring to turn around.

Turn around and he may shoot.

Then again, he may shoot anyway.

"Who the hell is Nick?"

Oh. Thank God. I released the breath I hadn't realized I was holding. Of course. I was being completely ridiculous. This guy wasn't Nick. There was no way this gross, disgusting creature was the dashing war correspondent Nick Fitzgerald. No way was this grumpy garlic-and-onions smelling gangster my handsome, funny ex-boyfriend inside. What was I thinking?

"Uh, nothing. Forget it. I was just . . . Did you call me Dora?" Of course, I had to be sure. Even if this guy wasn't Nick, maybe he knew Nick. Maybe Nick had been here already and had blown my cover.

"It's an expression, genius. Dumb Dora. As in 'stupid fucking bitch who evidently needs to be bought a dictionary for her fucking birthday.'"

Oh.

Wow. I don't think I've ever in my entire life been so happy to be called a bitch.

"Right, of course," I babbled as my hand slipped around the doorknob. My escape route revealed itself with a loud creak. "Sorry. My mistake. I'll just . . . get out of your hair now. Go wash up . . . lie down. 'Cause, you know, I'm obviously sick and all."

I stepped out of the room and yanked the door closed behind me. Leaning against the hallway wall, I let out a long sigh of frustration. This time travel stuff was hard. Day two and I'd already managed to run for my life from the cops, make out with the wrong man, exchange jabs with a talking rat, and throw up on a gangster's feet after refusing to suck on his toes. Could things get any crazier?

And the worst thing was, I still had zero clue as to whose body Nick was hiding in, and what his world-changing plan entailed. Great. I was doing a stellar job at this whole time travel secret agent thing.

I headed for the bathroom—didn't want to walk around with puke breath the rest of the day. I found toothpaste in the cabinet, encased in what appeared to be a lead tube. Now there was a health hazard if I ever saw one. Buy teeth cleanser, get a side of lead poisoning for free.

I debated whether to use it, then decided to take a chance. After all, one brushing couldn't hurt. And my breath smelled really, really bad. Besides, it'd be poor Louise that had to suffer the after-effects, not me.

I squeezed out a dollop and finger-brushed my teeth, not trusting the random used toothbrushes sitting on the counter. I didn't know which one, if any, belonged to Louise, and I wasn't taking any chances. In fact, even if I knew which one was hers, I also knew where her mouth had been, and was safer using a finger.

After washing up, I clumped down the narrow flight of stairs and opened the door that led back into the club and out to freedom. As I stepped into the main ballroom, a man jumped out in front of me, blocking my path. I looked up.

Sam.

"Hiya, again," he said cockily, taking off his fedora and bowing slightly. I raised an eyebrow. He certainly was a confident one, wasn't he?

"What do you want now?" I growled, annoyed that his very presence made all the hairs on the back of my neck stand on end and my fingers tremble. Lousy, traitorous fingers. I shoved them behind my back.

"How's your *boyfriend?*" Sam asked, a mocking twinkle in his devastating blue-green eyes.

"He's great, actually. Really great."

Or he will be as soon as he wipes all the vomit from between his toes. Not that I was going to inform Sam of that little technicality. I wondered if my breath still smelled bad. He was definitely close enough to know.

"Excellent." Sam grinned. "Glad to hear it. I adore hearing about couples who are deeply in love and not using one another for sex and financial stability."

I frowned. Wow, that was a brazen jab at Louise and her choices. Who did he think he was, anyway?

"Jealous much, darling?" I couldn't resist asking.

Sam glanced around the room, as if checking to see if anyone was paying attention to us. But the only people there were sidled up to the bar, mesmerized by their illegal gin and tonics. He turned back to me, grinning wickedly, and leaned in for a peck on my unsuspecting lips. I let out a cry of outrage.

"Hey, you can't do that!" I scolded, even though there was a part of me that couldn't help but be delighted. Truth be told, the quick brush of his lips was enough to light up every nerve ending in Louise's body. Kind of pathetic, when you thought about it. Yet also secretly delicious.

"I am Sam. I can do anything."

"Well, I am Louise. And you can't kiss me."

"I just did, baby." He grinned again, flashing a row of pearly white teeth. How did he manage to keep them so bright when laser whitening wouldn't be invented for decades?

"Well, it won't happen again."

"We'll see about that. I'm pretty sneaky, you know. I might just steal a kiss from you when you're not looking. Maybe at the party tonight, even."

"Uh, party?" There was a party? Tonight? Was this something I should know about?

A high-pitched female voice interrupted. "Of course, silly!" I whirled around and my eyes fell upon a real life flapper girl. She was about five-one, with jet-black bobbed hair, dark raccoon rimmed eyes, a powdered white face, and little red bow lips. She wore a loose-fitting tunic dress with a dropped waist and unlaced boots on her feet. How utterly adorable! She looked exactly like Catherine Zeta Jones in *Chicago*.

"Well hello, Daisy," Sam said, looking more than a bit disappointed. "Nice to see you again."

The little black-haired bombshell shot him a glare and then turned to me. "Louise, I've been lookin' everywhere for yah. Where *have* you been hiding?" she asked, grabbing my arm and pulling me away. Away from Sam. I couldn't help but glance back at him as she dragged me across the dance floor. He'd folded his arms across his chest and was watching me with an amused smile. When he caught my eye, he winked. I shook my head and turned away.

"Where are we . . . ?" I began to ask the flapper as we reached the other end of the ballroom.

Daisy stopped walking and released her hold on my arm. "Away from Sam, of course," she said. "I know you think he's the cat's meow and all, Louise, but you gotta stop letting him kiss yah like that. Especially in public. You finally got a decent fella. A daddy with dough. You wanna mess that up because you're carrying a torch for some ragamuffin like him?"

"I—" I wasn't sure how to respond.

"You wanna be a showgirl forever? Then you go pet Sam. In fact, you go on and have a petting party for two in his struggle buggy. Or do yah wanna live the life of luxury? The one we always talked about all these years? Then stay with the big cheese, Louise. He may be a flat tire, but he's got the rubes."

"Uh . . ."

Daisy laughed, probably at my pathetic attempt to be articulate when I hadn't the slightest clue what she was discussing.

"Okay, okay. I'll stop beating my gums," she apologized. "Butt me." She looked at me expectantly.

"Wha . . . ?" Butt her? What the hell did that mean? I was so lost it wasn't even funny.

"Hello? Anyone home?" she said, waving a red-nailed hand in front of my face. "A ciggy? You got a ciggy?"

Oh. *Butt* me. As in a butt. A cigarette. Bleh. Talk about remedial Slang 101. Even I should have figured out that one.

"Oh. No. Sorry."

She shook her head, as if gravely disappointed in my lack of tobacco. "Wait here."

I watched as she walked over to the bar and started

talking to the bartender. She was a little sprite who couldn't stand still for a millisecond, bobbing her head to some inaudible beat. Her nasal voice echoed through the nightclub. In short, she was exactly what I always imagined a flapper to be like. Almost scarily stereotypical.

Daisy skipped back over to me a moment later with a pack of Lucky cigarettes in her hand. She opened the box and held them out to me. I shook my head.

"Why on earth not?" she asked, lighting hers. I coughed at the plume of smoke she exhaled. With California practically making smoking a capital crime against humanity punishable by death, I hadn't been around a smoker in a while.

"I'm, um, trying to quit," I said. "Those things will kill you, you know."

Daisy looked at me as if I had just said I thought rabid, man-eating bunny rabbits were going to take over the world. Which I guess I understood. Back then supposedly no one knew that inhaling an unknown mixture of toxic chemicals on a regular basis could damage your body in any way, shape, or form.

"You're off your trolley, Louise," Daisy muttered. She took a deep drag and exhaled in my face. My eyes started to water. Nice. "If anything, ciggys are good for you. Help you lose weight." She patted her flat stomach. "You've seen the ad, right? 'Reach for a Lucky instead of a sweet.'"

I shook my head. As much as I would have liked to, there was no way I could start citing Surgeon General warnings or tell her I'd rather be fat than die of lung cancer. Guess history had to figure out the smoking thing on its own.

"Anyhow, let's blow this juice joint," Daisy suggested. "I know of a much classier place down the road."

I debated whether I should go with her, then thought, why not? After all, the more people I hung out with, the more chance I might be able to discover which of these suspects was actually Nick Fitzgerald in disguise.

Wouldn't it be funny if *Daisy* were Nick? I mean, there was no reason he couldn't have jumped into a girl's body, was there? If Special Agent Rogers could live as a rat . . .

But nah, Daisy had the vernacular down way too well. There would be no way Nick would have mastered twenties-speak so quickly, even if he was good with languages.

I followed Daisy over to a shiny black Ford and got in the passenger side door. It had a leather interior and the top was down, even though it was about twenty degrees out. She turned the key, put the car in gear, and we were off down the street, bouncing and swaying from side to side. Not much shock absorption in these things, evidently. The wind whipped through my hair and I grabbed at the dashboard to avoid being thrown from the car. My stomach started to go twisty again and I hoped our destination really was just down the street. After all, throwing up two times in one day would not be good for Spy Girl here.

"*Argh!*" I cried, as she swerved to not hit a car that had, for some reason, stopped smack dab in the middle of the road. Man, she drove worse than her *Great Gatsby* namesake, and I hoped there was no husband's girlfriend to run over, 'cause I sure as hell wasn't going to play Jay. I had enough to deal with in the next few days, without agreeing to go down for a murder I did not commit.

"Oh, I brought your costume for tonight, by the way," Daisy said, taking her eyes off the road to look over at me, much to my dismay. I grabbed onto the door handle as she turned back to the road, just in time to avoid smooshing a freaked-out squirrel. If they required driver's licenses back then, hers would surely be revoked for reckless endangerment. I wondered how many gin and tonics she'd tossed back before getting behind the wheel. Guess there was no Breathalyzer or drunk driving laws to worry about.

Which just left that whole death-and-dismemberment thing.

Wait a minute! Her words sank in and, suddenly, I was more afraid of her words than her driving ability. And that was saying something!

"Costume?" I repeated. "Uh, what costume?"

"Yeah, you know, for the party," she said, shaking her head, as if in disbelief of my stupidity. "What's with you today, Louise? You're doing your act at nine, remember?"

I swallowed hard. Oh God. I had an act? An act I was performing at nine? An act I was performing at nine in front of real live people?

Talk about being screwed.

"I, um, actually am not feeling well," I said, placing a hand on my stomach. "I don't know if I'll be able to go on tonight."

Daisy laughed. "You slay me, Louise. You really do. Of course you're going on."

"But I think I'm sick. I threw up earlier."

"You'll feel better after a few mint juleps."

"But—"

Daisy yanked at the steering wheel, dumping the car with a screech on the side of the road. I nearly toppled out of the door.

"Goddamn, you are a sucky driver!" I cried, rubbing my arm angrily. I was going to be black and blue for a week.

"And you, Louise Rolfe, are a showgirl," Daisy retorted, wagging a red fingernail at me. "A showgirl with a show tonight. No, not only a show. A show at the swanky home of movie producer Don Wags. And I, your best friend in the whole world, will not allow you to miss your opportunity to show off in front of him." Her gaze softened and she reached over to squeeze my shoulder. "I know you're nervous, honey, but you'll be swell, I promise."

I sighed. Nervous didn't begin to explain it. Not to mention the fact that I wasn't sure what would happen to the known universe if I messed up this act. What if Louise was destined to go to Hollywood after being discovered at a party by this Don guy? There was no way he was going to discover her when she was me. I mean, I sang like Ethel Merman on helium and danced as gawkily as Baby in *Dirty Dancing*—pre–Patrick Swayze's dance lessons. Not to mention the fact that I didn't know any twenties tunes.

Then again, I *had* been queen of karaoke back in college. . . .

Daisy reached into the backseat and pulled out a beautiful beaded black dress. She handed it to me and I fingered the long black fringe. It looked like something out of *Chicago*. Or something Satine would have worn in *Moulin Rouge*. . . .

And that gave me an idea . . .

CHAPTER SIX

The white-washed home belonging to Don Wags, movie producer and party host, rose tall and proud against the shores of Lake Michigan. I stared at it, somewhat in awe. It was an utter monster. Bigger than your stereotypical twenty-first century McMansion, for sure. In fact, I'd bet my Tivo there had to be fifty rooms, at least. (And you can be sure I don't make Tivo bets lightly.)

Outside, an array of white sparkly lights climbed the majestic oak trees and wrapped around squat rosebushes. Inside, every room was ablaze with light; and tinny, cheerful jazz drifted out of the house, effectively sound-tracking the night like a Busby Berkeley flick. In fact, the whole thing was like something out of a movie, and I couldn't believe I was witnessing it all in real life.

At least two dozen shiny black automobiles with os-tentatious hood ornaments were parked alongside the long circular driveway. A few looked abandoned, as if the drivers, in their extreme haste to let the party games begin, had just killed the engines without any regard for where they'd actually left their cars. Parallel parking, it seemed, had yet to be invented.

"Here we are!" Daisy exclaimed, yanking the steering wheel to one side and landing half on the front lawn. But I didn't care about lousy parking skills at the moment. I was too grateful to have survived the trip all in one piece. Even though a hideous car accident might have been more fun than my upcoming debut.

Would they buy my pathetic act? Or would I be lynched, revealed as the fraud I was? I sank into my seat, suddenly not wanting to go inside.

"Get a wiggle on," Daisy scolded as she hopped out of the car and into the night. "We're already late."

We were "already late" because we had already wasted the entire afternoon bar-hopping. My first full day in 1929 Chicago and I could already pen my own Zagat's guide, thanks to Daisy. Of course, unlike her, I was swigging soda the whole time. No way was I going to allow myself to get tanked and say something stupid to give my twenty-first century self away. Daisy, on the other hand, had nothing to give away, evidently, and she drank accordingly. I couldn't believe the five-foot-nothing was still standing after the amount of gin she'd poured down her throat.

I grabbed my costume and exited the car. Walking toward the house, Daisy and I passed myriad people, lounging, dancing, drinking and smoking on the front porch, as if they didn't have a care in the world. Kind of crazy, since it was about twenty-two degrees out and half of them had evidently forgotten to bring their coats. Alcohol heated the blood, I guessed. The men all wore smart tuxes, and the women had on loose-fitting party dresses of white, beige, and black, all light and chiffony and not at all appropriate for winter. Many wore felt caps or straw hats on their bobbed heads, and almost all held cigarettes placed in long, elegant holders in their well-manicured hands.

"Hi, Louisey," one of them slurred gaily as Daisy and I stepped onto the porch. "Yourha missin' a great pahhhty."

"Ab-sho-lute-ly," chimed in the curly redhead next to her. "Itsha truly mah-velous event."

Wow. I shook my head. Was-ted. You'd never know from this scene that liquor was technically illegal. It was fascinating what an utter failure prohibition turned out to be. Made a girl wonder what would happen if they just ended the war on drugs in the twenty-first century.

I studied the crowd. Those lazy, drunken thirty-something-year-old guys leaning against the wall probably had been soldiers overseas just ten years before, risking their lives to fight for their country. And the women could have been nurses at the time, angels in white, bandaging and comforting their wounded and dying men. Or they could have been back home . . . making, um, rivets? Or whatever random war thing that Rosie the Riveter chick made to help her boys overseas. Though technically she might have been from World War II; I couldn't remember. Whatever.

In any case, these partygoers certainly weren't necking and dancing and drinking and smoking a decade ago. It was almost as if the war had scarred them so much that they'd blocked it from their minds and adopted a sort of extreme opposite hedonism to deal with the memories.

Sort of like someone else I knew. Minus the hedonism, of course. In fact, minus anything remotely fun. Hm. Maybe these people were onto something. They certainly did look like they were having a great old time. Not a care in the world. Maybe I should follow their example. Lighten up a little and try to enjoy my time in the twenties. After all, how many opportunities does one have to travel back in time?

Though, I suppose, this was all easier said than done, considering I was apparently the evening's entertainment. And of course there was that whole pesky "find Nick the Prick and stop him from changing history" thing I had to contend with. Saving the world didn't leave much time for a girl to kick back a few and let her hair down.

Daisy grabbed my hand and pulled me along. We entered the house itself and followed a long ornate hallway that opened into a huge ballroom. Dim chandeliers dripped from the ceilings. Champagne fountains cascaded on scattered tables. Waiters dressed in black tuxes wandered around with trays filled with drinks or fancy-looking canapés. And a five-piece jazz band—with . . . was that Louis Armstrong on the trumpet?—played gaily from a raised stage on the far side of the room.

"Wow, good turnout," Daisy marveled. "But then, everyone always ends up at Don's house, whether they were invited or not."

I nodded, scarcely able to take it all in. This was incredible. Absolutely amazing. I couldn't believe I was actually here, witnessing a 1929 gala firsthand. The sights, the smells, the sound. It was overwhelming to my mortal senses. I wanted to memorize each and every detail so I could go over it all in my mind when the stimulation ended. Maybe I could even write a history book when I got back to the twenty-first century. Or at least a time travel romance. . . .

I scanned the room, watching as couples teamed up to dance, holding their hands out like waltzing, then bobbing from side to side in what seemed a silly manner to me, but must have actually been cool in their scene. Kind of a twenties version of the Hustle.

I sighed. There was no way I was going to find Nick in a crowd like this. Perhaps it'd be better just to enjoy myself and revisit the mission in the A.M.

"Daisy, my baby!"

I stepped back as an extremely intoxicated thirty-something man with watery eyes and pasty skin leaped through the crowd to throw his arms around my friend. He looked as if he were actually going to crush her small, birdlike frame and she didn't appear pleased to be crushed. A moment later, she grabbed him by his shoulders and pushed him away from her.

"I thought you were moving back to France, Scott," she scolded. "For Zelda."

The man hung his head, looking slightly abashed. "I am. I am," he insisted. "Tomorrow morning. Really. But I couldn't leave without one more party, now could I? Especially not at Don's. Don throws the absolute best parties. Everyone says so."

Daisy rolled her eyes. "Yes. Of course. You came for the party. As usual, Scott, you're all wet."

He grinned. "Well, of course I also came to see you, my love." He placed a hand on her forearm. She shook it away.

"How many times do I have to tell you, Scott? I am not your love," Daisy said with a scowl. "You have a wife, remember? A wife named Zelda? Probably suffering away in France all by her lonesome while you chase women at parties and drink far too much hooch?" She shook her head. "Men. I swear to God."

I scratched my head, trying to figure out what was niggling at the back of my brain. This guy. He seemed so familiar. But why? Who?

Then it clicked.

Scott.

Zelda.

Oh my God.

"You're F. Scott Fitzgerald!" I exclaimed, my eyes widening in disbelief. "You wrote *The Great Gatsby*!"

The man turned to me, his skin deepening into a blush, and shrugged his shoulders. "Yeah. Terrible failure that was."

"Failure? Are you kidding me? There's not a high school in the country that doesn't—" I stopped short. What the hell was I saying? I couldn't explain to this guy how his book had become a worldwide classic. I couldn't tell him about the multitude of movies inspired by it, including the one with the drool-worthy Robert Redford playing Gatsby. He'd think I was nuts.

Too bad I couldn't, though, seeing the look on his

face. He really thought he was a failure. Very sad that the world would not recognize his genius 'til after his death. I wished there was some way I could reassure him that his literary masterpiece would be remembered forever and that he'd go down in time as one of America's greatest writers.

"Well, *I* loved it," I said, changing tactics. I could at least compliment him personally. "I thought it was brilliantly written."

"You did?" he asked, looking amazed. In fact, he actually stopped pawing Daisy for a moment to turn and look at me. "Really? You're not just saying that to make polite party chatter?"

"I never make polite party chatter," I insisted. "I loved the book. Now, let me ask you. When you wrote the scene where Daisy and Gatsby were—"

"Come on, Louise," the real-life Daisy interrupted. She grabbed my hand and started dragging me away. "Scott, we'll see you later. We have to get Louise all dolled up for her act."

"What, I couldn't I ask him a question?" I sulked, as she led me through the crowd. I couldn't believe I'd missed my one opportunity to find out what really was behind one of my favorite novels. "I loved that book."

Daisy laughed. "You're probably the only one in the country who did. Besides, I'm sick of him carrying a torch for me. He needs to go back to his sick wife and stop following me around."

I stopped short, something dawning on me. "So . . . you're Daisy?"

She rolled her eyes. "Last I checked."

"No, I mean, you're Daisy in the book. He named the character after you."

The flapper let out an exasperated sigh. "I guess. Maybe. He's crazy and usually drunk. You can't take anything he says seriously."

"Yeah, but how great is it to have a character in a book named after you? Doesn't that thrill you just the littlest bit?"

"It gives me the heebie-jeebies, if you must know." Daisy shook her head, leading me through a side door and into a small changing room flanked by large mirrors. "As does old F. Scott himself."

I gave up. There was obviously no convincing her that being the literary inspiration for one of America's most important books was reason to be impressed.

Daisy shut the door behind us and held out her hands. "Here you go," she said. "You can change here. You're on in about fifteen minutes."

"Great," I said, rolling my eyes. "Just super." Only fifteen minutes 'til doom. 'Til everyone figured out that I was a complete fraud. I'd at least hoped for a half hour.

"Louise, what's wrong with you?" Daisy asked, her big brown eyes studying me with concern. "You're usually excited about performing. And you're so terrif at it, too. I wish I could be half as good on the stage as you. You're better than Mary Pickford, even. You could be in movies if you stopped messing around with the fellas and moved to Hollywood like I'm always sayin'. You know it's true."

Right. Forget fooling the whole party. I couldn't even fool one girlfriend.

"Sorry, Daisy. I was just thinking."

"You think too much, Louise," Daisy said, pressing her lips together sternly.

"Yeah, yeah." I glanced into the mirror. Louise's face stared back at me. She really was a pretty girl. All blonde and doll-like, with little bow lips and sparkling blue eyes. No wonder all the guys chased her. Well, at least Sam.

Speaking of Sam, I wondered if he'd arrived at the party yet. Hopefully, he'd be more than fashionably late and miss my act altogether. After all, seeing my sure-to-be lousy performance might vastly change his opinion of Louise's charm.

Not that that would necessarily be a bad thing. Then, at least, I wouldn't have to worry about resisting his advances anymore. His oh-so-tempting, smoldering advances. I wouldn't have to worry about his lips pressing against mine, crushing my mouth. And I'd have absolutely no reason to be concerned about his long fingers deftly exploring my body in a way that made me go slightly insane.

I shook my head. I needed to get my mind out of the Sam gutter and back on my impending doom . . . er, act.

Anyway, Daisy was right. I was completely overthinking this whole thing. Worrying about nothing. This was the twenties. I didn't have to do a Britney Spears dance routine, and no one cared if I had a voice like Celine Dion. (Of course, I couldn't lip sync like Ashlee Simpson, either.) These kids didn't even have MTV. (Or any TV to speak of, really.) Not to mention they were all so wasted, probably no one would even notice a few screwups from the night's entertainment.

And so what if they did? Missing a few notes would

never convince anyone I was a spy girl sent from the future to stop her ex-boyfriend from messing with the St. Valentine's Day Massacre. They'd probably just assume Louise Rolfe had had one too many glasses of champagne.

Yup. I could do this. I could fool them. I even had the perfect song. If only I could remember all the lyrics. . . .

I realized Daisy was staring into the mirror at me.

"What?" I asked, suddenly feeling self-conscious for no good reason. "Do I have pie on my face or something?" (I'd wolfed down three slices at the nearby diner on the way here. After all, I figured calories didn't count when you were using someone else's body, and I planned to take complete advantage. Poor Louise would probably weigh three hundred pounds when I was through with her.)

"Oh. No," Daisy said, her face instantly turning beet red. She quickly exchanged her fascination with the mirror for one of the floor. "You're fine. Sorry. Do you want me to get out of your hair or something?"

"Sorry," I said, feeling bad to boot her. Still, if I was going to pull this off, I needed all the practice time I could get. Which now was down to about seven minutes, including the costume change. "Do you mind if I have a little alone time? I've got to go over my song."

"Sure. No problem. I'll beat it," she said, her face falling. I cocked my head in confusion. The girl suddenly looked as if someone had just run over her pet hamster. What had I said? "I'm dying to go Charleston anyway."

"Uh, okay. Have fun," I said, more than a bit puzzled. What was her problem? I'd just asked for five minutes privacy, not the end of our friendship. Jeesh. Talk about overly sensitive. Was I missing something here?

Throwing me a halfhearted grin, Daisy turned to exit, shoulders slumped and dragging her feet.

I sighed. "Daisy?" I called out after her, not wanting to see her go away upset, even if I had no idea what I'd done to make her so sad.

She stopped, not turning around. "Yeah?"

"Thanks for the pep talk. It means a lot that you believe in me. Even if I don't always show it."

"Yeah?" Her voice sounded hopeful.

"Ab-so-lute-ly," I twanged, just like I'd heard others do. I was definitely getting the hang of this twenties speak.

"Good." Daisy turned around, her smile looking more real this time. "'Cause I do. I really do think you're terrif."

I laughed. "You're pretty terrif yourself. Now go Charleston." I turned back to the mirror. "I have an act to prepare for."

CHAPTER SEVEN

"And now, for this evening's entertainment—the one, the only, the sassy superstar of the south side. The vamp vixen of Victor Street. I give you, Miss Louise Rolfe."

The tuxedoed emcee put his hands together, urging the audience to start clapping as the spotlight shifted to me, over on stage left where I stood waiting in the wings, trembling like crazy.

I drew in a breath. I knew I should have had a few cocktails to steady my nerves.

Donning my biggest smile, I strutted out on the stage. God, there were a lot of people at the party. And every pair of eyes was fixated directly on me and my very skimpy, skintight outfit. Thank goodness I wasn't in my own skin. My big butt would have sent people screaming from the ballroom before my voice even began to offend their eardrums.

Stop thinking, Dora, and start singing!

I cleared my throat and took the mic off the stand. Here went nothin'.

> *"Come on, babe, why don't we paint the town?*
> *And all that jazz?"*

My voice sounded a bit on the trembly side as I recited the first lyrics of the only twenties song I knew. Not that it was an actual twenties song, I didn't think, but hey, *Chicago* the musical was set in the twenties and we were in 1929 Chicago, so I felt it was somehow appropriate. Better than that "voulez vous couchez avec moi" song from *Moulin Rouge*, which was the only other show tune I could think of with such short notice.

The only hitch was, I wasn't sure I actually remembered all the words to this one.

> *"I'm gonna put . . . blush . . . on my knees.*
> *And roll my . . . thigh highs . . . down.*
> *And all that jazz."*

That didn't seem quite right to me, but then, hey, the crowd wouldn't know the words either, so I guessed I could safely fudge them, right?

Right.

> *"Start the car*
> *I know a . . . totally cool . . . place*
> *Where the . . . cosmopolitans . . . are delish*
> *and you don't need mace."*

111

Much to my delight, the band behind me started picking up the melody in that clever way that always happens in the movies. At first this freaked me out a bit—like, how can they possibly play a song that's yet to be composed?—but then I decided not to look the gift accompaniment in the mouth. After all, I had more important things to ponder. Like, could I actually pull this off?

"It's just a . . . really loud bar
Where you'll fight and get a scar.
And all . . . that . . . jazz."

I strutted around the stage, channeling Catherine Zeta Jones, making up words as I went. This was kind of fun, actually. I scanned the crowd. They seemed into me, too, bobbing their heads and swaying from side to side.

They liked me! They really liked me! Maybe I was better than I thought. Maybe when I got back to the twenty-first century I could create my own act. Go on tour. Make millions.

"Put Aveda gel in your hair
And wear your Jimmy Choos to the fair
And all that jazz!"

Gaining courage, I pranced backwards over to the piano, placing my hands behind me and leaning up against it like the sexy singing siren they all thought I was.

And then I got an idea.

112

They wanted a show? Well, I was going to make love to the piano, baby. I could lie on top of it and roll around, just like Catherine did in the movie. Or Michelle Pfeiffer in *The Fabulous Baker Boys*. The audience would go wild. And long after I had returned to the twenty-first century, these party guests and I would remember me as that sexy soloing sister on the piano.

> *"Hold on, dude*
> *We're gonna bunny hug*
> *I bought some Excedrin*
> *Down at Eckerds Drug."*

For those of you who have never done so, it turns out hopping backwards onto a piano isn't as easy as one might expect. Especially when it turns out the piano in question has its cover open, and one hasn't turned around to notice this before making one's move.

Therefore, instead of sliding onto it and slinking around, I ended up falling inside. And as my butt made contact with the piano's interior plate, obscene musical sounds that should never come out of a jazz piano echoed through the hall.

Oops.

"What the hell are you doing?" the piano man hissed at me. If he were a gentleman, like Billy Joel, he would have stopped playing and gotten up from his seat to help me out of my precarious situation. However, it turned out, he was a card-carrying member of the "show must go on" school of thought and therefore he continued to play, the piano hammers slamming against my butt as I struggled to free myself.

To make matters worse, I soon realized the fringe of my dress had somehow gotten tangled in the strings.

"And all that . . . jazz!" I sang out as I tugged on my dress. Hey, if Piano Man was going to keep playing, I sure as hell wasn't going to stop singing.

I could hear laughter erupting from the hall as I fought with the dress. I would love to tell you they were laughing with me and not at me, but I'm afraid that would be a dreadful lie, as I was definitely not chuckling with mirth at this point in time.

I tugged again. No dice. The dress was stuck fast. If I had to stop the show and get someone to come up here and cut me free, I was literally going to die of embarrassment.

"And all that . . . freaking jazz!" I muttered, using all my body weight for one last furious yank.

The good news was that the last effort worked to free me from my piano prison. The bad news was it also worked to send me crashing out of the instrument and onto the stage floor, face first, in a very undignified sprawling position.

Well, one thing was for sure. Louise was definitely not getting her big Hollywood break while I was caretaking her body. She'd be lucky if she escaped the ER.

More laughter came from the peanut gallery. Losers. I'd like to see them come up here and try this. I lay on the stage, considering my next move. Should I jump up, run stage left, and disappear into the night? That seemed like the completely rational solution.

But no, I couldn't do that. I had too much pride to give

up now. Besides, it couldn't get any worse. I would finish my song. Rally, and end on a high note.

Scrambling to my feet, I turned to face the audience, defiant though red-faced, and started the next verse, singing as loud as my vocal chords would allow, if not necessarily in tune.

"Find a six-pack
We're playing fast and loose
And all that jazz.

Cause in the woods
Is where you'll find . . . bear and moose
And all that jazz."

I sang my heart out, making up verse after verse, not caring if the words made absolutely no sense whatsoever or what the audience was thinking of them or how badly my screwup could affect the future as I knew it.

I just sang. And sang. And sang.

And eventually, after what seemed like a millennium of torturous verses, I came to the last.

"No, I'm no one's wife.
But I've got a hell of a good life!
And all . . . that. . . . ja-ee-azz!"

I ended the song with a huge sweeping bow and the crowd went wild. Absolutely wild. Clapping and cheering like crazy. I half-expected Arsenio Hall "woots" to erupt from the back of the room.

Wow! They loved me. I was a hit. Even after the Great Piano Incident That Shall Henceforth Not be Mentioned Until the End of Time, they still dug my act.

I grinned triumphantly, wiping the beads of sweat from my brow. I couldn't believe I'd actually pulled it off. I'd fooled everyone in the room into thinking that I was not only a girl from the 1920s, but a girl from the 1920s who could sing and dance. (There was no way I could have pulled that off in 2006!) How amazing was that? I couldn't wait to tell The Rat. This would *have* to impress him, even if he'd rather die than admit it to my face.

I bowed again, almost not wanting to leave the stage.

"Encore!"

Until I realized they didn't want me to leave either.

Gulp.

Luckily for me there was another act after mine, and so I didn't have to come up with something completely different. After all, while I knew I could get away with "All that Jazz"—Nick had refused to rent *Chicago* on DVD with me, insisting it was a chick flick—I couldn't be sure he wouldn't recognize other twenty-first-century songs if he was at the party. For example, my reverting to my college karaoke staples of "Girls Just Want to Have Fun" and "The Safety Dance" might clue him in that I was not who I appeared to be.

So the enthusiastic crowd allowed me offstage, but not before giving me a rousing round of applause. I almost felt bad for the plate-spinning guy they had up next. No one could top my brilliant performance.

Heh. Well, okay, maybe I was overstating just a tad. But at least I hadn't fallen on my face. Well, only that once, but remember we're not to mention that anymore.

I slipped offstage and into the shadows, relieved to be out of the spotlight. I found a side door at the far end of the ballroom that led outside. I was roasting hot from dancing, and the crisp air felt nice kissing my shoulders and face. I saw a cobblestone path leading down to the lake and decided to follow, to see what was down there. To have a few moments of alone time to clear my head before going back into the party. After all, I still had a mission to accomplish, now that I'd gotten that pesky singing out of the way.

"Boo!"

A whisper in my ear caused me to nearly jump out of my skin. I whirled around, raising my hands in a Tae Kwon Do position. Then I lowered them and released my breath as I realized who had come up behind me.

Sam.

"Don't sneak up on me like that!" I growled, not quite sure whether the instant goose bumps on my skin were caused by my being startled or turned on by his proximity.

"Why not?" he asked coyly, circling round to come up behind me again. I shifted to face him.

"Because it's rude."

"I never claimed to be polite."

"It's also childish."

"I never claimed to be a grownup, baby."

"Don't call me baby." Oh, jeesh, now I sounded like the chick in *Tank Girl*. Michelle Pfeiffer in *Scarface*.

117

"Do you prefer doll? Dame? Moll?" He asked with a sparkle in his kaleidoscopic eyes. "Darling? Dear?"

I couldn't help but laugh. "How about, oh I don't know, my name?"

"Ah, yes. Louise. Louise, Louise, who is the bee's knees."

"Cute."

"I know I am."

"Modest, too."

"Never."

He glanced from left to right, then suddenly grabbed my hands and leaned in to give me a quick peck on the lips. I leaped back, surprised.

"And . . . brazen."

"Oh yeah. I'm a big, bad rebel of love, baby," he mocked in almost an Elvis-like voice. "Er, not baby. Sorry about that. Habit."

"S'okay. It's just that my ex used to call me that and well, it's left sort of a sour taste."

"And I just want to be sweet to you."

"Argh!" I groaned. "What's with all the cheesy lines, man?"

He laughed, running a hand through his hair. "Not working, huh?"

"Hardly," I snorted.

"How about this then?" He wrapped a hand around my waist and yanked me close, so my body was flush with his. My knees trembled as I looked up at him, instantly caught in his smoldering gaze. He really did have amazing eyes. The kind that changed color depending on what he was wearing. Currently they were a vivid green with flecks of amber. Gave me the image of a storm-tossed sea.

I could feel every muscle in his chest, his breath on my face. He smelled slightly musky. Slightly delicious. I swallowed hard, making a halfhearted attempt to squirm away. But he was having none of that; he had me captive and he wasn't about to let go.

"Uh-uh, beautiful. There's no escaping this time," he said, almost apologetically, pulling me even closer. In this position I could feel his desire against me; this guy wasn't playing games anymore. He wanted me. Badly, from the feel of it. The idea caused my nipples to harden, scraping against my costume as I struggled. Stupid no-bra-wearing flappers.

With his free hand he captured the side of my face. Our eyes met, mine still defiant and annoyed, his wide and fascinated, his pupils darkened with lust. No more lazy grins and saucy winks. Now he looked dead serious. And drop-dead sexy, if we're being entirely honest. I drew in a shaky breath. It should be illegal for one man to be so hot. At the very least he should come with a warning label.

He dipped his head to kiss me. But this was not meant to be a gentle kiss, not a wisp of butterfly wings and rose petals this time. No, this kiss was more of a crush, a crush of his mouth against mine. His lips demanded my total submission. It was what they called in romance novels a "punishing kiss" and I wondered what I'd done wrong. (Mainly so I could do it again. And again!) An all-consuming fire scorched my insides as he took my lips, devouring them with a fierce intensity that made my toes curl. I moaned, surprised even myself by the desire he'd evoked, and he took advantage of my parted lips to claim the rest of my mouth.

But I wasn't about to let him have free rein without any resistance. My tongue matched his, sparring, defending, dancing in a battle I wasn't sure I wanted to win.

His left hand grabbed fistfuls of silk as he clawed at my back, still effectively keeping me pinned to him. The fingers of his right hand lowered from my jaw to clamp possessively around my neck until I began to wonder if he'd leave bruises. I began to wonder if I'd mind if he did.

My hands took on a mind of their own and I wrapped them around his waist, my nails digging into the small of his back. He let out a groan and involuntarily thrust against me, pressing himself into me as if he were desperate to be inside. I found myself widening my stance to feel him better and rejoiced in the tingling sensation his proximity invoked. Every nerve ending was standing at attention, rejoicing at this man's touch. This was the kind of guy who could make a girl see stars before she was even fully undressed.

He loosened his hold on my neck and dragged his hand downward, palm heavy and flat as it ran over my breast, ribcage, and tracing my pelvic bone with greedy fingers.

"God you have a hot body," he murmured against my mouth.

I wanted to tell him it wasn't mine, but that seemed hardly appropriate and a good way to spoil the mood. No, I wasn't to let a little technicality like body-snatching time travel ruin the moment.

He cupped my bottom, kneading it with his hand while his mouth strayed from mine and began trailing kisses across my face, finding my ear. I shivered as his tongue licked at the lobe, holding it in between his teeth and taking tiny bites. He let out a hot breath and the whoosh of air tickled my every extremity. I gasped and clung tighter to him. The power he held was almost frightening.

It'd been so long, *too* long since I felt this good. Why had I been content with celibacy for nearly a year? Why had I decided I didn't want this kind of ecstasy? These exploding bursts of starlight? Perhaps I fancied myself waiting for the right guy. But that was stupid. Sam was definitely the wrong guy. And he had no problems making me feel oh-so-right.

Stop analyzing, Dora! Stop thinking. Enjoy the moment.

He led me over to a nearby rock, setting me down on it and getting on his knees in front of me. It should have been cold. There was snow on the ground, for God's sake. But I felt nothing. In fact, I was burning.

His mouth abandoned my ear, layering kisses along my neck, then lower, until he reached my breast, lightly pecking at the nipple through the beaded fabric, making me groan. Then, evidently not content to fight the silk barrier, he reached up to yank the straps off my shoulders and the flimsy dress fell to my waist. Now his mouth found what it sought, laving my nipple with his tongue, biting lightly, then dragging his teeth across the rock-hard peaks.

It was pain. It was pleasure. It was everything in between.

"Gah!" I cried, definitely not at my most articulate. Liquid lightning coursed through my veins and my whole body reacted with a hard shudder.

He looked up, his eyes teasingly light. "You okay?" he asked with a grin. He evidently knew what he was doing to me and loved it. Cocky son of a bitch. I had the urge to play harder-to-get, but realized I was well beyond that point. He could easily have me. And he already knew it.

"Y-yeah," I managed to spit out. "I-I'm good."

He smiled and went back to his task: licking, caressing, nibbling, biting. I swallowed hard. The sensations I was cataloging were nearly overwhelming at this point and we hadn't even gotten to the actual sex yet.

My hands were restless, so I dug them into his hair, rejoicing at the long silky strands. My brain was mush. My body was melting. My heart was—

A crash in the bushes and the tinkling of broken glass followed by giggling laughter slammed me back to reality.

"Uh, do you think this is really the best place to be doing this?" I whispered, glancing around the clearing.

Sam looked up at me. He grinned. "You got a better place in mind, baby?"

I shook my head. "But this just seems so open. Exposed. What if someone sees us and reports back to Machine Gun?"

"Awh, where's your sense of adventure?" Sam teased.

"Uh, right. There's adventure, then there's being on your knees with the butt of a semiautomatic weapon at the back of your head."

"Touché." Sam scrambled to his feet and fumbled to help me pull my dress back up onto my shoulders. He attempted a blasé smile, but I could see the strain against his pants and the sweat dampening his temples. It was taking every bit of effort for him to cease and desist. Of course it was the same for me. I couldn't remember a time being so turned on.

"Sorry," I whispered. "Spoilsport, I know."

"Nah, you're probably right," he said, raking a hand through the hair I'd just tousled. He looked around the clearing, his eyes resting on a neighboring mansion. He turned back to me with a devilish glint in his eyes. "How about there?" he asked, pointing at the house while raising his eyebrows in challenge.

I followed his hand to examine the suggested rendezvous more carefully. It was a large Tudor mansion, nestled in a grove of pine trees.

"There?" I asked, not quite following. "Doesn't someone live there?"

"I'm sure. So what?"

"Well, don't you think that someone might object to hosting our own sexual Olympics on the premises?"

"Nah, they're at the party."

I furrowed my brow. It was tempting, but . . . "Are we talking confirmed party sighting or total conjecture?"

Sam grinned and grabbed my hand. "Total and utter conjecture, baby," he said, dragging me off my rock and toward the house. "Come on. You know it's more fun when you might get caught."

I considered this as I relented, allowing him to lead me across the clearing. It *had* seemed more fun when I might get caught in the back of my high school boyfriend's mom's station wagon. The one with the wood paneling on the side. And it *had* seemed more fun when Nick and I might have gotten caught in some random corner in downtown Baghdad for a quick make-out session between assignments. But that was the old Dora. The one who sought out that kind of adventure. The one who liked the adrenaline rush of running for her life.

The new Dora played it safe. She went to work at her mindless job each day, exploiting the dumber American viewers by airing inane advertisements disguised as news features stories. She went home after work to her cat and her TV. She defined the eighteen- to forty-nine-year-old demo who was "too stressed for sex." Especially dangerous sex.

What has become of me? I don't even recognize myself anymore. Then again, maybe that's because technically I haven't been born yet.

I squared my shoulders and firmed my resolve. You know what? Fuck the new Dora. The old Dora wanted to *be* fucked, and I was going to give her the chance. God knew when she'd get another opportunity. Especially with someone so goddamned sexy.

Besides, my brain reminded me as we cautiously tiptoed through the yard and toward the darkened house. *This was just sex in a stranger's house. Not like what you went through last year.*

We got to the house and Sam put a finger to his luscious lips, reminding me both to be quiet and how much I wanted to continue kissing him. Then he walked over to a bottom-story window and hooked his hands underneath the sill. The window lifted easily.

"What about—?" I started, then stopped. No ADT

alarm system to worry about in the twenties. "Uh, never mind."

Sam raised the window and gestured me toward it. "After you, milady," he said with a mock bow. I giggled and grabbed onto the base of the window as I attempted to climb in. Not so easy with a short dress on, but I was pretty sure Sam would be seeing the undergarments I was exposing very shortly anyway, so what did it really matter? He gave me a little boost, his hands on my bottom, and I rejoiced in the fact that those hands would soon be ravaging my body once again.

The house was pitch-black, and I wasn't sure at first which room I'd entered. But I managed to quash the rising fear of the dark rather quickly by thinking about what I was about to do in this particular darkness. There was nothing to fear here. Just a man who wanted me as badly as I wanted him.

I heard a thump as Sam came through the window, and a millisecond later felt his hands grasp my shoulders and push me roughly backward. With a cry of surprise, I lost my balance, thankfully falling back on a bed. (A bed? On the first floor? Maybe we were in the maid's quarters. Hopefully she'd been invited to the big party, too. Or given the night off.) Without pause, Sam climbed on top of me, pressing his knee between my legs and clamping his mouth over my own. He pinned my arms above my head with one hand, claiming dominance. Complete control. I squirmed against him, unable to resist chasing the sensation coursing through me. God, he felt so good. God, it'd been so long.

His kisses were rougher now, his fingers fiercer in their

exploration. With his free hand, he grabbed at the neckline of my dress, tearing at the silk 'til he'd rent it from my body. I had a brief panicked thought about what the hell I'd wear back to the party, then shoved it out of my mind and concentrated on the sensation of his hands on my breasts. Tugging, teasing, flicking, tweaking. He splayed his thumb and forefinger so he could service both at once, rolling the nipples around until I was pretty sure they would fall off my body they were so rock hard. The sensation was like liquid fire coursing through my body, lighting every last nerve ending.

No longer content to let him have all the fun, I wrestled my hands free and reached up and pulled off his tuxedo jacket, yanked his bow tie, and started unbuttoning his shirt—not caring that the buttons were popping off and flying around the room. If he could rip my dress, I sure as hell was allowed to destroy his shirt.

His chest was even better than I'd imagined, and believe me, I'd imagined quite a bit. Rock-hard muscle, six-pack abs. A light dusting of black hair trailing down into his trousers. A trail that I, like Hansel and Gretel with their bread crumbs, was desperate to follow.

He rolled me over so I was on top, straddling him, my dress riding up to my waist. I pressed myself against him, feeling how much he desired me with every thrust. I buried my face in his shoulder, nipping at his skin, licking at the beads of sweat. Salty, yet oh so sweet.

"God, I want you," I whispered in his ear.

The instant the words left my lips I regretted them. That was probably way too forward for a twenties girl to say. I lifted my head to look at him. To gauge his reaction.

He grinned, and for a moment I was relieved. But then he lifted his hand, his index and middle finger forming bunny ears and wagging up and down twice.

The sign of "ditto."

A sign I knew all too well. One that, at this very moment, nearly had the power to shut down my heart. To spin my world off its axis.

Oh. My. God.

"Ditto," he said.

Oh fuck.

It was a gesture I knew, all right.

A gesture jokingly made by one man and one man only.

Nick "The Prick" Fitzgerald.

God fucking damn it.

It had been our private joke ever since we'd watched *Ghost* on DVD and something he knew drove me crazy. I'd say something loving, something sweet, expecting him to say something equally as endearing back. Instead he'd say "ditto" or wag his fingers. I'd usually playfully swat him in response.

This time I kneed him in the groin.

"Argh!" he cried. "What the fuck?"

But I was already off the bed. Desperately clinging to the shreds of my dress, I stumbled out of the window and ran through the woods, as fast as Louise's legs would carry me. I could hear Sam calling after me, calling after Louise, but I didn't turn around.

Turn around and he may break your heart.

Of course, he may break your heart anyway.

I ran. My heart pounded. Tears streamed from my eyes.

I couldn't believe it. Why hadn't I seen it from the beginning? It all seemed so obvious now.

Sam was Nick.

Nick was Sam.

And I'd almost had sex with him.

I'd almost enjoyed having sex with him.

I didn't know what was worse: that I'd almost had sex with Nick/Sam, or that Nick/Sam had almost had sex with Louise/me. Of course he had no idea that Louise/me was really me, which meant that he really liked Louise. That he was more than over me and ready to decade-jump just to fuck another woman.

Okay, fine, sure, if you wanted to be technical it was I who broke up with him. And it had been a year ago. And he had every right to be dating other people.

But I didn't want to be technical. I wanted to be completely irrational and cry my eyes out. 'Cause it hurt. It hurt to know that another woman could turn Nick on as I used to.

Okay, fine, so that "other woman" was technically still me, but not really. I mean, sort of.

Oh god, this was so confusing.

All the moments of making love to him crashed back in waves of unwelcome memories. The moments of tender caresses, the times of nearly violent passion, even the quickies that meant nothing at the time but I would die to have the chance to experience again. Every encounter was special. Priceless. A celebration of our love for one another.

And now he'd rather screw a complete stranger.

Another choking sob wrenched from my throat. I

guess I'd somehow always entertained the notion that he was up there, anchoring the news in Los Angeles, desperately sad and wishing on first stars and penny fountains that I would come back to him someday. I'd wanted to imagine that he felt incomplete without me by his side and wished to God I would change my mind. That I'd forgive him. I wanted to imagine him thinking that he would always hold a torch for me and could never really love again.

Evidently not so much.

When we first broke up he'd begged me to come back to him. He'd sent flowers. He'd even written poetry. Macho, self-assured, alpha reporter Nick had actually written beautiful verse, dedicated to me. I remember his brother delivering it to my door, begging me to give Nick another chance. But I'd been too angry. I was in no mood to hear explanations and excuses. There was no way in hell he could justify what he'd done.

Yes. I'd been stubborn. Angry. Enraged. Full of hate. I'd blamed him for all I'd suffered while captured by those Iraqis. Blamed him for the scars I saw in the mirror each day, both physical and emotional. I'd thought I was going to die in that prison. All because of him and his little whore.

Have you seen Nick Fitzgerald? I remembered asking every new prisoner during my month of incarceration; desperate for information, missing him, longing for him, holding out hope that he was doing everything he could to rescue me.

The reporter? Yeah, sure. At the bars. With some Iraqi chick, they'd all reply.

Yes, while I was in prison. In the dark. Suffering, scared. During all this, Nick, it seemed, had found a new girlfriend with whom to carouse. He had probably met her earlier. She was probably the reason he hadn't shown up to the hotel bar that day. The day I got caught, he'd been too busy banging his new girlfriend.

The knowledge hurt worse than any of the knives. The gunshot wound. Had they asked me that day if I wanted to die, I would have gladly said yes.

You know, up until now, I'd really thought I was doing pretty well moving on with things. I thought I'd healed. Rebuilt my pathetic new life in San Diego. But seeing Nick, even in the body of Sam, made it all come rushing back. My heart felt squeezed in a vise. My painful breath stuck behind a lump in my throat. My stomach hurt. My head hurt. I could quite possibly drown in the amount of tears my eyes were currently shedding.

This sucked.

Of course Sam was really Nick. It made perfect sense. That was why I was so attracted to him. Why I felt that instant ease kissing him. Touching him. Wanting him. And here I'd thought I was being pretty good—finally able to move on and feel attraction for a man other than Nick.

Machine Gun was right. I really was a Dumb Dora.

God, what was I going to do now? I still had to save the world, even if I couldn't save my heart. And that meant I had to hang out with Nick/Sam some more. I had to convince him not to change history. But how could I do that? Just looking at him was going to make me fall apart.

No, Dora, you're stronger than that. You can do this.

I swallowed hard, shook my head and brushed the tears from my eyes. Dora the Explorer was okay. I could do this. Just because Nick broke my heart didn't mean I was going to stand around and let him break the rest of the world.

CHAPTER EIGHT

"Louise! What's wrong?"

I looked up to see Daisy flying at me, a distraught look on her already pancaked-white, bow-lipped face. Great. The last thing I needed right now was for someone to see me in a torn dress, bawling my eyes out in the middle of the woods, alone. How had she found me out here? And how was I going to explain myself now that she had?

Don't mind me, I just almost accidentally screwed my ex-boyfriend. No, of course I didn't recognize him right away. He's hiding in someone else's body, you know.

"Nothing. I'm fine," I said, in a vain attempt to assure her that everything was hunky-dory. Not that I thought for one second she'd buy my act. Mainly because while the raccoon eye motif may have looked cool when applied hours earlier, now, after a near-sex experience and a massive crying jag, I probably resembled Tim Burton's Corpse Bride. And there was certainly no hiding the big rip in the front of my dress. Damn Nick and his alpha male fetishes. I had lost more articles of clothing that way. . . .

Daisy shook her head, then grabbed me by the hand, pulling me onto my feet. She wrapped an arm around my waist and led me down the path. She didn't speak until we came to a small caretaker's cottage.

"It's too cold out here," she said by way of explanation as she pushed open the door and led me inside.

I shivered as I stepped over the threshold. In my grief my body had hardly registered the chill. Now it hit me full force, making my head hurt and bones ache.

I watched dully as Daisy grabbed a log and tossed it into the fireplace. She crumbled up a few newspapers and lit a match. Soon, smoke funneled up the chimney from the small but comforting fire.

"Louise, sit down. Take a load off," she scolded, walking back over to me and leading me to the couch. I followed, seeming to have no will of my own. Was this what shock felt like? Was I in actual shock over seeing Nick again?

Daisy sat down beside me, grabbing my hands in her own, much warmer ones. "Okay, now tell me what happened, Louise. You're shaking and I know it's not just 'cause you're cold. Did a fella mess you up or somethin'? Was it that guy Sam? I told you he was no good. You need to stay away from him. I told you that."

I shook my head, unable to speak. She was more right than she could ever know. No-good Sam/Nick. I should have stayed away. Far, far away. Like back in the twenty-first century far away. Maybe even twenty-first century Tibet far.

Daisy reached up to brush a lock of hair from my eyes, still studying my tear-blotched face. "Louise, I keep telling you. You don't need to be hanging around some guy who'd rough you up like this." She rummaged through her beaded purse, pulled out an embroidered handkerchief, and handed it to me. "You're too good for this life. Me, well, maybe I deserve it. I don't know. But you . . ." She shook her head. "I saw you on stage tonight. You were terrif. Really terrif. I'm sure Don thought you were the cat's pajamas. Why, I bet he's already got you cast in his next picture. You'll be a star, Louise. A real star."

I smiled through my tears. "You're sweet," I told her. And I meant it. Louise was lucky to have such a supportive friend. Even if she was a chain-smoking, tough-talking flapper who didn't get *The Great Gatsby*.

Daisy laughed. "Just don't tell anyone," she said, wrinkling her button nose. "Would ruin my reputation."

"Your secret is safe with me."

We laughed for a moment, then fell silent. The flames licked at the logs and the fire crackled. In the distance you could still hear the tinny sounds of jazz from the party, which evidently was raging without us. I wondered if Nick had gone back to search for me. To find out why I'd reacted the way I had. Or maybe the kick to the groin was enough to dissuade him from future advances. That wouldn't be a bad thing, I guessed.

I released a long sigh. How could I have gotten myself into that situation to begin with? How had I let my hormones lead me by the nose instead of concentrating on my mission? Now I had to convince a guy who not only hated me in the twenty-first century, but was not my biggest fan in the twentieth either, not to change history.

It seemed somewhat impossible.

"Are you ready to tell me what happened?" Daisy asked in a comforting tone. She really was a good friend. Louise was lucky to have her.

I shrugged. "It doesn't matter. It's really no big deal."

Daisy opened her mouth, as if to say something, then closed it again. After pausing for a moment, she said, "Can I tell you a story then?"

"Okay. Sure," I said, shifting myself to a more comfortable position on the sofa. After all, it was better to let her ramble on than to field more questions about how I'd ended up in the woods with my dress torn. "What about?"

"My mother," Daisy said, motioning for me to push over to make room for her petite frame. She sat down beside me. "God rest her soul."

I raised an eyebrow. This should be interesting.

"We grew up in the slums of Chicago. My father never had a proper job. Ten kids and no food to feed 'em half the time. It was a lousy lot in life, for sure. But instead of my father trying to better himself, to get a real job or somethin', help out his family, he took it out on my mother." Daisy shook her head. "The poor woman put up with years of abuse from him. Dinner was cold? Bam— clock her in the head! That was his way. And yah know what? It was her own fault. She was as bad as him. 'Cause she didn't do nuthin' about it. Nuthin'. She just let that palooka use her as a human punching bag anytime he felt like it. He'd go out to the juice joint every night and come back corked and smelling like whores. Usually confessin' that he'd gambled away the week's grocery money again."

"Ugh," I said. I thought about my safe, suburban upbringing. My loving, gentle father who was still married to my sweet, church-going mother after thirty-five years. The caring and support and encouragement they gave me all through my childhood. I'd never wanted for a thing. I couldn't imagine what it'd be like to grow up as Daisy had. To have nothing. No one. To feel unsafe in your own home. No wonder she was bitter toward men.

Suddenly, I missed home with a vengeance. The little New England town I'd grown up in. The old saltbox house my parents still lived in. When I returned from Iraq, they had begged me to come home. To let them take care of me while I got on my feet. But I had been too proud. I'd thought I could do it all on my own.

If/when I ever got out of this mess, I was definitely going to pay them a visit. Even if just to let them know how much I loved and appreciated them.

I turned my attention back to Daisy.

"And my mother," the flapper was saying, staring off into the fire, "did she stand up to him? Tell him he was a no good bum and should get out and never come back? No. Not at all. Instead, she'd just cower." She turned back to me. "Oh, Louise, how she'd cower in front of him. It woulda made you sick to watch. Made me sick, I'll tell ya that. Especially when we got a little older and he started in on me and my sisters. I ran away when I was fourteen and I vowed then and there that I would never let a man keep me down like she did."

Daisy took the handkerchief from me and used it to dab at the corners of her own black-rimmed eyes. "Sorry," she said. "The memories always get me." She sighed. "Anyway, the reason I'm tellin' you this is that we ain't like our mothers. We're moderns. We got freedom now. We don't need to attach ourselves to the first guy who comes along. We can make our own money. We can live our own lives. Who wants to settle down in a house with a white picket fence when you can run off to Hollywood and star in pictures? We could do that, you know? We could get on a train right now and head to California." She jumped to her feet and started dancing a silly dance. "We could be movie stars, Louise. We could be anything."

I laughed appreciatively. This was certainly a lesson I hadn't planned on getting while visiting the 1920s. But she was right. Women had been long oppressed throughout history and now, as the twenties roared, they were just coming into their own. Sure, they'd made a lot of mistakes along the way, but they were their mistakes to make. And now they were almost free. They could hold jobs (though perhaps not great ones). They could vote. They could smoke and dance and marry the guy they chose to. Or no guy at all, if they preferred.

All were things I completely took for granted back in the twenty-first century. I could learn to stand on my own two feet and be my own person. And in the future, if I wanted to share my life with someone, I could. But I would never have to give up my self-respect and autonomy to do so.

I wished I could tell Daisy some of this. To instill some

hope in her about the future. But I remembered what happened to Michael J. Fox's future girlfriend in *Back to the Future 2* when she saw her past self, and I didn't want to be scraping the little flapper's jaw off the floor with my fantastical tale of time travel.

"You're right, Daisy," I said, scrambling to my feet. She was still dancing her goofy dance, so I grabbed her and playfully twirled her around. Then I started dancing too, mimicking the strange waltz I'd seen at the party. We bobbed from side to side, giggling like schoolgirls. I wasn't sure my torn dress would survive the abuse, but I didn't care. After all, it belonged to Louise, not me.

"See, we don't need men!" Daisy crowed, twirling me around this time. I spun away from her and then back again, laughing.

"Nope. To hell with men!" I cried triumphantly, raising my fist in the air. "We are women! Hear us roar!"

While confidently roaring, I managed to trip over the coffee table and fell, taking Daisy down with me. We collapsed onto the floor, still giggling.

"Ow!" I cried, laughing and rubbing my knee. "Maybe I need a man after all. A man doctor!"

Daisy snorted, reaching over and rubbing my knee with her hand. "Poor baby," she cooed. "Want me to kiss it better?"

"Is everyone in this place going to insist on calling me baby?" I groaned. I was beginning to feel like Jennifer Grey in *Dirty Dancing*. "I mean, I get why the men do, but . . ."

I started trying to scramble to my feet, but Daisy suddenly placed a firm hand on my shoulder. I looked at her, cocking my head in surprise at her gesture and the sudden serious look on her face. Her eyes were large and round and staring right back into mine.

"What?" I asked, feeling the inexplicable need to blush. Why was she always staring at me like that? "Do I have lettuce in my teeth or something?" Not that I had eaten any lettuce. Like I said before, I was all carbs all the time while I was living on someone else's metabolism.

"Uh, no. Sorry." She shook her head and scrambled back to her feet. "We should, um, get you cleaned up. Let's go back to the house."

"Oh-kay," I said, scrunching my face in confusion. What the hell was that about? She didn't suspect something was wrong, did she? That her best friend was different somehow?

She couldn't see Dora behind Louise's eyes, could she? I hoped not. 'Cause that would put me in serious trouble.

"Hi honey, I'm home!" I called to The Rat as I entered my apartment and shut the door behind me. It was past eleven P.M. and Mrs. Landers had taken it upon herself to give me an in-depth lecture on the evils of staying out late. According to her, the night air itself could get you knocked up and hooked on drugs if you weren't careful. Who knew?

"Dinner's on the table, sweetie," The Rat called back in an equally sarcastic voice from his position on the armchair. He had somehow managed to turn the radio on and was listening to some lively sounding jazz. "God, radios suck," he muttered. "My kingdom for the Playboy channel."

I rolled my eyes, not dignifying his desire for softcore porn with a response. Too bad he wasn't serious about that whole dinner on the table thing, though. I was starving, and pretty sure that Domino's delivery wouldn't be invented for another few decades. In fact, there wasn't even a Wendy's "Eat Great, Even Late" drive-through I could hit. Damn this decade. You never realize the pure bliss of super value menus until they're taken away.

"What a day!" I said as I kicked off my shoes and collapsed onto the bed. I stared up at the ceiling, trying not to listen to my growling stomach. I should have eaten more of those appetizers at the party and not burned so many calories with my near-sex activities.

The Rat shot me a suspicious look. "When you say, 'What a day!' do you mean, 'What a day—I can't believe how easy it is to change history? You'll never guess how much I screwed up the world in fourteen short hours!'? Or 'What a day—I accomplished my mission, got my ex-boyfriend to agree not to wake up Bugs Moran, and the world as we know it is safe and sound until the next time the Time Warriors decide to try and mess with something.'?"

"Uh . . . somewhere in between?"

"Ah. What a day—I actually screwed around and drank too much gin and didn't accomplish a gosh darn thing."

"No!" I protested, perhaps a bit too strongly, sitting up. "I accomplished . . . things."

"Things?" The Rat jumped down from the chair and scampered over to the bed. He twitched his nose at me. "Define 'things.'"

"Um, well, I met with Louise's boyfriend. That Machine Gun guy." I grimaced. "You wouldn't believe what he wanted me to do, though."

"I hope whatever it was, you not only did it, but you did it with a big freaking smile on your face and said, 'Thank you for the opportunity to serve you' afterwards."

"Dude, it was sucking on his fungus-filled toes!"

"Mmm. Peanut butter and toe jam sandwich, eh? So, how'd it taste?" His tail twitched back and forth.

"I didn't do it!" I screwed up my face in disgust. Maybe the idea didn't sound too bad to a rodent, but just thinking about it made me sick to my stomach all over again. "I'm sorry, Ratty, but there's only so much I'm willing to do for my country."

"Fine," The Rat said, crawling up onto the bed, his little feet clawing the duvet for traction. "So you didn't suck on his toes. Did you please him in other ways, perhaps?"

"I . . ." Eesh, this was embarrassing. "I . . . threw up on his feet."

"Wow. If I could reach, I'd be slapping my forehead with my paw and making Homer Simpson '*d'oh*' noises right about now."

"Whatever, dude. You have no idea how bad he smelled."

"Right. I get you. When given the choice between, say, saving the world and disturbing your olfactory glands, you say bye-bye the world every time, right?"

"You know, I'm not telling you anything else if you're going to hassle me at every step," I said with a frown. "I mean, could you at least save the condemnation 'til I'm done with my story? Don't worry, I'm pretty sure you'll get other opportunities to poke fun at my shortcomings."

"I would be willing to bet very expensive cheese on that fact," The Rat agreed. "Fine. Go on. You puked on a guy with a penchant for automatic weapons. How else did you screw things up today, darling?"

I sighed. "Well, do you want the good news or the bad news?"

"God. Please don't make me choose."

"Fine. The good news is I figured out whose body Nick has snatched."

"Really?" The Rat actually looked impressed. Somewhat. "Nice work." He paused. "Uh, what's the bad news?"

I swallowed hard. (And I'd thought the puking thing was embarrassing?) "I almost had sex with him."

"Uh . . ."

"And . . . then I kicked him in the balls and ran out of the house."

"Oh dear."

"It wasn't really my fault though!" I protested, not liking the horrified, disappointed look on The Rat's twitchy little face. He really was expressive for a rodent. "I didn't figure it out 'til halfway through, when he did this stupid thing that Nick used to always do."

"Uh-huh."

"Do you have any idea how freaky that was? To be halfway ravished by a handsome stranger and then find out that the handsome stranger in question is actually your ex-boyfriend who you hate and are never speaking to again?"

"No, but one time I hooked up with this chick at a bar that turned out to be a man. . . ."

I raised my eyebrows. "I am not even sure how to respond to that."

"Hey, I was drunk. And the dude definitely looked like a lady." The Rat shrugged his little shoulders. "But let's get back to your misadventures here. You had him in your bed, half-naked and vulnerable, and . . . now you've lost him?"

"Look. You don't have to worry. I'll find Nick again and apologize for kicking him. At least now I know what he looks like. And where he hangs out. I'll find him and make sure he doesn't screw up the St. Valentine's Day Massacre." I sighed. "Somehow."

"You'd better, princess. Tomorrow's February Twelfth. You've got just two days left."

"Plenty of time."

"Uh-huh." The Rat didn't look convinced. But then again, neither was I.

"Tomorrow," I said, in my best Scarlett O'Hara voice "is another day."

I grabbed my nightclothes and headed to the bathroom to change, ignoring Ratty's squeaky suggestion that I strip down in the bedroom to make up for the absence of Skin-e-max. He claimed it wouldn't be a big deal since technically he'd be gawking at Louise's body, not mine. Impeccable time travel logic, but I was so not buying it. I pulled the bathroom door firmly shut behind me, locking it for good measure.

Alone at last, I stared into the mirror. I'd really done a number on the body I was borrowing. Louise looked like hell. Makeup smeared, dress ripped, bite marks on her neck, and small bruises on her arms where Nick had grabbed her/me. She was going to be so pissed come February Fifteenth when she got her body back. Pissed and deeply confused.

Where was Louise, anyway? I wondered. Was she inside this body somewhere, deep in a coma-like sleep, praying that I didn't screw up her life too much while I controlled her every move? Or had we swapped bodies? Was she walking around San Diego as I spoke? If so, she'd better not go get anything tattooed. Or close down the all-you-can-eat Chinese buffet and make me gain fifty pounds. I should have left her detailed instructions on my five-mile jogs and carb-free lifestyle. (Uh, not that I had a five-mile jog/carb-free lifestyle beforehand, but she didn't need to know that.)

I sighed and sat down on the edge of the tub. What was I going to do? In two nights, Machine Gun was supposed to take me to a hotel room where we were to wait out the St. Valentine's Day Massacre. That didn't give me much time.

Why did the FBI pick *me* for this? How could they have possibly decided I was the best person for the job? Couldn't they have gotten Nick's billionaire brother to come back and persuade him? After all, those two were thick as thieves. Or maybe his best friend, Mike? Either of them would have been better choices in my opinion. For starters, Nick actually didn't hate their guts.

How had I got myself talked into this? Stupid guilt-ridden changing history speech. How could I have fallen for that? I was a complete narcissist to actually believe that I had the power to save the world.

And because of my vanity, now the world was pretty much doomed.

I shook my head, trying to rid myself of negative thoughts. They wouldn't help me. As the shrinks said, they were self-defeating. No, I needed a plan. Unfortunately, I was very sucky in the plan department. And I knew Ratty wasn't going to be much help in the matter. Nick probably would have been able to come up with a brilliant plan, but since he was the one I was planning against, I could hardly ask him to formulate one for me this time.

Nick. Sigh. Just thinking the name caused high-def visuals of our near encounter to flood my brain once again. Not that it hadn't been playing on endless loop since I had left the party. His mouth on mine. His hands exploring every inch of me. Hot flesh against hot flesh. Half of me wished I didn't realize it was him until after we'd gone all the way. At least then I would have gotten an orgasm or two out of the deal, even if it would have probably messed me up even further.

You know, I thought I'd been doing so well moving on with my life. Now I realized I was back at square one. As much as I hated the guy, I still had strong feelings for him. I still wanted him. I still cared for him. I still loved him very much.

I'm such a Dumb Dora.

CHAPTER NINE

"Jiminy Cricket! It must be nice to have your conscience go on extended vacations, allowing you to ignore the fact that you've got only two days left to save the world and instead giving you a few extra moments of shut-eye."

"Ugh. It's still dark out," I groaned, ignoring the voice in my ear and pulling the covers over my head. "You're worse than a clock radio set on an all-polka-all-the-time station."

"Yup. And I'm not equipped with a snooze button, either."

"Or an off switch."

"I'm always on, baby," The Rat crowed.

"Believe me when I say that little fact has certainly not escaped my notice." I peeked out from under the blankets. "What time is it, anyway?"

"You think they make rat-size pocket watches?"

I gritted my teeth. "So you are *assuming* it's morning and not, say, the middle of the freaking night?"

"Look, you're the one with the mission to save the world, not me. I was just doing you a favor. Figured you might want to get an early start. Silly me."

"Fine. I'll get up." Reluctantly, I rolled out of bed and stretched my hands over my head. I'd be happy to get back to the twenty-first century just to get a good night's sleep. Two nights on a mattress that was definitely no Sealy Posturepedic was two too many. Luckily it was Louise's back I was damaging, so thankfully I wouldn't need to see a chiropractor when I got back.

I headed to the bathroom and grudgingly began my new morning routine. I was never one of those girls who took a million years to get ready to go out, but the fact that Louise only had a bathtub and not a shower slowed my preparation time a bit. Not to mention the extensive flapper-appropriate makeup routine. But even still, by the time I slipped on my Mary Jane shoes the sun was just peeking over the horizon.

"I can't believe you woke me up at five A.M.," I muttered. "No one's even going to be awake when I get outside. I mean, Machine Gun is a mobster. Surely he's more of a night owl than an early bird."

"Maybe you'll catch him before he goes to bed," The Rat suggested, oh-so-innocently.

I glared at him and grabbed my coat and hat and opened the front door.

"Bye, darling," I cooed in my most sarcastic tone. "Don't wait up."

"Where are you going, anyway?"

I paused at the door. "Not that it should make any difference to you, but I'm headed to the club."

"Going to see Machine Gun?" The Rat asked. "And not Nick?"

"Yes."

He snickered.

"What?" I cried, not liking the defensiveness in my voice. I knew exactly what he was going to say before he opened his little mouth.

"Wimp."

I pressed my lips together in displeasure. "Dude, I am *so* not a wimp. I'm on my way to see an infamous historical bad guy. Public Enemy Numero Uno. Absolutely nothing wimpy about that. In fact," I added, patting myself on the shoulder, "I think it's rather brave of me if you want to know the truth."

"Oh, come on," groaned The Rat. "You're not fooling anyone. You'd rather go sweet-talk a guy who whacks people for a living and wants you to suck on his toes than face your ex-boyfriend again." He squeaked with laughter. "Man, that Nick must really be something to have you so freaked out. Seriously, I'd give my Beer of the Month subscription to know that guy's secret."

"It's not that," I protested. Even though, of course, it was exactly that. In fact, Ratty had hit the nail right on its proverbial head.

After stirring the whole thing around in my brain the night before, I'd come to the conclusion that it'd be a hell of a lot easier to convince Louise's mobster boyfriend not to listen to Nick than it would be to convince Nick not to change history. And as a not-unrecognized bonus, that way I wouldn't have to interact with Nick at all and I'd still get the job done.

It was the perfect plan, I felt. Especially since I truly believed that setting eyes on Nick again would cause me to melt into a pile of Jell-O, and it was well known to be very difficult to convince anyone of anything when you were reduced to a glob of gelatinous goo.

"Fine, fine. Do it your way, princess," The Rat said, still sounding way too amused for my liking. "But when your plan doesn't work, don't come crying to me. I'll only say, 'I told you so.'"

"Right. Well, I'd be disappointed with anything less." I sighed. "What are you planning to do today, anyway?"

"Me?" Ratty snorted. "I'm going back to bed."

Of course.

The sky was just pinkening with dawn and the street-lights still glowed dimly as I walked down the snow-lined street. The wind cruelly ripped into me, and I hugged my coat tight against my body. When I next went back in time, I'd request a summer assignment. Or at least one that took place in the tropics instead of the Windy City in February. Not that I was ever in a million years agreeing to this type of gig again, mind you.

Luckily the club wasn't far, and I managed to make it there without turning into a complete Popsicle, though my teeth were extremely chattery and I was quite positive my lips had turned blue. I walked up to the front door, ready to open it, when someone pushed through from the other side. I jumped back to avoid being hit and was surprised to see it was Daisy who burst forth from behind it.

Even more surprising, she was still wearing her party dress from the night before. Curiouser and curiouser.

"Hey, Daisy. What are you doing here?" I asked, giving her a once-over. She didn't look so hot: no makeup and dark circles under her eyes. Her whole look screamed "Walk of Shame," and I wondered if she'd hooked up last night, and if she had, with whom? I didn't know anyone actually lived in the club. Except maybe Machine Gun himself. But she wouldn't hook up with her best friend's fellow.

Would she?

"I might ask you the same question," Daisy retorted a bit too strongly, shuffling her feet and not meeting my eyes. Wow. *Holy guilty conscience, Batman. Maybe she was doing the dirty deed with Machine Gun. Poor Louise.* "It's awfully early, don't you think? I can't remember a time seeing you up before noon."

Grr. I knew it! I'd *told* Ratty it was too early for Louise to be traipsing about. Here he was all worrying about me messing up history, and then he goes and sends me out at the crack of dawn, making Louise's best friend all suspicious.

"Yeah, couldn't sleep," I lied. "How about you? Get lucky last night?" I couldn't help but ask the question with a sarcastic twinge in my voice. I mean, here Daisy had been playing sweet, supportive best friend. Was she really stabbing Louise in the back, sleeping with her guy this whole time?

Daisy cocked her head, looking confused. "Lucky?" she repeated. Then she adopted a rueful grin. "Is that what they're calling it these days?"

Whoops. Had to be careful of those twenty-first centuryisms creeping into my vocab. Unfortunately, my mind blanked and I couldn't think of another way to put it off the top of my head. At least not another way that wouldn't sound overly offensive. What I really wanted to say was, "Hey, did you screw Louise's boyfriend, you skanky ho?" but that hardly seemed appropriate under the circumstances. I wasn't here to fix Louise's love life, after all. Yet, at the same time, I couldn't help feeling a bit protective of my host body.

"You know what I mean," I said, attempting to keep the venom out of my voice. "All that talk last night about no-good men, and now I find you headed home after being out all night. Makes me wonder if you went and found some no-good man to share your bed with or something."

Daisy's face flushed deep crimson and she stuck her hands in her coat pocket, kicking a rock with her shoe. "You know, Louise, sometimes you can be a real bitch."

I could be a real bitch? She was the one screwing around with another girl's boyfriend! I bit my lip to stop myself from launching into a full-on scolding. It didn't matter, I told myself. The only thing that mattered was the mission. Still, for some reason, the betrayal stung a bit.

"Sorry. I was just teasing," I said, trying to sound sincere. I wasn't sure it was working though. "You know me."

"I've got to scram," Daisy muttered, evidently not ready to accept my apology. "Catch you later."

She pushed by me and headed down the street. I watched her go, not quite sure what to do. Then I shrugged. What did it matter? I wasn't here to straighten out Louise's soap opera life, that's for sure. And besides, technically wasn't Louise cheating on Machine Gun with Sam? Maybe they had a mutual arrangement or something. Maybe they were swingers. It was their lives, after all. Who was I to judge?

I opened the door and walked into the club. The lights were on and a couple of cleaning men were mopping up the floor. The place reeked of cigarette smoke and I wondered if they had a way to air it out or if it always smelled like this. The same bouncer as yesterday greeted me inside the entrance.

"Wow, never seen you up before noon," he remarked, raising his bushy eyebrows. "Unless you haven't been to bed yet?"

I squeezed my hands into fists. I was going to kill Ratty when I saw him. *Kill* him. Slowly—with much pain and suffering. You know, I could have easily slept in an additional seven hours and no one would have batted an eye. So not fair.

"Ha, ha! Yes, you know me," I said. "Still up from the night before. Sleeping is so overrated, don't you think?"

He laughed appreciatively, buying my act. "You here to see Jack?"

"Yup. If he's up. I mean, I don't want to wake him."

"Should be." He laughed. "As you know, the guy never sleeps."

"Heh. Right. Good old Machine Gun. Always counting sheep and never falling asleep," I said with a big fake laugh to cover my dumb comment.

"You can just go up," the bouncer said. "I've got to stay by my post. Watch these fly-boys." He pointed over to the usual suspects at the bar who evidently thought six A.M. was the perfect time to start boozing it up. Sad, really.

I thanked the bouncer and walked through the club to the back door. I remembered from yesterday that his apartment was off his main office. An overly observant reporter brain sometimes came in handy.

I got to the door that led into his apartment and knocked twice. I realized my hands were shaking a bit. Hopefully he'd forgiven and forgotten that whole puking incident. . . .

"Who is it?"

"Louise," I answered. "I came to see you."

"What the hell you knocking for, baby? You know you can just come on in."

Well, that sounded positive. Maybe he was the type that didn't hold a grudge. I wrapped my hand around the doorknob and turned it. Locked. Great.

"Uh, it's locked, baby," I informed him.

"Use your key."

Grr. Why couldn't anything be easy? "I, uh, left it at home," I fibbed.

"Get the one out of the hiding spot then."

Oh jeez. Now I had to figure out where the spare key was hidden? Why couldn't the lazy bastard just come to the door? I glanced around the hallway. If I were a key to a mobster's bedroom, where would I hide? I scanned the hallway.

153

"What's taking you so long?" Machine Gun cried from behind the door. "Come on in, baby. I missed you."

Grr. Why did every little thing have to turn into a whole production?

"Just a second, baby."

My eyes fell on an ornate statue of the Virgin Mary, on a pedestal in the far corner of the hallway. Aha. I approached the statue, picked it up and examined it. Sure enough, there was a shiny key underneath.

Huh. Well, that wasn't a very good security system if I could figure it out. Then again, he probably had a handy stash of semiautomatic weapons on the other side of the door to keep him safe and sound. The key was just to keep honest people out.

I unlocked the door and entered the room. Jack's suite was just as ornate as his office. The wallpaper was red and gold, with lavish jewel-toned Italian paintings hanging from the wall. Botticellis, I believed, if memories of my art history classes weren't doing me wrong. The mobster sat under the covers in a huge king-size sleigh bed that took up the majority of the room. I shuddered to think of the acts that had probably been performed in that bed. Performed by my host body, to be exact. Ew.

"So, what are you doing here?" the gangster asked, sitting up in bed with a perplexed look on his growly, unshaven face. He wore no shirt and I was afraid of what he wasn't wearing underneath the covers. "Not that I'm not happy to see you. But it's so early. You never come here this early."

"I couldn't wait to see you," I said, walking over to the bed and sitting down on the side. "I felt so bad about what happened yesterday. I wanted to apologize. I hadn't been feeling well, and . . ."

He smiled and reached over to tousle my curls. Curls I'd spent half an hour trying to tame, I might add.

"Don't worry your pretty little head about it, doll," he said. "In fact, fuhgetaboutit," he added, channeling Tony Soprano. Or maybe Tony Soprano was channeling him, since Machine Gun had obviously been born first. "You're my best girl. It's all water under the bridge, far as I'm concerned."

Phew. As long as by "water under the bridge" he didn't mean "water under the bridge that I'm going to drown you in after fitting you with cement shoes," I was saved.

"Thanks. I'm glad. The last thing I wanted was for you to be mad at me."

I guess it made sense for him to forgive me. After all, according to the history books, Louise was his blonde alibi. His ticket to getting away with murder. And getting away with murder probably ranked higher than saving face on a foot-vomit mishap.

"At you? Never."

"Good," I gushed. "I was so worried you weren't gonna take me to the hotel tomorrow night. That we weren't going to celebrate Valentine's Day together."

He reached out to paw my shoulder, trying to grab on and pull me over to him. I inched further down to the foot of the bed. So not happening. I wouldn't suck on his toes, and I sure as hell wasn't going to curl up in bed with him. Or do anything else remotely romantic or sexual, for that matter.

"Nope. Besides one little adjustment to the plan,

everything's on schedule," he said, giving up his pawing for the moment, much to my relief. But relief ended quickly when his words sunk in.

Adjustment?

Uh-oh.

"Adjustment? I thought you said the plan was in place. That nothing would change. You said, and I quote, 'What's set up by me and Al stays set up.'"

"Sure. I mighta said that." Machine Gun shrugged. "But somethin's come to my attention since then. So I made a little change. It ain't a big deal, Louise, baby. It's just a little insurance. To make sure Bugs shows up so we can kill him."

My shoulders slumped. Great. I was too late. Nick must have already been here. Already talked to Machine Gun about how they needed to ensure that Bugs Moran woke up on time.

Yeah. He probably went upstairs to talk to the gangster right after Daisy and I left the club yesterday. Convinced him he should change his plan. Figure out a way to ensure Bugs would be in the right place at the right time. I knew as well as anyone how convincing Nick could be when he wanted.

Way more convincing than me.

I stifled a sigh. Ratty was right. I sucked. And now the world as we knew it was going to end, solely based on my suckiness.

If only I'd known Nick was Sam yesterday at this time. I could have told Machine Gun not to listen to him. Or stopped him in some other way. But no, I had to waste time shopping with Daisy. Singing and dancing on the stage. Flirting and almost having sex with my ex-boyfriend, whose goal it was to screw me and then screw the world.

Bleh.

"You don't have to change the plan, do you, baby?" I asked. It was time to turn on the Dora Mega-Charm. Not that I, um, had any Dora Mega-Charm to speak of. In fact, truth be told, I was severely lacking in the charm department.

Then again, my inner Glass Half-Full Chick argued that maybe Louise had some charm reserves I could dip into. After all, the girl had done something to win over this gangster guy in the first place. . . .

Yup, it was time for a little twenties vamping, with a dash of good old-fashioned (new-fashioned?) twenty-first century psychology thrown in.

I brought my hand to his chest and dragged my index finger down his sternum, stroking him softly. He let out of a soft moan of pleasure. "I mean, it was an awfully terrif plan," I said in Louise's most throaty voice. "One that you thought of all by yourself. Why ever would you let anyone talk you into changing it?"

"Well, Louise, I'm not one of those guys who doesn't listen to my boys. If someone suggests something that I think is a good idea, I listen to that good idea. And then I take action, if I think it's called for. It's good business. You know how it is, don'tcha?"

"Huh." I frowned, pulling my hand away. "I didn't know you were a pushover, baby."

Jack's indulgent smile morphed into a frown. "A pushover?" he growled, sitting up in bed. "You'd better watch what you say, girl. You don't know nuthin' from nuthin'."

"Yes, I do, actually. I know that a good plan doesn't need to be changed," I replied in my most stubborn voice.

"Mary, Mother of God, what did I do to deserve such a woman?" Jack asked, glancing over at the Madonna painting across the room. He turned back to me. "Look, girl. Why don't you just go home and pack your bags and stop thinking about the plan, okay? We're still going to the hotel. We're still going to the theater. We're still celebrating St. Valentine's Day together. Your part of the plan hasn't changed, and that's all you need to worry about."

"Well then, what part changed?" I asked, knowing I was pushing my luck but seeing no alternative. Maybe if he told me about how he was going to wake up Bugs, I could convince him it wasn't necessary.

He let out a small growl. "Louise, you're trying my patience. I told you. It's just a small thing that has to do with Bugs and making sure he shows up to the warehouse. I shoulda never even mentioned it, really."

Grr. I was right. Nick had somehow managed to convince the mob leader that Bugs wouldn't show up on time without a little persuasion. And McGurn had bought it, hook, line, and sinker. And now he'd changed the plan solely because of Nick's suggestion. Just as the FBI had said would happen. Grr.

I wondered how Nick had done it; what verbal persuasion he'd used to convince Al Capone's number one right-hand man that his plan was better. It was almost impressive, if it wasn't so frightening. My ex really could sell ice cubes to Eskimos. Or pasta to Italian mob bosses.

Sigh. Okay, well, what's done was done. Time for Dora to make it, uh, undone. And there was only one way I could see to do that. One thing that I had that Nick didn't.

Breasts. Perhaps the most powerful weapon on earth.

I let out a breath. The FBI better give me a freaking medal if I pulled this one off. Maybe even a purple heart. Sure, I hadn't been injured in battle, but I was making extreme oral sacrifices for the cause.

Yup. I was gonna do it. I was gonna suck on his toes.

"I don't know what Sam said to you, baby," I cooed, crawling down to the foot of the bed and pulling up the covers, mentally preparing myself for the disgusting act to follow. I'd better not puke this time; that would ruin everything. "But you can't tell me you really think Bugs won't wake up on time. That he'll miss the massacre. That's completely ridiculous. He'll wake up. The guy's totally up with the sun." I drew in a breath through my mouth, mainly so I wouldn't have to smell his sweaty feet. Then I leaned forward, closing my eyes, ready to seal the deal.

But something caused me to stop before my mouth made contact with his toes. I opened my eyes and looked up. Jack "Machine Gun" McGurn was staring down at me, head cocked, eyes squinting, an utterly bewildered expression on his unshaven face.

Uh . . .

"What the hell are you talking about?" he asked in a slow, even voice. "What do you mean, you don't think Bugs will wake up on time? Do you know somethin' that I don't know? Did someone tell you somethin', Louise? And what does Sam have to do with any of this?"

All the blood drained from my face. "You, uh, haven't talked to Sam recently?" I asked. Wow, it was really hard to swallow with such a huge lump in my throat.

"I haven't seen the guy in days. He's not even a part of this. I'm using an outside crew for this operation."

Oh, crap.

"So maybe you should tell me what the hell is goin' on, Louise," McGurn said, tight-lipped. "What makes you think Bugs won't wake up on time? And what connection does Sam have to all of this?"

"No, you misunderstood me." I laughed nervously. "I said Bugs *would* wake up on time. Absolutely would. You don't have to worry about him waking up, because he will . . . most definitely . . . wake . . . up."

Oh God. I had a bad feeling I'd just messed up big time. Spoken too soon. Should I toe-suck? Maybe it would distract him. . . .

Machine Gun scrunched up his face, and I could practically see the brain cells inside his big head trying to fire up. Damn it! Me and my big mouth. I'd been so sure that Nick had already been by. That he was the one who had changed the plan. But now it looked like I'd been wrong. Completely and utterly wrong. Not to mention the slight possibility that now I'd just inadvertently suggested that the bad guy go do exactly what I'd been sent back in time to stop him from doing.

God. I was too stupid to live. Seriously. Way, way too stupid to live.

I looked over at McGurn. He was still lost in thought. I had to save this. Somehow. Some way. Oh, man, Ratty was going to be so pissed at me.

"Oh, Jackie, I was just flapping my gums. You know me. Can't help but give my opinion, even when it's not asked for. I'm sure your plan is perfect. I'm just being silly. Bugs will totally show up on time. And then you can shoot him and he'll be dead and Al will be so proud of you. And—" *Come on, Dora, keep it up!* "And we'll celebrate. With . . . champagne. Really good champagne." I beamed my best smile at him, then leaned down to get closer to his toes. "But now, baby, enough talk. Close your eyes and let's make you feel all good inside. I can do that for you. You know I can."

But before I could make contact, McGurn pulled his feet away. I didn't know whether to be relieved or disappointed. "No, no, wait." He waved a hand at me. "You've actually got a good point, Louise. I mean, what if Bugs don't show up? He's a notoriously late sleeper. He'd be late to his own funeral—that's what they like to say about Bugs, you know? And if he don't show up on time, well, the whole thing would be a bust." He looked down at me, a big smarmy grin on his face. "You know, Louise, for a dim-witted showgirl, you can be pretty smart sometimes."

"Uh, no, I'm not. I'm really not smart. In fact, I'm

dumb. A Dumb Dora, remember?" I desperately tried to backpedal. Me and my big mouth. Me and my stupid big mouth. "Forget I said anything."

"No, no, this is good," McGurn insisted. "We can send someone over there. Your friend Daisy, maybe. Have her . . . entertain him for the night. Then make sure he wakes up in the morning on time. It's a good plan. I'm grateful to you for thinking of it."

"No, really. You don't have to—"

I stopped, midsentence.

Did he just say . . . ?

"Daisy?" What the hell did any of this have to do with Daisy?

"Yeah, Daisy." McGurn shrugged. "Why not? Everyone loves Daisy. She's a good girl. Not a bad looker, either. Bugs will love her."

I sat up at the foot of the bed, confused as hell. "Do you think she'd do that? Agree to sleep with the guy just 'cause you asked her to?" I couldn't imagine the vivacious flapper allowing herself to be used like that. Especially by a guy. I mean, she was so anti-men. What kind of hold did McGurn have on her that would make him think she'd agree to this kind of plan? Was he blackmailing her or something?

"Why wouldn't she?" McGurn asked, scrunching his thick eyebrows together. "Our little whore isn't developing morals all of a sudden, is she? She'd better not be getting religion or somethin'. It would be a serious inconvenience to my whole operation."

"Whore . . . ?" I mouthed. Oh. My. God. Suddenly everything started sliding into a sick, screwed-up place.

"Sorry. Does that word offend you?" Jack grinned, not appearing the least bit apologetic. "How about . . . our little professional? Is that better for you, Louise? Don't wanna offend your delicate sensibilities and all."

I could barely focus on his words. My mind was spinning too fast. Daisy was a prostitute? That sweet, big-hearted, pretty girl was actually a *Pretty Woman*? It seemed impossible, yet . . .

I'd just caught her leaving the club, still dressed from the night before. I'd thought it was a walk of shame. Maybe it wasn't so shameful after all . . .

"*You* slept with her last night!" I cried incredulously. The second I voiced the accusation, I regretted it. After all, what did I care who McGurn was sleeping with? It wasn't like he was actually my boyfriend. And it wasn't like Louise wasn't busy hooking up with Sam on a regular basis. Machine Gun's sex life was a complete red herring in this case. And I had more important fish to fry.

"Yeah, so what if I did?" he asked, folding his arms across his chest, a frown on his face. "You gonna make somethin' of it, Louise?"

Grr. How dare he be so smug about it? He should be apologizing, at least. Or making up stupid excuses that no one would buy except a girlfriend who desperately wanted to believe that her man wasn't a complete and utter A-hole. But no. This guy felt no shame for his extracurricular bedroom antics. No shame at all. And that pissed me off.

"Hello?! Earth to Machine Gun. Come in, Machine Gun." I waved my hands in front of his face. "You have a girlfriend, remember?"

He shrugged. "I also have a wife."

My mouth dropped open in my utter disgust. God, what a scumbag! He had a wife? A *wife*? Ugh. I wanted to smack him. But that wouldn't help the whole saving the world thing, so I restrained myself. Barely.

But still! How could Louise be so stupid? Sleeping with a guy like this? Was she really so desperate to get into his wallet? Didn't she even have the least bit of respect for herself?

You know, I should write her a letter. Something for her to read when she takes back possession of her body. Explain to her that she doesn't have to live this way. Daisy was right. She should run off to Hollywood. Or something. Anything except hang around a married, prostitute-banging gangster just because he had a little dough. The girl definitely needed to find a little R-E-S-P-E-C-T, that was for sure.

I shook my head. Lecturing my host body would have to come later. Right now I had to stay focused, change the subject back to the matter at hand.

"So, *any*-way," I said through clenched teeth. "You really think it's a good idea to send Daisy in to make sure Bugs wakes up on time?"

"Yeah." McGurn nodded, looking a little relieved at the subject change. Lucky bastard, getting off the hook so easily. "Think of it as . . . insurance. We all need a little insurance in our lives." He reached down to rumple my hair again. Annoying. Especially since flatirons were years away from being invented and I was going to have a heck of time getting those curls presentable again.

"You're a genius, doll. I'm a lucky man to have you around. Real lucky."

Lucky indeed. I was sick of everyone else being so goddamned lucky. When was it my turn to roll the dice? Of course, I'd probably get snake eyes the way this time travel trip was going.

What was I going to do? Thanks to me and my big mouth, McGurn was now totally and utterly convinced that this was the best course of action. And from the look on his face, I was pretty sure I wasn't going to be able to talk him out of it.

But maybe I could work on Daisy . . .

A lightbulb lit up above my head like always happens with cartoon characters. I jumped off the bed, then leaned down to kiss him on his slightly sweaty forehead.

"I'm lucky to have you, too, sweetie," I cooed. "But now I've got to get going. Things to do, people to see. All of that."

McGurn frowned. "You don't want to stay a bit?" he asked in a whining, hopeful tone. "Have our own little petting party under the covers?"

It took all the power I had not to wrinkle my nose in disgust. Ew, ew, ew. I mean, the idea of jumping into bed with him would have disgusted me before I knew he'd just slept with a prostitute and had a wife on the side. Now it was just horrifying.

"I'm sorry, darling," I said, hoping my voice sounded more believable to his ears than it did to mine. "But I have to go. I'll make it up to you later, I promise." I beamed at him. "Besides, you just had Daisy, right?

Didn't she satisfy your little toesie-woesies?" Inspired, I reached down and tickled his feet, promising myself I'd sterilize my fingers as soon as I left the room.

He giggled. Actually giggled. "Stop that!" he cried, swatting me playfully. I forced myself to not roll my eyes. For a big-time people-killing Chicago-controlling gangster, he really was a silly little boy when it came to his feet.

Can we say *freak*?

I stopped the tickling. "Okay, dearie, I'll see you later," I said. I headed to the door, more than ready to make my exit.

"Don't stray too far," McGurn called after me. "We've got to check into the hotel tomorrow. It'll be a nice romantic Valentine's Day. Just the two of us."

My shoulders slumped. I was really running out of time, wasn't I? Soon it would be just the twelve of us: me, him, and his ten fat, smelly toes.

"Terrif," I muttered. "Can't wait."

CHAPTER TEN

No matter how dim-witted Ratty might have thought me, Observant Reporter Girl did thankfully have the common sense to note where Daisy lived when we'd stopped by her place yesterday. (I'd waited in the car while she ran up to change before the party.) So it was no trouble at all once I left the club to hail a taxi and head across town for an impromptu visit. The two of us had to talk.

For a lady of the evening, Daisy lived in a pretty nice spot. When I visited yesterday, I'd assumed it was a residence hotel, with its cheery brick façade and green awning over the shiny red door. Now I wondered if perhaps it was actually the Illinois equivalent to the Best Little Whorehouse. Could be either, I guessed, depending on whether Daisy was more of a takeout or delivery type of girl.

I immediately felt bad for making cracks about Louise's friend. Daisy had been nothing but sweet and supportive to me. Who was I to judge her lifestyle? There were only a few ways for a woman to make a living back in the 1920s. And it wasn't like she could have gone to college and become a doctor or something. Even secretarial school must have cost a few bucks. Bucks Daisy didn't have because she'd had to escape her abusive father when she was fourteen.

I paid the cabbie and walked into the building, wondering what I was getting myself into. The lobby was dark and quiet at this early morning hour. A few couches faced a dying fire, and a coffee table between them held the empty glasses and full ashtray remnants of a party the night before.

"Well, well, well. Look what the cat dragged in."

Startled, I whirled. A tiny Asian woman with a wrinkled face and gray streaks in her long black hair stood behind me, arms crossed over her breasts. She was wearing a silk bathrobe and didn't look at all pleased with my presence.

"Uh, hi," I said brightly. "Is Daisy here, do you know?"

The woman's face darkened and she set her lips into a pursing frown. "This is how you greet me, Louise Rolfe?" she said in an overly angry tone. "You think you can just waltz back in here after eight months and pretend like nothing happened? You think I'd forget?"

"Huh?" Oh, great. I'd evidently inadvertently walked right into some bees' nest. Did Louise used to live here or something? Maybe she'd skipped out on the rent when McGurn set her up with her new digs.

"I'm, uh, sorry," I stammered. "I'm just here to see Daisy."

"You're not seeing anyone, darling, until I get my money."

I sighed. *Thanks a lot, Louise. As if things weren't difficult enough. Now I have to deal with your back rent.*

I fished into my purse. "Uh, how much do I owe you?"

"You should know. You stole it from me in the first place."

Ugh. Louise, I'm so going to kill you, girl.

Well, technically I wouldn't, since murdering her wouldn't be so hot for me, either. Maybe I'd just, uh, pig out later—have a big fat carbfest or something. Make her gain a ton of weight. That way I could literally have my revenge and eat it, too.

"It was eight months ago, lady," I said. "Cut me some slack."

"Two hundred eleven dollars and eighty-three cents."

Damn. I had like a buck fifty in my purse. I didn't suppose she'd take American Express either. Not that I had an Amex on me. And I certainly couldn't hit the ATM. What did people do before plastic?

"I, uh, don't have it now," I admitted. "But I promise to come back later this afternoon if I can just see Daisy for two seconds."

The woman smiled, but not in a happy-go-lucky bunny rabbits and roses sure-I-believe-you-and-will-catch-you-later kind of way. More of a, say, oh-I've-got-an-evil-idea-that-you're-going-to-hate-and-I'm-going-to-love type of smile if I had to describe it. And I was so not looking forward to finding out what that evil idea that I was going to hate and she was going to love was.

"Actually, since you're here, you can pay it back in

trade," she said in a smug voice. "In a lucky coincidence, Mr. Brown is upstairs right now. And we all know you're a favorite of Mr. Brown's."

Oh.

My.

God.

I stared at her, horrified, realization smacking me across the face. And here I'd been judging Daisy for being a prostitute. Was I one as well? Was I a hooker? A whore? A Julia Roberts without a Richard Gere?

Things fell into place. That's probably how Louise knew Daisy. And how a showgirl hooked up with a married mob boss. He was probably a former client who decided to go the rent-to-own route after sampling the wares.

Ew. I suddenly felt itchy. Dirty in Louise's skin. Thinking about where she'd been. What she'd done.

Ew, ew, ew.

I drew in a deep breath. Panicking wasn't going to help me. I needed to keep a calm head so I didn't end up in Mr. Brown's room.

"Actually, I've retired from the whole working-girl biz," I said, trying to sound nonchalant. "Got a full-time gig now as a girlfriend, you know. And I don't really think my old man will appreciate me sharing the goods with Mr. Brown."

The madame, for I guess that's what she was, rolled her eyes, took deliberate steps over to the hotel reception counter and reached under the bar.

Then she pulled out a shotgun.

Fucking hell. This was going from bad to worse.

"You have three choices, dearie," she said in a calm, overly sweet voice. "You can pay me what you owe. You can go visit Mr. Brown. Or you can be shot from here to kingdom come." She raised the gun, pointing it at my heart. "It really doesn't make much difference to me."

I swallowed hard. The look in her eyes told me that she wasn't playing games. I could really get shot here. Game over.

I held out my hands. "Uh, wait," I begged in a trembling voice. "You don't want to do that. Really. I'll, um, go see . . . Mr. Brown. Or something. Please!"

She paused for what seemed an eternity. Maybe she had already decided shooting me would be her best option. That'd be my luck. I squeezed my eyes shut. I couldn't believe after all I'd been through that this was where it was going to end.

And then what would happen? Would I wake up as Dora? Or would I be buried in Louise's body? And what would happen to the future now that I'd so miserably, stupidly failed the past?

But just as I resigned myself to an unceremonial death in a Chicago bunny ranch, a voice prompted me to open my eyes and whirl around.

"How much does she owe you?"

Recognition and relief allowed me to let out the breath I was holding. The call-girl cavalry had arrived, just in the nick of time.

Daisy was still wearing the same outfit. Had she been out turning a breakfast trick while I was talking to McGurn?

"Daisy, thank God you're here," I said. "This woman was going to shoot me if I didn't pay her."

"Shut up, Louise," the flapper said curtly. She turned to the madame. "How much does she owe you, Mrs. Grundy?"

The Madame lowered the gun, looking almost disappointed she wasn't going to get to shoot me. "Two hundred eleven dollars and thirteen cents."

"Fine." Daisy fished in her purse and handed over a wad of bills. "There's two hundred twenty there at least. That should settle her account with interest."

Mrs. Grundy greedily took the money and started counting. Daisy rolled her eyes and grabbed me by the hand, leading me toward the stairs.

"Thank—," I started to say. She put a hand over my mouth and nodded her head in the upstairs direction.

We reached her apartment and she unlocked the door and led me inside.

Her place was small and plain, but cute and well taken care of. Not like what you'd expect in a flophouse. Like my apartment, it was a studio; a queen-sized bed with a wrought iron headboard sat on one end and a kitchenette lined the adjacent wall. A navy blue upholstered couch faced a large radio.

I studied the bed for a moment, unable to help wondering what kind of acts had been performed on it, then berated myself for thinking such things. Daisy had just saved my life. I had to stop with the whole judgmental thing.

Daisy pulled a chair out from the kitchen table and offered it to me. "You okay?" she asked, studying me with concerned eyes.

I shrugged, sitting down at the table. "As well as can be expected, I guess, after nearly getting shot and killed."

Daisy laughed. "Yeah, well, you're the one who's off your trolley, Louise. I can't believe you showed your face here after what you did to her. She's got every right to shoot you."

I was dying to know what Louise did, but of course I couldn't ask. "Well, thanks for coughing up the cash," I said instead. "I'll pay you back, of course."

"No problem, doll." Daisy smiled. "Anything for you." She turned to the kitchen. "I'll put on some tea."

"Thanks." I could definitely use the caffeine after my near-death experience. Of course, a Starbucks triple venti sugar-free vanilla nonfat latte would have done me better, but I'd take what I could get.

As she bustled in the kitchen area, filling the teapot with water and placing it on the stove, I pondered how I would explain what I needed her to do. What if she asked a lot of questions? I wouldn't be able to answer them. What if she got suspicious and went back to Machine Gun and told him what I'd told her? He'd think I was a traitor. That I had connections with the North Siders and was actively trying to save Bugs Moran. That would not be good. I'd better hope Daisy and Louise were damn good friends.

"So, Daisy . . ."

"One second." Daisy walked back to the table, two steaming mugs of tea in her hands. She handed one over and sat down across from me. She set her tea down and met my eyes. "Look, I know why you're here. And I'm sorry. I never thought you'd get up that early to catch me leaving."

Ah, she thought I was mad that she'd slept with my boyfriend. Well, I guess I should play mad. After all, it would seem more realistic. And I'd been mad earlier.

"Yeah. I was pretty shocked to learn my best friend was having sex with my boyfriend, if you must know."

"Yeah, but better it was me, right? You know he's going to hire some dame to suck his toes when you're not around. I mean, he's Machine Gun McGurn. So, better that it's your friend who won't try to take him from you than some other girl."

I didn't know what was worse. Her ridiculous logic or the fact that she'd basically just admitted to wrapping her mouth around his disgusting feet.

"I just wish you had told me."

"I would have. But I thought you'd probably kick him to the curb if I did. And he's good for you, Louise. He's got money. A lot of money."

"Money isn't everything."

"No? Well, maybe not, but it's certainly nice to have. You've never lived on the streets, Louise. You don't know what it's like to have no money."

My heart went out to the little flapper. She really was one of those stereotypical hookers you always saw in the movies. The ones with hearts of gold beneath their corsets. But Daisy didn't have to "put on the red light," as Sting would say. There were other options.

"Maybe not, but I know that the trade you practice isn't going to support you for the long term. What are you going to do when you get older?"

"Shoot myself?" Daisy laughed hoarsely, in a way that made me wonder whether she was joking. "Blackmail one of my clients? Don't worry. I'll figure out something."

"Why don't you start now? Go to Katie Gibbs or something. You've got some money saved, right?"

Daisy frowned. "You know that money's for California, Louise. For when you finally agree to leave this dump with me. I've saved enough for two train tickets to Hollywood, with enough left over to get an apartment for at least a month. And by then, we'll be movie stars." My heart broke for her. Her outer shell said tough street chick. But inside, she was so naïve. So innocent. She really thought it would be that easy. To show up in Hollywood and become a star. More likely she'd end up turning tricks for B-movie actors who would try to pay with bad checks.

"Look, I didn't come here to lecture you on your career choice," I said. "I came because I found out Machine Gun is going to ask you to do him a favor. And as your best friend, I'm asking you not to do it."

Daisy cocked her head. "A favor? What kind of favor?"

"He's going to ask you to go sleep with Bugs Moran, this North Side gangster."

"I know who Bugs is, Louise," Daisy said. "But why on earth would Machine Gun want me to sleep with him? I thought they were sworn enemies."

"I'm, uh, not sure," I lied. "Just, when he asks you, I

want you to agree to do it, get him to think it's all set. Then, on the night you're supposed to go, check into a hotel or something. I'll pay."

"Uh, o-kay," Daisy said hesitantly. She took a long sip of tea. "But why?"

I knew she was going to ask that. Damn, what should I tell her? What possible reason could Louise have to not want her hooker friend to not turn a particular trick?

"Because, uh, he has, uh . . . the clap," I said, divine inspiration hitting at the last possible moment. "Nasty guy. You wouldn't want to catch that, now would you?"

"No. Of course not." Daisy still looked a bit puzzled. "But I still don't understand why Machine Gun wants me to sleep with Bugs at all. Is something going down I should know about? Does it have to do with Capone? I heard Al went down to Florida this week. Are they planning something I should know about?"

I shrugged. "You know Machine Gun. He never tells me the inside mob stuff. But I just wanted to make sure you were safe. That's all that matters to me."

"Awh, baby, that's so sweet." Daisy rose from her chair and walked around the table. She took my hands in hers and pulled me to a standing position.

Uh . . .

"I really appreciate you looking out for me, doll. We women have to stick together."

"Exactly," I said. Why was she still holding my hands? And, uh, standing very close to me? Had she never heard of the three foot-bubble rule?

"I love you, Louise," she murmured. Then, before I

could properly respond, she stood up on her tiptoes and pressed her mouth against mine.

Oh. My. God.

For a moment I didn't know what to do. Was this just some sisterly gesture? Maybe this was something women in the twenties did. An innocent—

Her tongue darted out to lick my lips.

Then again, to quote the great Britney Spears, "not that innocent."

Oh dear.

What should I do? What would Louise do? I'd never thought in a million years to ask the Men in Black whether Louise's best friend was a lesbian. Or if Louise was even remotely bi-curious. For all I knew, maybe Daisy and Louise locked lips on a daily basis.

Even so . . .

I reached out, placing my hands on her shoulders, and gently pushed her away. She looked back at me with such a confused, lost puppy dog face that I realized without a doubt this was her first foray into girl-kissing. And I was the lucky girl who got stuck breaking her heart.

I sighed. "I'm sorry," I said. "You're beautiful and sweet. But I just can't . . ." I trailed off. What more could I really say? There was no way to make this easier. Less awkward. "I'm not, you know . . ."

"I thought . . . I mean, I hoped . . ." Daisy scrunched her little doll face in frustration. "God. I'm such a Dumb Dora. To think that someone like you . . ." She trailed off, her big brown eyes filling with tears. "Don't tell anyone, Louise. Please don't tell anyone. I'd rather die than let anyone know."

She sank into the chair, putting her head in her hands and started sobbing away. My heart ached for her and I longed to take her in my arms and offer her a comforting hug. But I was worried the gesture would be taken for something it wasn't, and the last thing I wanted was to confuse the girl any further.

Poor thing. It was difficult enough for women to love women in the twenty-first century. But now, in the twenties, it must have been damn near impossible. For her to get up the courage to even make a move, to kiss her best friend and hope that the best friend wanted to kiss her back . . . Well, that must have been the hardest thing she'd ever had to do. I had to let her know I saw it as an act of courage rather than an act of weakness.

"It's not a big deal, sweetie," I assured her. "I understand. And just because I don't feel the same way doesn't mean you should be embarrassed. It's perfectly natural."

Daisy shook her head, tears streaming down her face. "What are you talking about? Natural? It's not natural! It's an abomination of nature. I'm a freak." She scrambled to her feet and paced the kitchen, stomping in frustration. The neighbors below were going to be so pleased. "I've tried and tried to fall in love with men. I've necked and petted fellas who everyone says are perfect catches. But I've never felt a thing for them. The only time I feel goofy is when I think about other women." She paused, looking over at me, her eyes black with smudged makeup. "When I think of you, Louise, I think . . . I think I'm in love with you."

178

After finishing her rant, the young flapper burst into a fresh set of tears. Concerned, I started to stand up, but she put out a hand in a gesture to stop.

"No. Please. You'll only make it worse."

"But, Daisy . . ." I had to let her know it was okay for her to feel as she did. That she couldn't help being born with a particular sexual preference, and that she needed to embrace who she was and not fight it to the point where she made herself sick. I wanted to assure her that she would find someone someday who shared her interests. Who would love her for who she was and want to make her a special part of her life.

"I've got to . . . You've got to go!" Before I could get a word in, Daisy made strides to the front door and yanked it open. She gestured for me to leave.

I considered arguing the point further, convincing her that all was okay, but then decided she probably needed some alone time to nurse her embarrassed confusion before facing me again. If she'd been feeling that way about Louise for a long time and finally picked this morning to make her move—well, my rejection was bound to mess her up for a while, poor thing.

Why was it we humans always ended up causing each other so much pain? Life evolved into a series of miscommunications and unreturned desires. You liked him, he liked the girl down the street, who liked someone else entirely. And we danced the dance, played the games, and allowed ourselves to get hurt over and over and over. And to what ultimate gain? Was there a light at the end of this tunnel? Was there hope that two people could find each other and truly be happy for a lifetime? Was there a person out there with whom you'd feel completely content and who would also feel completely content with you?

Was that even possible? Rational?

Or were we chasing rainbows and mirages and risking our hearts and wasting our lives on this game called "love" for absolutely no reason at all?

"Well, that didn't go as well as I'd hoped," I said to The Rat as I walked back into the apartment.

"Mess everything up again, honey?" Ratty asked. He was lying in the middle of the bed, cleaning himself. Yes, *there*. Ew. I turned my head, not wanting to look.

"Do you, uh, mind not licking yourself on my bed?" I asked.

"Hey, you'd do it too, if you could reach."

"Actually, no. No, I wouldn't."

"Mm-hm. Right. So what happened? How'd you effortlessly succeed in fucking up the world before eight in the morning?"

"You're the one who got me up early."

"And good thing I did. Sounds like you're going to need all day to fix your screwups."

I sighed and sank down into a stiff, upholstered armchair. (I so wasn't getting back on the bed until I changed the sheets!) "Well, it's really not my fault. . . ."

"Right. Uh-huh. Neither was Mrs. O'Leary's cow to blame for the Great Chicago Fire. But do go on and explain why not."

So I did. I told him about meeting Daisy mid-walk of

shame. About going up to McGurn's room and learning the plan had changed. (I sort of left out the part that it was my fault he now wanted Daisy to wake up Moran; The Rat had enough ammunition on me as it was.) Then I got to the point in the story where Daisy kissed me.

Ratty sat up. "Talk about burying the lead," he cried. "She's a lesbian? How freaking awesome is that? Did you two get it on? Did you giggle as you ripped off each other's clothes?"

I sighed. "It was just a kiss. There was no clothes ripping."

"Was there tickling? Maybe, say, with a feather duster?"

"And you say *I'm* distracted from saving the world."

"Fine. Destroy my fantasy. Thank you very much. You could have made something up, you know." Ratty pouted. "I'd never have known the diff *and* it would have killed the monotony that is my day to day rodental existence."

"I'm sorry," I said, lacing my voice with sarcasm. "Maybe I misunderstood my mission: I'm supposed to entertain you, not save the world."

"You're doing a lousy job at both, so I suppose it doesn't matter which you concentrate on at this point."

I opened my mouth to argue, then realized that unfortunately he was right. I really had ruined everything. Worse than he realized, even. How had I been so stupid to blurt out the part about waking up Moran? I mean, what had I been thinking?

I decided to get off my high horse. Sure, it was humiliating to grovel before The Rat, but at this point I didn't know what else to do.

"So I'm stuck," I confessed. "I don't know how to change Machine Gun's mind. I don't know if Daisy will honor my request not to go see Moran and wake him up."

"I suppose not. Though if you had torn her clothes off and given her multiple orgasms she probably would have. Now, who knows?"

"I'm trying to be serious here!"

"Okay. You're right. Sorry." The Rat jumped off the bed and scampered over to me. "So let's look at our options now. You've tried to talk to Machine Gun, but he won't listen. You're not sure you'd be able to convince Daisy of anything unless you pour chocolate sauce on her body and lick it off."

I shot him a glare. He chuckled.

"Sorry. Couldn't resist," he said. "So that leaves one person."

"It does?"

"Who are you forgetting? Who's the guy you keep claiming is the most charming, convincing person you know?" He paused. "Besides me, of course."

"Are you talking about Nick?" Ugh, I was afraid he was going to bring him up.

"Give the girl a gold freaking star. Go to the head of the class."

"What can Nick do?"

"He's in the body of one of McGurn's men, right? If you befriend him, maybe you can convince him to get McGurn to change his mind again."

"But that doesn't make any sense. Nick's whole

mission—the whole reason he came back in time to begin with—was to wake Bugs up."

"The right woman has convinced many a man to abandon their purpose, honey. You think Paris gave a damn about anything when he stole Helen of Troy away from Menelaus? Or Romeo cared a lick for his family when he fell for Juliet? It's obvious Nick wants you. If you can seduce him, maybe he'll agree to talk to McGurn. After all, wasn't that the plan to begin with? To convince him not to change history? You're the one who tried to go the roundabout route. Look where that got you."

I released a frustrated sigh. He was right. Of course he was right. But go out and seduce Nick? That was asking an awful lot. First off, I had no idea if Nick would even be receptive to any advances I'd throw his way. After all, getting kicked in the balls by a woman you were trying to have sex with can be kind of a deal breaker. He probably hated Louise's guts right about now.

Then again, Nick always was stubborn. And when he went after something, he never gave up 'til he got it. If he wanted Louise, surely a little kick wasn't enough to dissuade him from his prize.

"You're right," I said, giving in. "As much as I don't like the idea of having to interact with him, it's the only thing left to try."

"Good." The Rat nodded his approval. "Just, whatever you do, don't let him know that you're really Dora."

"Right. I understand. That's the last thing I want, anyway." I couldn't imagine what Nick would do if he found out who I really was. Though I did wonder . . .

No. I shook my head. It was much better to stay in character. Get the job done. Go back to my life as single girl in San Diego, Dora Duncan. This way I'd not only be saving the world . . .

I'd be saving my heart.

CHAPTER ELEVEN

I watched from the bar, sipping my water and keeping a low profile as Nick entered the ballroom. He stormed across the shiny wood floor, his steps quick and his mouth turned down in a frustrated frown. His meeting with the big boss must not have gone as well as he'd planned. Funny. I would have thought he'd be happy that I'd oh-so-conveniently already changed McGurn's plans to include the Bugs Moran wake-up call that he'd been sent back eighty-something years for. Then again, Nick had always been a do-it-yourself type of guy; he was probably pissed off that his job had been made redundant by my idiocy.

Tommy the tuxedoed bouncer approached him, holding out a box of cigars, but Nick waved him off. He mumbled something I couldn't make out, then grabbed his coat off a hook and pushed open the front door.

I drew in a breath. Here went nothing.

After giving him a few seconds of a head start, I

slipped off my barstool and walked slowly toward the exit. I'd decided it'd be much better to approach him outside the club, away from McGurn's spies. Speaking of . . .

"Going somewhere, Louise?"

I whirled around and saw Tommy had come up behind me. He set the cigar box down on a nearby table and folded his burly arms across his chest.

"Uh, out for a smoke," I said, the first thing that came to my mind. Hopefully he wouldn't ask to bum a light as I had neither ciggys nor matches to back up my story.

He furrowed his eyebrows, looking honestly confused. "Why don't you just smoke inside?" he asked.

D'oh. That was dumb. I forgot it'd be another eighty years before society denounced smokers as evil demons and relegated them to the circle of Hell that was Out in the Freezing Cold.

"I need a breath of fresh air," I amended, crossing my fingers he'd buy the idea of a smoker needing fresh air while poisoning her lungs. Although he didn't know about the poison part, of course.

Tommy frowned. "Jackie says you're not supposed to leave the club," he explained. "He says you and him got some hotel to go to tomorrow night to celebrate Valentine's Day and it's very important that you stick around. He told me to make sure you did."

I rolled my eyes. "Yeah. That's *tomorrow* night," I said, emphasizing the word. "As in the day after today? I think I'm okay to go outside for a quick smoke this afternoon, don't you? I'm pretty sure I'll make it back through the door within the next twenty-four hours."

Tommy scratched his head. Evidently my day-of-the-week logic was a bit too complex for him to grasp. McGurn hadn't picked him for his MENSA eligibility, that was for sure.

"I don't know. Jackie said—"

"'Jackie said, Jackie said,'" I mocked gently. "Jeesh. I know he's your boss and all, Tommy, but really! Do you have to ask the guy for permission to use the bathroom?"

He frowned. "No, but—"

"You know, Tommy, I'm disappointed," I said, sighing deeply. "I always thought of you as a smart guy. The type to take charge. Make important decisions all on your own. I had no idea you were just another one of Jackie's flunkies."

Tommy's face darkened. "I ain't no . . ." He cocked his head and I could practically see smoke coming out of his ears. "Whatever it was you called me. I ain't that."

I shrugged. "Okay, if you say so."

"I ain't," he insisted. "Jackie trusts me to run things down here. He lets me make . . . decisions."

"Yeah, right. Sure he does," I patronized, petting his arm. "Just like the one about me going outside for a smoke." I pulled my hand away. "Why don't you go upstairs and ask him for permission to let me go outside?"

"I told you. I can make decisions. I don't need to ask Jackie." He looked enraged. The male ego sure was a fragile thing.

"So . . . ?"

"You can go out for a smoke. I'm deciding. Just come right back." He puffed out his chest in pride over his manly decision.

I wanted to puff mine out over my feminine wiles, but

instead I just grinned. "Ooh, I just love a take-charge man," I cooed, standing on my tiptoes to kiss him on the cheek. "Thanks, darling. See you in a minute."

I dashed out the door before the bouncer could change his mind. I had to say, I was pretty proud of myself. Sure, Tommy wasn't the sharpest tool in the shed, but I still gave myself major points for being able to talk my way out of the situation. Something I used to always leave for Nick to do.

Speaking of, hopefully I wasn't too late to find the guy. I looked up and down the street.

Bingo!

I spotted a lone figure, just turning the corner down the end of the road. Yes! I hadn't lost him. I hastened down the street, trying to catch up. It was really cold out, I suddenly realized, and I'd been so eager to escape Tommy the Brain that I'd forgotten to grab my coat. I hugged my arms around myself in a useless effort to get warm. Hopefully wherever Nick was going wasn't far.

He turned the corner and I continued to stalk him. It was kind of fun, in a way. Reminded me of the old days when we used to do reconnaissance in Baghdad. Of course, back then we were on the same side.

I got to the corner, then stopped as I realized he was nowhere to be seen. I scanned the street. The blinding white sun reflecting off the snow made it difficult to see. Where the hell did he go? I picked up my pace, hurrying down the road to the next cut-off, hoping I could still catch him.

"Looking for someone?"

The voice from behind made me nearly jump out of

my skin. I whirled around. Nick stood there, hands stuffed in his overcoat pockets, eyebrows raised in amused smugness.

Damn. He'd caught me. He must have sensed being followed and ducked into one of the alleyways.

"Uh, just taking a stroll."

"Without your coat?"

"I'm not cold," I retorted. "In fact, I dare say it's rather balmy out here."

I was proud of my answer, but less so when my body decided to betray me with a wracking shudder.

Nick chuckled. "Yes. Balmy. I see." He gallantly pulled off his heavy wool coat and proceeded to drape it over my shoulders. At first I thought about shrugging it off, but my body wasn't about to let me discard this kind of free warmth.

As he swathed me in the coat, his fingertips grazed my shoulder blades and I immediately forgot all about the cold. In fact, I suddenly burned hotter than a Fourth of July picnic. The idea that his touch could do that to me made me frown. How annoying: even now that I knew Sam was really Nick, it didn't stop me from getting completely turned on by the guy! In fact, if anything, knowing Nick was under there made things all the worse. I shivered again, this time more with desire than cold.

Satisfied with the coat placement, Nick turned to look at me. His blue-green eyes studied me with an intensity that made my legs go all gooey.

What was he thinking? Was he wishing he could just throw me up against the wall, pressing hard against me? No words, no casual introductory caress, just his body

189

claiming mine? Taking what he wanted without asking first?

Uh, not that something like that would appeal to me on any level. . . .

"What?" I asked finally, averting my eyes from his. His stare was making my heart beat too fast.

"Your lips are blue," he noted, reaching out to press a finger against them. I had the inexplicable urge to bite the finger, but was thankfully able to restrain myself. "Come on, let's get you inside."

I wanted to refuse. To tell him I'd rather eat a snake. Mainly because I was so pissed at myself for wanting him so badly. But I couldn't do that. I had to get him to help me fix history. My libido would have to behave itself for a little longer.

He put an arm around me, clamping his hand on my shoulder, and led me down the street. It would have been natural for me to wrap my arm around the back of his waist, but I resisted the urge. The less I touched him the better.

What had I gotten myself into? How was I going to convince him to help me? It seemed much simpler when talking to The Rat back in my room. Now, I had no idea how to even start the conversation.

Hey Sammy, dear, want to help me save the world?

I shook my head. I'd just have to bide my time. Keep my cards close, wait for the right opening. Besides, I had to get him in my good graces first, before I could move in for the kill.

Soon we came to a small bar tucked away in a nondescript alleyway. Like with Machine Gun's place, there was no sign, just a burly, heavy-coated bouncer at the door.

"Want to try this place?" Nick asked. "I've never been, but it seems nice and out of the way. Probably won't run into any of your boyfriend's thugs here."

"Sure," I said with a shrug. It was kind of funny, now that I knew Nick was inside Sam's body, to see him try to act like he knew his way around 1929 Chicago. In reality, he was probably just as lost as I was, feeling his way around, hoping he didn't get caught in a mistake. It gave me an odd feeling of power. For once, I was in control. I held all the cards.

We stepped inside the joint. It was a small place, nothing like Machine Gun's lavish speakeasy/dance hall. This was more of a dive bar, really, with a few rickety tables and chairs, a small stage and a bar on the back wall. The kind of place you'd expect peanut shells on the floor. Nothing fancy, but there was an oil burning stove radiating heat in one corner, and that was good enough for me.

Nick led me over to one of the tables and I sank into a seat, soaking in the warmth. I shrugged his coat onto the back of the chair.

"Want a drink?" he asked.

I shook my head. "Water's fine."

I actually could have used a drink—or maybe seven. But I worried about imbibing alcohol around him. A few sips and I'd lose my edge. And with what I had to convince him of, I needed all the edge I could get.

"Awh, come on. Have a drink," he cajoled. "I hate to drink alone."

I frowned. He really thought he was something, didn't

he? Even in someone else's body. Always had to get his own way.

"Water," I repeated, then pressed my lips together firmly.

He rolled his eyes. "You know, babe, sometimes you remind me of my ex-girlfriend. She was just as uptight and high-strung as you are. Never could relax. Enjoy life."

What?!

How dare he? I narrowed my eyes and glared at the jerk across the table. I wasn't uptight! I wasn't high strung! Sure, in Iraq I took life more seriously than he did. I didn't go out and party with the soldiers the night before we had to work. But that didn't make me uptight or high-strung.

Did it? Evidently Nick thought so. Was that why he'd gone off with that Iraqi girl while I languished in prison—because he thought I was unable to have a good time?

I huffed. Uptight. Puh-leeze. Just 'cause I was responsible and took my job seriously and didn't think my time in Baghdad was some Sandals vacation. It was easy for him to be the life of the party. He already had a great career. A good track record with the network. I had to scramble. To prove myself. And that meant long hours and hard work. Sure, I didn't have as much time to hang around the bar with the other correspondents. It didn't mean I didn't know how to have a good time in the right situation.

"You know, life isn't just one big pub crawl," I growled. He gave me a funny look. Oops. That didn't sound very 1920s, did it? I needed to start thinking before just spouting off random twenty-first centuryisms around him. Not that he had a shot in hell at guessing that I was really his ex-girlfriend, sent back in time to stop him from committing another St. Valentine's Day Massacre. But still, I didn't need to rouse his suspicions or I'd never get what I wanted out of him.

Luckily he lacked the technology to fire up Wikipedia to see when the phrase "pub crawl" was coined. For all he knew, it could have been a standard part of the twenties vernacular.

"I never said it was," he replied at last. "But it's not a funeral, either."

I had the serious urge to reach over the table and strangle him—or kiss him senseless. One of the two. But I restrained myself on both ends. My mission was to get him to help me, and that meant I had to sweet talk him, not piss him off or molest him.

"Fine. I've changed my mind," I said. "I'll have a gin and tonic." I paused, then added bravely, "But hold the tonic."

He wanted to have a good time? I'd show him I could have a good time. Besides, maybe a drink would help me relax. I could then get out what I had to say without as much bumbling and hesitation.

Nick raised an eyebrow, but nodded in response. "Excellent choice, Madame. I'll be right back," he said, reaching over to pat me on the forearm. I grimaced, as even the most casual of touches shot electricity through my bones. Stupid traitorous Roaring Twenties body. If only I was myself, his touch would do absolutely nothing to me. In fact, it'd probably feel slimy. Disgusting.

Yeah, right, Dora. You keep telling yourself that.

I watched as Nick approached the bar, leaning onto it casually, with his typical alpha male arrogance. Even here, he really thought the world was his oyster, didn't he? That confidence he exuded: it used to charm me. Now it just annoyed the hell out of me. How dare he be able to act so free? So happy and unbothered?

Forget that, I told myself. *It doesn't matter.* He was a jerk. I was over him. The only reason I was here was to convince him to help me save the world. Finito. End of story.

The plan formed in my mind. We'd have a few drinks. He'd loosen up. I'd flirt and sweet talk my way into his good graces. Then I'd spring my request. I wasn't exactly sure how I'd phrase it—neither Ms. Manners nor Ann Landers ever did cover "how to ask your ex-boyfriend to help you save the world." But I was confident I'd be able to come up with something when the moment presented itself.

In the meantime, I'd show that bastard I knew how to have a good time.

Nick returned with our drinks and handed me mine. "Here you go, princess," he said. "Straight up. Hope you can handle it."

I scowled at his sarcasm, taking the finger of gin and tipping it back, sucking down the contents in one gulp. I clanked the glass back down on the table. Handle it, indeed. I'd show him I knew how to handle it. He wanted to see Louise have a good time? Well, send in the clowns, baby. This was about to become a rip-roaring party.

"Uh," he said, taking a small sip of his own drink. "You . . . want another?"

"Yes. But I'll get it." I rose from my seat and headed to the bar, my stomach already warm from the first round. I'd never been much of a drinker, really. Not after my sister and I robbed my parents' liquor cabinet in junior high. Having your stomach pumped at twelve can really convince you to lay off the booze.

But this time, I had something to prove. So I ordered two shots, downed one and brought the other to the table. It spilled a bit as I set it down.

"For a girl who only wanted water, you seem to have suddenly developed an unquenchable thirst for gin," Nick remarked.

I groaned. "First you criticize me for not drinking. Now you're on my case for drinking too much? There's no winning with you, man."

He laughed. "No judgment here, baby. Just observation." He lifted his drink. "To you, Louise," he toasted. "The prettiest girl in the room."

I scanned the bar. "Uh, hello? I'm the only girl in the room."

"Well, you win by default then, don't you?" he said with a wink.

"Thanks a lot."

"My pleasure." He tipped back his drink. "Me, I'm the compliment masta," he said with a swagger.

I giggled at his silliness, then berated myself for doing

so. I shouldn't be falling for this. Stupid alcohol. If I were sober I wouldn't find him the least bit funny. In fact, I'd find his confident arrogance extremely annoying.

I mean, really! How could he just sit here, in someone else's body, eighty-something years in the past, looking so cool and collected and in control? Effortlessly flirting with the first girl who came along? Here I was, trying to save the world, and to him—just like in Iraq—this was just one big time-travel Club Med.

The idea infuriated me. Why didn't he feel the pain and longing I did? Why wasn't he mourning the loss of our relationship? Why was I the only one in the room still ready to burst into tears at a moment's notice?

Because he doesn't know it's you, you idiot! My oh-so-gentle brain stepped in to reality check me.

Well, that was true, I supposed. He didn't have the complete 411 on the situation as I did. And I was willing to bet he'd be acting a tad differently if he knew who was looking through Louise's eyes across the table.

And besides, if I was being completely honest here, I knew Nick's talent at false bravado better than anyone. How good he was at hiding his true feelings from the world. He could be hurting like mad on the inside; he'd never let on to a stranger.

I flashed back to those rare nights in Iraq after he'd had a few too many drinks. We'd go back to our hotel and he'd start crying. Crying for all that we'd seen. The bloodied babies. The blackened flesh of dead women and children who happened to be in the wrong place at the wrong time. He'd cry for humanity and all that was lost.

That was the Nick I fell in love with. The one he kept

hidden from the rest of the world. The one he was keeping hidden from Louise now. He didn't love Louise. He wasn't even being honest with her. He was just playing his part in the game.

As I should be playing mine.

Okay, then. I firmed my resolve. I could do this. I just had to think about it as he did: that it was only a game. Sure, the stakes were pretty high, but still. Better to bet on the world than my heart.

With perfect timing, the bartender dropped the needle on the record and the cheery sounds of vibrant jazz drowned out any opportunity to have a deep discussion.

As David Bowie would say, "Let's Dance."

I sucked down my third shot (no sense just leaving it on the table where someone could spike it or something) and jumped up from my chair. My foot caught under the table leg and I almost tripped.

Hm, maybe that last shot wasn't such a good idea.

I managed to right myself and grabbed Nick by the hand. "Come on!" I cried. "Dance Party USA!"

Nick stared at me as if I had two heads, then shrugged and tipped back his drink. He stood up and led me over to the tiny dance floor. He wrapped his arms around my waist and soon we were swinging to the beat.

We weren't very good. After all, neither of us were actually from the 1920s or had any idea what we were doing. At the same time, we both had to fake that this was something we did all the time. It made for some amusing moments, as well as some painful ones when Nick inadvertently stepped on my toes. He never was a very good dancer, even in modern day.

Still, at the same time, it was kind of fun. What had I been so worried about? So sad about? The music was bright and cheery, Nick as Sam was dashing and sexy. What more could a flapper chick want?

Maybe one more drink . . .

I broke away from Nick, motioning to the bar. He raised a skeptical eyebrow and, for a moment, I thought he was going to try to cut me off. As if he had a chance. He wanted someone fun? Someone not uptight? Well, tonight was his lucky night.

A few more couples entered the bar as I downed another gin. Even though it was only early afternoon, they seemed quite intoxicated, laughing and joking as they grabbed drinks and then started dancing.

I watched them as I headed back to Nick, envious of their carefree smiles and easy laughter. What would it be like to be them? To hang out afternoons in bars without a care in the world?

Since I was watching them, I was not watching where I was going. I suddenly tripped over who knows what and lurched forward, right into Nick. I grabbed his arms so I wouldn't splat on the floor, and as a result my third gin sloshed down his white shirt.

D'oh! Even in Louise's body I was still the clumsiest person in the universe.

Nick sighed and shook his head, staring down at his now-dripping shirt. "Maybe you should slow down, kiddo," he said. He grabbed a white cloth from a nearby table and dabbed himself with it. "I mean, just a thought."

"Don't be silly," I said, plucking the napkin from him and playfully wiping it down his chest. "I'm sooo not drunk. I just tripped. The floor is totally uneven. Made out of, like, lawsuit-waiting-to-happen-wood or something." I ran the napkin down the contours of his perfectly sculpted abs. "Ooh, you really have a nice chest," I cooed. "I love the six-pack."

"Uh, thanks," he said, prying the napkin from my fingers and throwing it in the trash. "Nice of you to say."

I scowled at him. What was his problem all of a sudden? He was normally so hot and bothered to get into Louise's pants. And now that I was paying him actual compliments he was backing down? Puh-leeze. What a loser. Loser with a capital L stamped on his forehead, in fact. He should be honored to be getting compliments from such a sexy siren as Louise. After all, she was the cat's pajamas.

"What's your problem, man?" I demanded. "Are you, like, still mad 'cause I kicked you last night?"

"It isn't my fondest recollection of an evening," he admitted. "Next time, a simple, 'I think we're moving too fast and I'd like to stop' would be quite effective."

I felt my face heat. If only he knew . . .

That's it! I should tell him! I should totally and utterly and completely tell him the truth. The whole truth and nothing but the truth, in fact! I mean, think about it. What if I just came out and told him I was Dora? Explain why I was here. What I had to do. Wouldn't that be the simplest solution? Just go ahead and spill all the beans and then tell him why it was so important that we didn't change history? Would he listen? Would he believe me? Would he agree to do what I said?

No. I forced my racing thoughts to make a pit stop. This was the alcohol talking. I wasn't being sensible.

I couldn't tell him who I was or why I was here. As The Rat had said, that would ruin everything. He'd end up pissed off and more determined than ever to make sure he accomplished his mission and changed history. Just to spite me.

No, it was better to go the subtle route. Play the seductress and get him to think he was abandoning his mission for the love of a good woman. A good random fun-loving flapper woman, not his uptight, high-strung ex-girlfriend.

The music changed and the other couples started cheering. I recognized the tune: "Yes, Sir, That's My Baby." A twenties classic.

"The Charleston!" I cried. "I've always wanted to learn to Charleston!"

Nick cocked his head and scrunched his eyebrows. "You don't know how?" he asked incredulously.

Damn. Bigmouth strikes again. The gin was really making me Loose Lips Lola. Of course Louise would know how to Charleston. There was no way she wouldn't know.

"Well . . . do you know it?" I asked, turning the tables on him, knowing the answer before he could open his mouth.

He blushed. Ha! Got him. "Well, I haven't d-done it in a few years," he stammered.

I laughed, glancing over at the other dancers. They

looked like they were having a blast! Suddenly, I wanted nothing more than to join them. To stop worrying and caring and hurting so much and just start dancing.

Ground control to Major Louise. Please put mission on pause. I was going to take five and have a good time.

"I bet they'd teach us if we asked," I suggested. Before Nick could protest, I approached the dancers. "Can you teach us the Charleston?"

"Ab-so-lute-ly!" cried one of the female dancers. She must have been about eighteen. All flapper'd out with her requisite black bob, fringed green dress, and Mary Jane shoes. "You'll be hip to the jive!"

She motioned to her two guy friends to clear away the tables and chairs. Then she headed over to the bartender and asked him to start the song over from the beginning.

Yes sir, that's my baby.
No sir, I don't mean maybe.
Yes, sir, that's my baby now.

"Okay. Now, first yah step back with your right foot," she instructed. "And then you kick back with your left."

I mimicked her movements. Okay, got that.

"Then you step forward with your left foot. And kick with your right."

"OK. Step with my left, kick with my right."

"Then repeat."

"Forward right, kick left. Forward left, kick right." I was getting this. If only in my gin-fueled buzz I could remember which was left and which was right.

201

I glanced over at Nick. He seemed to be getting it a little easier than me. But then, he was still on drink number one.

"Now you're on the trolley!" our instructor praised, clapping her hands. "Time to add arms."

Oh, shoot. I forgot about the arms. This was going to throw off my coordination big time.

"Arms out," the girl said, holding hers raised in example. "Then bend at the elbows." She walked over and bent my arms and positioned my hands facing up. "Now swing your arms from the right to the left." She watched for a moment. "No, no, your other left. That's right! No left!"

I tuned her out. I was doing it! I was dancing the Charleston. In the actual 1920s. How cool was that? I felt like a real flapper now. Woo!

"Hey, this is fun!" I cried. The flapper grinned and started dancing herself. Her two guy friends joined in and soon the place was rocking out like a mini-jazz rave.

I glanced over at Nick. He'd stopped dancing and was leaning against the far wall, taking in the scene. Oh, no he didn't! If I was able to have fun in the 1920s, he was going to, too.

"Come on, Sam!" I begged, dancing over to him. "Swing those arms. Step those feet."

He gave me an amused look, but shook his head. Spoilsport. I grabbed his arms and pulled him away from the wall. For a moment it was just me dancing and him standing there. Then, as the music played on, he gave in and started bobbing a bit. Then came his feet. And finally he was swinging with me. Totally getting into it, grinning like an idiot.

This was, until somehow I managed to trip (stupid floorboards again!) and fell into Nick's arms. He laughed and kissed the top of my head before righting me. Then we continued dancing and he spun me around. We were probably terrible. Probably a shame to our twenties bodies. But it was just so darn fun. I couldn't stop laughing.

Soon we were dancing as good as the guys from the movie *Swingers*. I half-expected a Big Bad Voodoo Daddy song to come on and for someone to tell me that I was "money."

"Woo-hoo!" I cheered. "This is fun!"

There's just something about dancing. It's one of those activities that sticks you in the here and now. When you're dancing there is no past. No present. No future. There's just you and the music.

And the guy who wraps you in his arms.

The song ended and the next one up was a slow ballad I didn't recognize. The other dancers, exhausted and sweaty, abandoned the floor and lined up on stools at the bar where they ordered more drinks.

Nick and I were alone on the dance floor. It was totally a movie moment, and I half-expected some spotlight from above to illuminate us as we suddenly broke into a tango. Instead, Nick pulled me close, placing a hand around my waist and taking my other hand in his. I could feel every contour of his body as he pressed against me. It was a waltz, sweet and quiet. And my feet barely touched the ground.

"This is more my speed," he whispered in my ear.

I laughed appreciatively. I wasn't exactly complaining about having him this close, either. It felt nice. Good.

I suddenly wanted him with a vengeance. So what if it was under false pretenses. So what if he thought I was someone else. I was supposed to be seducing him, right? I was supposed to put myself in the position where he would change history for me.

And besides, it wasn't even like I would be having sex with a stranger. This was Nick. I'd slept with him a billion times already. Technically it wouldn't even be another notch in my belt. Just sex with the ex.

Satisfied with my justification, albeit gin-soaked logic, I grabbed his hands in mine and looked up at him, trying to send him sultry bedroom-eyes vibes. Vibes that would make him unable to resist swooping me into his arms and—

"Are you okay?" he asked, cocking his head. "You look a little . . . constipated."

O-kay. My sultry bedroom eyes were perhaps not as sultry as I had imagined them to be. I should have practiced in the mirror first. But fine. I guess a girl couldn't be subtle in this day and age.

"Let's goh to your plathe," I suggested, realizing suddenly my words weren't forming as easily as I would have liked. Maybe that last gin had been a mistake. Oh well, who cared, right? I didn't need my tongue to form words; I had other plans for it tonight. And I was sure it was still up for that sort of business.

Nick studied my face with all-too-serious eyes. "You want to?" he asked, slowly, carefully. "Are you sure?"

I laughed. "Shorr, I'm shorr."

"'Cause truthfully you seem a bit . . . I guess intoxicated would be the proper word." He scratched his head, still watching me carefully. "I don't want you to do something you're going to regret in the morning."

I groaned. This was ridiculous. For the last few days all he'd tried to do was get me in bed. Now here I was making the offer straight-out and he was hesitating? And for what purpose? 'Cause I'd had a few drinks? I mean, hello? Since when did a woman having a few drinks make a man not want to sleep with her? For a lot of guys that was their whole MO.

"Look, buddy," I said, draping my arms around his shoulders and tipping into him with what I hoped was a sexy lean. "Do you wanna make love or not? 'Cause if you do, you have exactly ten seconds to sweep me off my feet and carry me out of this bar. Otherwise, I change my mind." Nick's eyes widened. Heh. I knew he, like most guys, could never resist an ultimatum. Especially one that involved sex with a hot girl.

"And you swear you won't . . . kick me anywhere remotely uncomfortable this time?"

"Yup." I winked and nodded my head up and down, trying not to let it loll backward as it seemed wont to do for some reason. "Ten, nine, eight . . ." I counted.

"And you won't run off into the night halfway through?"

"Cross my heart—seven, six—hope to die—four, three . . ." Oh, shoot. I think I forgot a number. This counting ultimatum was a bit more tricky than I'd thought.

"Five . . . two . . ."

"All right then," he said, still sounding a little hesitant. He grabbed his coat and swathed me in it. Once bundled up, he reached down and scooped me into his arms. "Here we go."

I cooed in delight as he cradled me like a baby, his hands tucked under my back and my knees. I leaned my head into his shoulder as he carried me out of the speakeasy, off into the sunset like some pirate romance hero, ready to ravish his virgin bride. I could hear the other patrons cheering and voicing their approval back in the bar. I smiled, rejoicing at the sound of his heartbeat in his chest.

Now *this* was romance.

I lifted my head to study him, wanting to better assess his current level of turned-onness. Had I morphed him into jelly with my sultry seduction?

Hm. I frowned. It was hard to tell, actually, if those beads of sweat were from him lusting after me or . . . lifting me.

I leaned in to place a wet kiss on his mouth. Mmm. His lips were so soft. So delish. So—

"Um, Louise?" I could feel his mouth struggling to form words from its trapped position under my lips. "Itth kinda hard to walk with you kithing me like that."

I pulled my head away, a bit offended. How dare he reject my oh-so-valuable kisses? No-good, ungrateful bastard. I considered kicking him again, then reassessed. To be perfectly honest, I guess I could kind of see how blocking his vision would hinder his forward movement. And since we were talking about movement that was carrying me to his apartment where I could kiss him plenty and have my wicked way with him, I guessed I could wait.

"Okay, no problem, baby," I whispered, flopping my head back on his shoulder. "Carry on."

He stopped. I raised my head, stifling a groan. What now?

"And, um, you don't expect me to carry you the whole way, do you?" he asked hesitantly.

I frowned. Wow. Some romance hero he was turning out to be.

"I mean, it's seven blocks," he said apologetically.

I rolled my eyes. Seven blocks? Please. Would Sir Lancelot not have carried fair Guinevere over hill and dale? Would brave Paris not carry fair Helen across the very sea? And here I had this poor slob masquerading as my hero objecting to carrying me seven blocks.

Romance was truly dead.

"Fine, whatever," I muttered, climbing down from his arms and planting my feet back on the ground. Wow. My knees felt kind of wobbly. "These boots were made for walkin'."

Nick shot me a confused look and I realized my mistake. Quoting Nancy Sinatra was probably not the best way to stay in character.

Luckily, a sudden clattering in the bushes prevented any potential interrogation. Nick shot me a look and put a finger to his mouth. He pulled out a gun from inside his jacket and motioned for me to get behind him. Wow, he had an actual gun? Did twenty-first century city boy even know how to use one of those?

"Is someone there?" he called out. "Show yourself."

He headed over to the bushes and scanned them closely. I waited under the street lamp, realizing I was a sitting duck. Was someone following us? Maybe Tommy the bouncer wasn't so stupid after all. Or maybe McGurn hired someone to trail me.

Nick returned to my side, shrugging his shoulders. "Probably just a cat," he said, though his voice told me he didn't buy the feline theory for a second. "Nothing to worry about."

"Are you sure?" I asked. The last thing I needed was to have some stoolie go back to McGurn and tell him I went home with another guy. And not just any other guy—one of his own men. Sure, *he* was sleeping with everyone under the sun, but I didn't believe for one second he'd be cool with his girlfriend doing the same.

"Yeah. But let's get you to my place quick," Nick said, putting an arm around my shoulders and hustling me down the street. "Just in case."

"Okay," I said, still a bit shaken. I'd already seen McGurn order the execution of a boxer who didn't go down in a fight. I couldn't imagine the death sentence Nick and I would face if we were caught. Was this really worth it? Was there another way to get Nick to go along with my plan? One that didn't involve betraying an infamous twentieth-century mobster? One that didn't involve the possibility of a very painful death?

I shook my head. It was too late now. I had to go through with this.

The sun had set and we walked in twilight down the snow-lined street. An eerie quiet settled over us. Even the honking of horns and police sirens faded into the distance. I glanced over at Nick. He looked uneasy. Uncomfortable. I wondered what was going on in his head and whether or not I should ask him about it.

We arrived at his apartment five minutes later. He lived in a four-story, crumbling brick building that had definitely seen better days. Guess being a mob henchman was on par with being a mob girlfriend, digs-wise.

He led me down a cobblestone walkway and held open the door for me. I stepped inside the lobby. Like with Daisy's building, there was a sitting area where several residents were lounging and smoking. They all waved to Nick as we walked by, a couple of the older men not-so-subtly winking at him, as if to congratulate him on his prize—aka, me.

Of course I felt more a booby prize when I managed to trip over a toy that someone's little brat had left on the floor. I went sprawling forward, grabbing onto anything that would break my fall. Unfortunately, this turned out to be a table with a colorful bouquet of geraniums sitting on top. The flowers, the water, and vase all went tumbling to the ground with me.

Now I had everyone's attention.

"I'm all right." I waved to them, scrambling back to my feet and grabbing handfuls of flowers to stuff back into the vase. "Nothing to see here."

Nick shook his head and wrapped an arm around my shoulders, leading me up the stairs again. This time I managed to make it to the top, though I did trip on the rug in the hallway. But to be fair, who puts a rug in a hallway?

"God, you're drunk," Nick remarked as he put his key in the lock and pushed open his door.

"I'm fine! I'm not drunk!" I protested, not sure why I felt the need to defend my blood alcohol content.

"Mm-hm."

We stepped inside his apartment and I scanned the room. Typical bachelor pad. Sparse and utilitarian. Probably Sam's style. Nick was way more into his creature comforts. Even in Iraq, he'd managed to make his hotel room look cozy and inviting.

He led me over to a stuffy maroon couch and sat me down. Then he sat down beside me, way too far away for my liking.

Speaking of cozy—or technically not so cozy. I glanced over at the guy who was supposed to be jumping my bones right about now. Instead, he was literally twiddling his thumbs, staring down at them with an intensity that made me wonder what the hell he was thinking.

Well, fine. I obviously needed to be the one to get this show on the road. I crawled across the couch and climbed on top of him. My dress was riding above my knees. Then I leaned in to kiss him.

His lips were stiff and resisting. I pressed harder.

I felt his hands around my shoulders, pushing me aside. He stood up. I stared at him.

"What the hell is wrong with you?" I demanded. This scene of seduction was not going as well as I'd hoped and I had no idea why.

He sighed. "Do you want a drink?"

"Shoore, I'll take a mint julep," I agreed.

"I was thinking more like a black coffee."

"Oh." I sighed. He certainly was being a spoil-sport. "Yeah. Whatever."

He disappeared into what I assumed was the kitchen and pulled the door shut behind him. I kicked off my boots and pulled my feet onto the couch, trying to get comfy. What was wrong with him? The guy was all hot to jump me the other day and now he was being a total prude. Stupid Nick. What, did he all of a sudden develop a conscience or something?

"I can't do it."

Nick's voice in the kitchen made me pause. Who was he talking to? I crawled off the couch and after steadying myself from the spins, crept toward the kitchen to see if I could hear more.

"She's too drunk. I'm not going to take advantage of her in this state. I don't do that."

Take advantage of me? What was going on here? Was he on the phone? Or was there someone in the kitchen? Was there a simple explanation for this, or some X-Files–size conspiracy that I didn't know about?

I leaned on the kitchen door, propping it open just a crack. I peered inside. It was a tiny kitchen with a large stove taking up most of the space.

Nick wasn't on the phone. But there was no one in the room, either. In fact, it appeared as if he was talking to himself. Weird. What was up with that?

"I'm sorry, but you'll just have to wait. If I'm going to seduce a girl, she's going to be sober enough to make her own decision. I won't take advantage of her."

Well, that was very knight in shining armor-ish to say. But I still felt like I had vacuumed up a big piece of the puzzle here. Had someone told him to seduce Louise? Was that why he'd been following me around, always trying to hook up? I had assumed he just liked the girl. Maybe there was something much more nefarious going on.

I leaned in further, hoping to catch more of the conversation. Unfortunately, I leaned a bit too far and my weight caused the door to swing wide open and for me to fall through into the kitchen. My palms hit the tile floor and my knee banged against a cabinet.

"Ow!" I cried, both in pain and embarrassment. I really was a terrible spy.

Nick raised an eyebrow. "Um, are you okay?" he asked, leaning over to pull me up by the arm. I knew I was probably blushing a deep shade of purple as I nodded in the affirmative.

"Come on, let's get you in bed," he said, leading me back into the living room and through a set of French doors that opened into a cozy bedroom with a double bed. He pulled down the duvet and sheets and patted the mattress.

"Stay here, my little drunk princess," he said. "I'll get that coffee."

I snuggled under the blankets as he headed back to the kitchen. Maybe he was right. Maybe I wasn't in good enough shape to engage in sexual relations with the guy my ex-boyfriend had body snatched. Especially if said ex-boyfriend was on some kind of counter-mission that involved seducing the girl I had body snatched. I needed more information. To find out what Nick was up to. The FBI thought it was just waking up Bugs on time. But what if they were misinformed? What if there was more to the Time Warriors' plans?

It was all so frustrating. To be here, in Louise's body. To have Nick so close and yet so far. I wished I could just tell him the truth. Tell him who I was and why I was there. Find out the whole story on the Time Warriors and impress upon him the importance of not changing history.

Would he listen to me if he found out I was really Dora? Or would he become more determined than ever to accomplish his mission?

"Here you go," Nick said, entering the room with a tray with two steaming mugs. "Wasn't sure if you liked cream in it or not."

"Black, thanks," I said, sitting up to take the cup of java off the tray. It smelled delicious.

Nick set the tray on the nightstand and crawled into bed beside me, angling his body so he was facing me. "You okay?" he asked in a gentle voice after I'd taken a sip.

"Yeah," I said gratefully. "Sorry about before. One too many gins, I guess."

"One too many? Seven too many." Nick grinned and reached over to brush a lock of hair out of my eyes.

"Yeah, yeah."

"You're cute. You know that?" he asked softly. "Such a little spitfire. You totally remind me of someone."

I almost choked on my coffee. "I do?" I asked, trying to will my voice to remain calm. "Who?"

Nick raked a hand through his hair. "Uh, no one, really. Well, my ex-girlfriend," he said, his face reddening.

Heh. I reminded him of his ex-girlfriend. Funny that.

"Oh, the uptight chick?" I asked, taking another sip of coffee. "What's her story?"

"Heh." Nick laughed. "I shouldn't have called her uptight. She was just . . . focused. Driven, I guess you could say." He sighed and rolled over onto his back so he was staring up at the ceiling. "I met her over in Ira—uh, France," he said, catching himself just in time. "During the war."

I leaned over on my side, propping my head up with my arm. So he was going to try to retell our story as if it happened during World War I. Fascinating. I couldn't wait to hear his version.

"Ah, so were you a soldier?" I asked, all wide-eyed and innocent and oh-so-ready to play along. "In the Great War?"

"A journalist, actually. Foreign correspondent."

"And she was . . . ?"

"Also a journalist."

"Really? Huh. I didn't realize women could be journalists." Heh. I was so going to give him a hard time. Watch him squirm.

"I mean, she was a nurse," Nick corrected, his face turning bright red. "But she was kind of an unofficial journalist. She wrote letters home. And they were, uh, published in her hometown paper."

"I see." I nodded. "A letter-writing nurse. Gotcha."

"Yeah. She was great," he said, ignoring my sarcasm. "Full of passion and enthusiasm. So ambitious. Risking her life, always going after the—uh, really sick patients."

I stifled a giggle. "Liked danger, did she?"

"Well, she wanted to prove herself, I think. Which was silly, 'cause she was amazing and everyone knew it. Especially me."

Amazing. He had thought I was *amazing*. I frowned. *So what happened, buddy?* I wanted to ask. *Did the amazingness wear off? Was the Iraqi chick you dumped me for even more amazing?*

"I thought you said she was uptight and high-strung. Those don't seem like very amazing qualities to me."

He chuckled ruefully. "I told you, I shouldn't have said that," he amended. "She could be . . . overly serious at times. She was so driven. So determined to prove herself. Her ambition robbed her of some of the joy she could have otherwise been experiencing in life. Sure, things in . . . France . . . weren't all sunshine and roses. The situation was at best bleak. But if you didn't seek out the moments of joy, the blackness could swallow you. I'd seen it happen to many good, uh, nurses. And I didn't want it to happen to her. I wanted to protect her innocence and give her some small peace in her heart." He swallowed hard. "She was so beautiful when she laughed. I wanted to find a way to keep her laughing forever."

My heart throbbed in my chest and tears threatened the corners of my eyes. It took every ounce of willpower I had not to throw myself into his arms. But there was more to this story and I had to hear it.

"So what happened? She's your ex, right?" I managed to say. "Why'd you break up?"

Nick released a deep sigh, rubbing his face with his hand. "I screwed up," he admitted. "I let her down. A stupid, stupid mistake that I'll never forgive myself for. I failed her and something horrible happened because of it. And no matter what I did after that I could never get her to forgive me." He shook his head. "Not that I blame her. I probably wouldn't have forgiven me either."

"What happened?" I asked, barely able to breathe. I couldn't believe I would finally find out, firsthand, the whole story. Even if it was disguised as a World War I soap opera.

"It doesn't matter, does it?" he asked, shrugging his shoulders. "It was a long time ago." He reached up to touch his eye with the back of his hand. I stared at him. Was that a tear he was brushing away? Was strong, arrogant, alpha Nick the Prick actually shedding a tear over me? I couldn't believe it.

Part of me wanted to press him. To find out exactly what went down. Why he had betrayed me and then let me rot in prison while he partied with another girl. But another part, a weaker, more vulnerable part, still wasn't quite sure I was ready to know.

"Anyway, why don't you try to get a little rest?" he said gently, obviously wanting to change the subject. "You'll feel better in the morning."

I wanted to protest. To hear more of the story. And I still had to talk to him about the whole waking-up Bugs thing. Which, of course, was the whole reason I'd met up with him in the first place.

"But—"

Nick put a finger to my lips. "No buts," he said in a soft, teasing voice. "Sleep now, princess. We'll talk in the morning." He reached over and switched out the light and settled onto his side, back toward me.

I sighed. Sleep. As if I could sleep after that whole inadvertent confession. I wanted to jump up and do cartwheels. To laugh. To cry. To scream. To tie him to a chair and interrogate him further. I wanted to do all of that and more.

Because, for the first time since I was captured in Iraq, I was beginning to think I might be able to forgive him.

Maybe.

CHAPTER TWELVE

I woke up in his arms. Somehow during the night we'd shifted into one another, melting into each other's unconscious embrace, his heavy arm draped over me and his body spooning me close. I could feel his slow heartbeat against my back and his warm breath tickled my ear. He felt so good. So warm. So safe. I never wanted to move again. In fact, even if someone had told me they were serving Oreo cookie ice cream in the next room, I'd probably have stayed put. And Oreo cookie ice cream was my absolute favorite.

My thoughts drifted back to what he'd said the night before. Did he really care about me as much as he claimed? I didn't want to believe him, but at the same time, why would he lie? There was no reason, nothing to gain by telling Louise his true feelings. After all, he had no idea that I was inside her body. That he was actually confessing to the one person who really needed to know.

Was it true what he'd said? Had I been so angry so long for no reason? It still didn't explain everything. He never said why he didn't show up the day I was captured. Never mentioned the other woman that people saw him with while I languished in prison. But for some reason his unintentional confession made me want to believe for the first time that there had to be some kind of rational explanation for everything that had happened, some piece of the puzzle that had fallen on the floor and been eaten by the dog. There had to be some missing link that I didn't know about and had refused to believe existed.

Could I have wasted this last year hating him? Wallowing in self-induced misery for no reason except my own stubbornness and inability to uncover the truth? Sticking to principles that were founded on incomplete or even bad information?

It was a lot to digest here and now, when I also had so much more on my mind. I still wasn't any closer to making sure history played out as it was supposed to. Stupid me, getting too drunk to accomplish my mission. The old Dora would have never allowed herself to do that.

That said, it had been a blast. Downing shots and dancing like we hadn't a care in the world—I couldn't remember the last time I felt so liberated. Not even when Nick and I were a couple. As he had described last night, back then I was too worried about my job and the casualties of war to let my hair down.

You know, for a girl living in someone else's body, I was beginning to feel very comfortable in my own skin.

Speaking of skin, I had an itch on my leg. I scrunched down to try and scratch it without moving too much, without waking the man beside me before I had a chance to work out what I was going to do. What I was going to say. But he shifted at my movement and rolled over onto his back. Nick always was a light sleeper. I mourned his closeness, his comforting touch, the second he turned away.

I listened for a moment, trying to determine if he was still asleep. But his deep, rhythmic breathing had subsided and a moment later he gave definitive proof by clearing his throat. He was awake. No more time to weigh my options, to plan; I'd just have to wing it.

I rolled onto my side, propping my head up with my elbow, looking down on him. He opened his beautiful almond-shaped eyes, blinking a couple of times, and then smiled up at me.

"Sorry," he said, his ears reddening at the edges in a way that could only be described as adorable. "I must have rolled over during the night." He scrubbed his face with his palm. "I didn't mean to—"

"It's okay," I murmured, unable to resist reaching over to brush a lock of hair out of his eyes. The strands felt silky smooth and slightly damp. I studied his face. He really was handsome. And to know my Nick was inside— well, that made my heart soften all the more.

I had been so angry. So, so angry. I thought I was being strong. But maybe I was just being an idiot. And now, now I just wanted to let go. To collapse in his arms and soak in his strength. To allow myself to feel again. To be tender and not hard. To be sweet and not bitter. To be me. The me who had once allowed herself to love a man like Nick—a man who perhaps deserved that love after all.

"What?" he asked softly, his eyes flickering up to the ceiling, not able to meet mine. Gone was his outer bravado, and in its place was the Nick I remembered. The one behind closed doors that no one saw but me. He shut his eyes for a moment, then opened them, this time daring to look back at me. "What are you looking at?" he asked in a curious, almost little-boy voice.

I smiled. "You."

He chuckled. Pulling his arms out from under the covers, he wrapped them around me, pulling me down into a warm embrace.

"You're sweet, Louise," he said. "A really nice girl."

Hm. There sounded like there was a *but* in there.

"But?" I asked.

He patted me on the back and then gently pushed me away so he could sit up in bed. I sat up, too, wondering what was bothering him. What he was going to say.

"You're beautiful. And you're fun. And you're fascinating," he told me. "And you remind me, as I said before, of my ex-girlfriend, which makes you all the more of a temptation." He raked a hand through his already tousled bed head. "But I can't do this. I can't start anything with you. I'm not ready." He stared across the room at the wall. "I'm still in love with Dora."

I stared at him, hardly daring to breathe. He was still in love with me? He'd give up his opportunity to sleep with Louise because he still felt loyal to me? After I'd discarded him and refused to hear his apology? After ignoring him and hating him for a year?

"I know it sounds stupid," he continued. "I mean, I know for a fact she hates my guts. After what happened in, uh, France, she'll never trust me again. We'll never get back together. I know that in my head, but in my heart . . ." He shrugged his shoulders. "In my heart I will always love that little girl. And there's just no way I can move on and start something new until I reconcile those feelings. Hopefully someday I'll be able to." He sighed. "But it's not going to happen anytime soon, that's for sure. And it'd be completely unfair of me to lead you on."

Was it possible for your heart to literally burst with love? At that moment it seemed likely. If only I had known the truth, how much Nick loved me this whole time. Why had I been such a moron?

Suddenly I realized I had to tell him. I had to let him know the truth. That I was actually Dora. It might take him a moment to digest the information. In fact, he might completely freak out and be pissed off at me for not telling him earlier, but I had to take the chance. I had to.

"I've got something to tell you," I said, gathering up my courage. "This may seem weird and totally bizarre, but—"

Before I could spit out the words, machine gun fire erupted in the morning air.

"What the—?" Nick bolted out of bed with a start. He looked around the room, then at me. "Shit. It sounds like they're in the building."

A sudden rap on the front door made me agree with him.

"Sam and Louise! We know you're in there," said a heavily accented Chicago voice on the other side. "Machine Gun wants to talk to you."

Talk, shmalk. Somehow, the mobster had found out that Sam and Louise had hooked up, and was warming up the executioner's chair. I was sure. I glanced over at Nick, whose eyes were wide with worry.

"I don't think he's really interested in talking, do you?" he asked quietly as he stuffed his feet in his shoes. Thank goodness we'd gone to bed in our clothes.

"Not likely," I replied, wishing for my own footwear. But I had taken off my boots in the living room, and I sure as hell wasn't going to ask mobster man to hand them through the door.

Damn it, why had I been so stupid, gotten wasted and ended up here at Sam/Nick's apartment? Why'd I passed out and stayed the night? Now I'd really gone and screwed up history. Instead of being Machine Gun's alibi, Louise would be his victim. And what if he got caught and went to jail for her murder? What if the St. Valentine's Day Massacre was cancelled altogether 'cause the boss who planned it was arrested for killing his own girlfriend? Life, the universe, and everything would be changed forever.

Of course, I'd be dead, so it'd make little difference to me. At least, I assumed I'd be dead. I really should have asked those FBI guys what dying in Louise's body back in 1929 would do to Dora in present day. I guess I never really considered that I would find myself in a situation like this.

"I know you're in there," the voice said, sounding a little pissed off that we hadn't just swung open the door and greeted him with a rousing rendition of *Kumbaya*. "I just riddled your landlady full of holes. You wanna be Swiss cheese too, then I suggest you keep stalling."

"Window," Nick instructed. "Quick."

I followed his pointing finger to the far side of the room, to a window that led out to the second-story fire escape. Together, we rushed over, Nick getting there first and wrapping his fingers around the frame to yank it upwards. Then he motioned for me to climb through.

"Always climbing through windows for you," I said with a laugh, not at all sure why I felt it okay to make jokes when I was about to get killed by a hail of machine gun bullets. Maybe I was learning to lighten up in the face of horrific situations.

"Less talking, more climbing," he scolded.

I started to scramble through the window. Stupid gangsters, interrupting my confession at the worst possible moment. Now I wasn't sure we'd live long enough for me to get the words out.

Boom!

All thoughts flew out of my head as an explosion suddenly rocked the apartment. The force of the blast threw me out the window and onto the fire escape. I landed with a sickening thud—face-first into wrought iron.

The force of the collision made me see spots, and for a moment I thought I'd black out from the hit. But if I blacked out, I knew I'd probably be caught. Or killed. I fought with all my might to remain conscious.

I managed to latch onto the fire escape bars and pull myself up to a kneeling position. I glanced back at the window, fear pounding in my heart.

Had Nick made it out?

Thick black smoke puffed out the window in sooty plumes, hampering my view. I knew that smoke, that smell, that look all too well from my days back in Iraq. They'd set off some kind of grenade.

"Sam?" I cried out, not knowing what to do next. The fire escape swayed dangerously under my weight. The force of the explosion must have knocked it loose from the wall. One false move and it could collapse completely, throwing me down two stories onto the unforgiving pavement below.

"Sam?" I yelled again. Had he gotten hit by the grenade? Oh god, what if he was killed! Would that mean Nick was dead, too?

I had to see. Placing one hand after the other, I crawled down the fire escape into the cloud of smoke. My lungs seized up from the dust and smoke, and I coughed my way blindly back down to the window. I knew I wouldn't last long sucking in this smoky air, but I had to make sure Nick was okay.

But a millisecond before I reached the window, the fire escape gave one last heaving groan and gave way, taking me with it. I crashed down into the alleyway, a big pile of garbage somewhat breaking my fall. Unfortunately, whoever had taken out the trash must have picked that day to throw out his Pet Rock collection or something, because those bags provided little cushion or relief from the hard pavement.

I was seeing stars left and right, but knew I couldn't black out there. Not directly under Nick's window, where the gangsters could see me. I spotted a lone doorway across the alley and started crawling toward it. My ankle panged in protest and I hoped it wasn't broken.

I reached for the door handle, looking back toward the apartment building one more time—much like Lot's wife must have done before she turned into a pillar of salt. Smoke billowed through the broken window, obscuring any chance of spotting Nick. If he were even still alive. Could anyone survive that grenade attack? And if he had managed, what would McGurn's men do to him once they found him?

I wanted to go back. To save him somehow, but I was just coherent enough to realize those kinds of heroics would only get me killed along with him. Better to hide and live to fight another day. At least that's what my brain told me. My heart begged I be much more irrational.

I managed to crawl through the doorway, pulling it shut behind me, then looked around. I was in a small, dusty storage room that looked like it hadn't been used in some time. I used my last reserves of strength to drag the heaviest box in front of the door, hoping that would convince McGurn's men I'd run away elsewhere.

Then I curled up in a pile of rags and let the darkness take me.

* * *

When I came to, I had no idea where I was or how I had gotten there. All I knew was my head hurt like crazy and my body felt like it'd been run over by a tractor trailer.

I forced my sluggish brain backwards, trying to remember where I was, what had happened. Then the events of the night before came raging back in a flood. Nick. McGurn's men. The grenade attack.

I sat up, shivering through my thin dress. The storage room I'd passed out in had no heat and I had no coat or shoes. The walk home was going to be a lot of fun. But first, I had to find out what happened to Nick. If he was okay. If he'd somehow escaped.

I pulled aside the box and opened the door. Sunlight streamed through, forcing me to squint into the alleyway. I must have been out for hours. At least that meant the gangsters probably weren't still poking around, looking for me. Sure enough, the alley was deserted. Only a rat (and unfortunately not *The* Rat) scurried by.

I looked up at Nick's window. It wasn't hard to identify. The blackened frame and cracked glass gave it away. My heart ached in my chest as I pondered the possibilities. What had happened to him? Had the gangsters got him? Or was he . . . ? I couldn't bear to think that thought.

Damn it, why had I allowed myself to pass out, left him up there to face the bad guys by himself? If Sam's lungs had collapsed—if his heart had stopped beating— what did that mean for Nick? Would he be shot back to the twenty-first century as soon as his host body gave out? Or was this game over for him as well?

My heart spasmed at the idea. Could Nick really be

dead? No. It was impossible. He'd been in a million tight jams in his lifetime. There was no way he'd allow himself to get killed while in someone else's body in 1929. He was too good for that.

Wasn't he?

I limped down the alleyway, determined to see for myself. I had to know. Each step was excruciating. My ankle throbbed. My ribs ached. It hurt to even blink my eyes.

I made my way into the apartment building. The place was deserted. I dragged myself up the stairs to his unit, praying, hoping, begging that everything would be okay. That he'd be there, waiting for me. Ready to tend my wounds because miraculously he'd suffered none of his own.

I remembered a movie I once saw. *The End of the Affair.* When a World War II bomb blasted a London apartment, the married heroine had promised God that she would never see her lover again, if only his life would be spared. Perhaps it would be worth making that kind of bargain myself. If only I believed something like that would work.

But when I turned the corner and saw what was left of the burned out apartment, I knew that Nick's life was beyond bargaining for. The grenade had done its worst. The place was gutted by flame. No one could have survived. There was absolutely no way.

I stared at the devastation for a moment, not knowing what to do. My body kicked into autopilot, concentrating on essential functions like breathing and keeping my heart beating. But there was little else going on, save a nonstop rapid repeating thought running on endless loop in my horrified brain.

Nick was dead. Nick was dead.

He had to be. No one could have survived this. All I could hope was that the real Nick was sent back to the twenty-first century. That Sam's body was just a dead, empty shell.

But how could I find out for sure?

Then I remembered the one person, well, rodent, who would probably know.

I had to get back to my apartment, pronto.

CHAPTER THIRTEEN

Shivering, terrified, and too freaked out to cry, I managed to steady my trembling hand to get the key into my lock. I wanted to know—*needed* to know—what would happen to Nick if Sam were really dead. And only one person, one rodent, had the answers.

I limped inside. "Ratty?" I called. My voice surprised me, hoarse and raspy. I guess from the smoke. "Special Agent Rogers? Are you here?"

The apartment was empty and silent as a tomb. Great. Rat Boy was probably off on a cheese binge or something. Just my luck.

I felt my knees wobble and just as I managed to close the door behind me, I lost it, collapsing to the floor. I let out a groan as my knees and then chest collided with hardwood. Walking back to my apartment had been too much. My body was bruised and my ankle throbbed. I considered crawling over to the bed. To at least pass out on something soft, but then decided it wasn't an achievable goal at the moment.

Instead, I closed my eyes and let the blackness sweep over me right where I lay on the floor. I thought of Nick. My darling Nick. He had to be alive. He just had to.

Then everything went black.

"Dora? Wake up! Are you okay? Do you see a white light? Don't walk into the light, Dora!"

"Argh," I moaned. All I wanted to do was sleep for like a thousand years, but an incessant voice kept squeaking in my ear. "Five more minutes, Mom."

"She lives! Hallelujah, praise the Lord!" the voice crowed. Then it added, "But, uh, please, never *ever* call me Mom again. That's just plain creepy."

Groggy, I opened one eye, then the other. I was still lying where I'd passed out, in the middle of the floor of my apartment. The Rat stood by me on his hind legs, not two feet away, his nose twitching anxiously. Had he really been worried about me?

"Wow, Ratty. I didn't know you cared."

"Heh. I don't really." The Rat plopped back down on all fours. "It's just that, um, if you die, I, uh, lose my bonus. And I really wouldn't want to show my face 'round town without that fat wallet in my pocket. Disappoint all the ladies."

"Ah. Of course. Silly me." I rolled over onto my back and then propped myself up to a sitting position. While I still smelled like a mixture of smoke and garbage, which was not a fragrance Chanel would be marketing anytime soon, I did feel a little better, actually. I was still tender and bruised, of course, but my ankle no longer throbbed and nothing felt broken. And after what I'd been through, I considered that somewhat of a miracle. Louise must have been drinking her milk. Good girl.

"So what the hell happened to you, anyway? I get back from a night out with this really adorable mouse named Missy—you should have seen her, by the way. Cute pink feet and a very sexy tail. Never had an albino chick before." Ratty beamed proudly at this studly accomplishment.

"Uh, congrats?"

"Right. So I get back and I find you lying on the floor, looking like you've been trampled by elephants. What the hell did you do to yourself this time? I'm thinking that convincing Nick to help you accomplish your mission didn't exactly pan out as well as you'd hoped?"

"Uh . . ." I rubbed my head, trying to remember everything that had happened. Suddenly it all came rushing back, knocking me down like a hurricane wind.

"Nick!" I cried, the memory of the charred embers and rubble smoldering in my brain. My heart panged and my next breath was painful. "Ratty, I think Nick—or I mean Sam—was killed in a grenade attack."

"Grenade attack? Are you sure?"

"No, but, well, we were in his apartment and—"

"You slept with him, didn't you? I knew it. I shoulda taken that bet with Missy."

"Will you listen to me for a moment?" I cried. "Something really horrible happened!"

232

"Sorry. Jeesh." The Rat scratched his ear with his back paw. "Please go on, sweetie. Was it good for you?"

Why was he being so flippant? I wanted to reach over and smack him upside the head, to crush him for his indifference and snide remarks. Nick could be dead and he didn't care one bit. What was wrong with him? Didn't he even have a shred of rodent decency? If not for Nick, how about for me?

I swallowed hard. "As I saying, we were in his apartment and these gangster men arrived. Demanded we come out and surrender ourselves. Said Machine Gun wanted to talk to us. We tried to escape and they threw a grenade. The whole place exploded. I was thrown into a pile of garbage and when I woke up, everyone was gone." Tears welled up in my eyes. "He was still in the room. I don't see how he could have survived the fire. And smoke. Oh Ratty, it was—"

"Good." The Rat nodded, looking very smug.

I stared at him, my mouth open. "What?"

"Good." He grinned. Actually curled up his whiskered mouth and grinned. I couldn't believe it. "If he's dead, then he can't screw up the future. Sure, the Feds would have preferred to catch him alive, put him on trial and all, but hey, this works, too. So now all you have to do is make sure things play out the way they should and then we can all go home and sleep with our wives."

"Wait. You mean . . . ?" I panicked so much I couldn't breathe; I literally couldn't suck in a breath. But I had to ask the question even though I was nearly positive the answer would stop my heart. "If . . ." I swallowed hard.

Oh, please don't let it be true! "If, uh, Sam dies while Nick's in his body, where does Nick go?"

The Rat shrugged. "Heaven? Hell? Nirvana? Reincarnated as a cow in India? That's one of life's great mysteries, right? Trust me, if I knew the answer to that I wouldn't be working Rat Duty at the Bureau."

My entire world spiraled out from under me. I couldn't speak. Then it was true. My worst fears had been confirmed. I'd been praying over and over that if the host body died then Nick would wake up from his time leap and be fine and dandy to anchor the evening news.

Evidently, not so much.

"So, if Sam's dead, that means Nick's dead, too?" I asked, my voice quavering. I had to be sure. "Like, he doesn't bounce back to his old body in the twenty-first century?"

"What, do you think you're made of rubber? There's no bouncing in time travel. The host body dies, you're toast, too. Don't worry, Nick knew that going into this whole thing. It's in the contract. The liability clause. The risk of death is part of the time travel high, they say."

I dropped my head into my hands, no longer feeling any physical pain as all my senses numbed in shock and horror. I couldn't bear it. I couldn't face the fact that the man I loved . . . the man whom I so recently had found out still loved me . . . was now dead. Dead and not coming back.

I had wasted a whole year hating him for no reason. A whole year spent away from his welcoming arms and soft

234

touch. A whole year of misery that could have been spent in pleasure.

And now he was gone forever. I'd never have the chance to love him again. To kiss his lips and run my hands through his hair. To tell him how sorry I was for being so stubborn. So stupid.

Before, he was dead to me. Now he was dead to all.

It was too much. A sob rose in my throat and I started shaking. My stomach heaved and I ran to the bathroom, bowing to the porcelain god in the nick of time. I vomited.

Coughing a few last times, on my knees, I grasped the sides of the toilet, unable to move. Nick was dead. Forever dead. And it was all my fault. If I'd forgiven him back in the twenty-first century, if I hadn't been so stubborn, he wouldn't have joined the Time Warriors. He wouldn't have traveled back in time. He'd be safe at the TV station, delivering the evening news the way he loved so much. Then he'd come home to our little ranch in the hills and we'd barbecue burgers and sit outside on the deck, sipping our glasses of pinot and complaining about gas-guzzling SUVs and the people who loved them.

Instead, I'd indulged in hate. In pride. In fear. And now I was nearly eighty years back in time, on my knees in a 1929 bathroom. Nick was dead and I only had a rat to console me.

Speaking of, I turned to see the little rodent had come up behind me. He sat up on his back legs and cocked his head.

"Hey, princess, what's wrong? You should be happy. If

Nick's dead, then he can't screw up history. So all you have to do is make sure Bugs stays away from Clark Street on Valentine's Day and you're all set. One more day and you can go back to your old life a hero. Maybe they'll even give you a medal. You never know."

"Is that supposed to be comforting?" I growled. The Rat took a hesitant step backward. I must have looked scary in my rage. "What do I care about my old life? The man I love is dead. Dead! And all you can think of is your stupid mission?"

The Rat twitched his nose. "Sor-ry," he said. "I didn't realize we had feelings for the guy again. Last I knew he was Nick the Prick and you hated his guts. Even though you did sleep with him."

I hung my head. "No. I *love* his guts," I sobbed. "Every single last entrail. And he still loves me. He told me so. Well, he told Louise, but obviously that means I heard."

"Huh," The Rat said, bobbing his head thoughtfully. "Well this changes everything, now doesn't it?"

"I'm such an idiot. I've screwed everything up." I exchanged my kneeling position for sitting Indian-style on the floor, rubbing my eyes with my hands.

I felt a clawing on my leg and looked down to see Ratty had scampered onto my knee. Ugh. I wanted to swat him away, but something in his face made me pause, a seriousness that normally eluded the smart-ass rodent.

"Are you telling me the truth?" The Rat asked slowly. "Do you love Nick?"

I sniffed. "Yes."

"And you'd do anything for him?"

"Sure. Though it's too late, obviously."

"It may not be, actually."

I stared at him. "What?"

"Are you sure Nick is dead? Did you see a body?"

"No, but . . ." I shook my head. "The blast. No one could have—"

"No one could have survived? How do you know that? Are you suddenly some grenade weapons specialist or something? You know, a few episodes of *CSI* does not a crime scene expert make." The Rat shook his head. "Jeez Louise, for a reporter you certainly jump to unsubstantiated conclusions. No wonder the media's in such disarray these days."

I stared at him. "But . . . the place was torched."

"By the grenade? Are you sure? Maybe it was torched afterwards. You ever think of that? Maybe they took Nick prisoner and then lit the match."

My mouth dropped open. In my grief I'd never given that scenario a single thought. But now that he mentioned it, it did seem quite possible. Probable even.

"So Nick could be . . . ?" I couldn't even say the words. I didn't want to hold out false hope. At the same time, it was certainly preferable to having no hope at all.

The Rat shrugged. "You won't know unless you check it out, right? Go back to McGurn. See if he has Nick prisoner. You've got nothing better to do, right?"

"But McGurn wants to kill me," I argued. "I think he believes I've cheated on him with Nick. He must have had me followed or something."

"Right. Well, I understand if you're too scared to go back there," Ratty said breezily. "Guess Nick will have to figure out a way to get out of prison himself. That'll give you time to hit the mall, anyway. Get some Jazz Age souvenirs for your trip back to the twenty-first century."

I didn't know what to say. What to do. Could Nick really be alive? Could he be incarcerated in a gangster's prison? This situation suddenly seemed too close to my own past experience for comfort. I flashed back to my days in the Iraqi prison. Bars. Cold. The agony I'd endured.

Was Nick being interrogated? Tortured? Would they hurt him? Kill him? My heart pounded in my chest as my head played out too many familiar scenarios.

I had to save him. Even if that meant risking my own life (as I now knew it did) to do so. I could feel the fear welling in my gut. But I couldn't let it win; I couldn't let it stop me from saving the man I loved.

"What do you propose I do?" I asked The Rat, squaring my shoulders and firming my resolve. I could do this. I knew I could. A new Dora had been born, like a phoenix rising from the ashes of Nick's building. I'd survived. And he would, too. I'd make sure of that.

"Well, if McGurn's got him," Ratty said with another shrug, "you're going to have to go to McGurn."

Great. I was afraid he'd say that.

CHAPTER FOURTEEN

I changed out of my nasty, bloodstained, garbage-smelling clothes, washed myself thoroughly, then changed into the sexiest little number I could find: a short white skirt and matching lacy blouse made of some kind of light chiffon material. To winterize the outfit, I found a white stole—rabbit fur, chubby, with a big fuzzy button on the front. Then I carefully applied my makeup. Red lined Clara Bow lips and big blackened eyes.

I stared at my reflection in the mirror. Unfortunately, there was no way to hide the ugly bruises dotting my arms. But besides that, I had to admit, I (aka, Louise) looked great. An angelic, porcelain doll of perfection.

Not that I was of the mind that McGurn would suddenly say, "Sure, babe, I forgive you for jumping into bed with one of my henchmen," and give Nick a Get Out of Jail Free card just because he dug my dress and kissable lips, but I figured making myself as attractive as possible couldn't hurt.

Of course, if Nick was already dead then this was all for naught. But I refused to consider that possibility. I was on a rescue mission and by sheer willpower, damn it, I was going to succeed.

"How do I look?" I asked Ratty as I stepped out of the bathroom. He gave a low whistle.

"Sex-y," he exclaimed, swishing his tail back and forth. Was that supposed to be rodent flirtation or something?

"Thanks." I laughed. Once in a while the tiny one wasn't half bad.

"Bet you wish you looked like that when you're in your own body," he added.

Then again . . .

"Whatever, dude," I said, shrugging on my coat. I refused to let him discourage me. I had a very important mission: to save the man I loved. "Anyway, I'm outta here."

"So what's your plan?"

I stopped. I'd been afraid he was going to ask that. "I don't have one," I admitted.

"What?" Ratty squeaked incredulously, his beady eyes flashing. "You're just planning to waltz into the club, demand to speak to McGurn and convince him that Sam should go free?"

"Something like that."

"Wow. I guess I should kiss that keeping-you-alive bonus good-bye."

I sighed. "Well, what do *you* suggest?"

"I suggest . . . ," The Rat said slowly, effectively drawing out the suspense. "I suggest that you come up with a good plan before you go down there."

I rolled my eyes. "You know, you're truly useless."

The Rat shrugged. "I've been called worse. Like, this one time—"

"Look," I interrupted. I'd just puked and didn't want another nausea-evoking story from him. "I appreciate your concern for your monetary gain, but I'm wasting valuable time here. Sam could be getting tortured right now. He's probably alone. Scared. Helpless."

"Like you were?" Ratty asked in a soft voice.

I stared at him. Every time I thought I had the little guy figured out, he'd suddenly surprise me.

"Look, Dora," the rodent said. "All joking aside here, I think what you're doing is very brave. Foolhardy and stupid, perhaps, but brave. Risking your life to save the man who may or may not have betrayed you in Iraq. That takes true courage."

How did he even know about Iraq? Had the FBI read my confidential file? Had they shared it with him? I hated the idea of this snide little creature knowing the details of my very private life story. My pain should not be his punchline.

"When you first came here you were a scared little mouse without a clue. You'd run before standing up to a fight. Now you're willingly heading into the lion's den." The Rat crawled over and petted me on the foot with his little paw. Suddenly he seemed very Yoda-like, and I half-expected a "do or do not, there is no try" or some other Lucasism to escape his lips. "I'm very proud of you, Dora."

"Uh, thanks." I ventured, still unsure how to react to this sudden soul-baring. I kept waiting for some derogatory crack. But none seemed forthcoming.

"Good luck," The Rat said, looking up at me with his twitchy face. "I know you can do it."

"You know what, Ratty?" I said as I reached for the door handle, ready to start my mission. "I think you might be right."

I arrived at McGurn's club a few minutes later, practically frozen to death. The weather had not become any balmier. In fact, I think it was colder than ever. I would have loved to make the suggestion for a Fourth of July Day Massacre next time around.

I entered the building, petrified, to say the least. What would they do when they saw me? Would they shoot me on sight? Did they think I was already dead?

No. They wouldn't. They needed me alive to be Machine Gun's alibi. To go to the hotel with him and fool the Untouchables into thinking he wasn't involved. It was way too late to recruit another girl for that gig, right?

"Louise!" Tommy greeted me at the door. His dim-witted face revealed his concern. Guess he wasn't the one throwing grenades earlier. "Where have you been? Jackie's been worried. He's sent out all the boys to look for you."

"Well, here I am, Tommy," I said, trying to act casual. My shaking hands and trembling voice kind of gave me away. "Can I go see him?"

"Of course. In fact, you don't got a choice. He gave orders that if you showed up I should bring you to him right away." Tommy glanced around the room. "Hey Joey, can you mind the door? I gotta bring Louise to Jackie."

The hefty, tuxedoed Joey nodded and took his place at the door. Tommy motioned for me to follow.

Even though it was only afternoon, the club was packed with people, the party in full swing. Evidently that raid the other day wasn't slowing business. Women and men dressed in silk and satin sipped champagne and danced merrily to a rockin' jazz band on stage. As we weaved through the crowd toward the back door, a couple people grabbed at my sleeve.

"Hey, Louise—when you gonna do an encore of your act at Don's?" one asked.

"Yeah, Louise, you were terrif," added another. "We want to see you again."

"Just don't make love with any pianos this time."

I laughed and smiled and said all the appropriate things, but inside my stomach was churning. This reminded me so much of when I was in Iraq. I'd watch TV from my hotel—my sister had bought me a VCR and would mail me entertainment shows, news, and soaps on tape. I'd sit and watch the programs and get furious. There was a war going on. People—American boys— were dying every day. And no one in the States seemed to care anything beyond whether Nick and Jessica's marriage was going to last or whose boyfriend Paris Hilton was stealing.

It was the same here in the twenties. The cities were corrupt, overrun by gangsters and bought public officials. Crime was rampant, murders were daily, and all anyone cared about was dancing and getting wasted. Reveling in the luxury they'd acquired. Spoils from a war that had resulted in over three hundred thousand casualties.

The man I loved was at best rotting in a jail cell, and at worst dead from a grenade explosion. And no one here would have cared, even if they knew.

But I did. I cared. And there was nothing wrong with caring. To hell with hedonism. With apathy. With living life for one's self. That just wasn't my style.

No, I was more the uptight, high-strung "save the world" type of girl, and you know what? I was not about to apologize for it.

We reached the far end of the room and Tommy unlocked the door that led to the offices. We climbed the stairs and he rapped sharply on McGurn's door, paused a moment, then knocked two more times, almost as if tapping out some secret code. I drew in a deep breath; my pulse quickened. This was it. In a few seconds, I'd find out whether Sam was dead or alive. And, of course, more importantly, whether Nick was dead or alive. Two sides to the most important coin in my life.

"Come in!" Machine Gun's voice boomed from the other side of the door. Tommy gestured for me to enter.

"I've got to go down to my post," he apologized. "But you'll be okay, right?"

"Sure. No problem." I smiled. *Yeah, right.* I bet even Tommy didn't believe that one.

I entered the room, my hands shaking like crazy. My heart felt three times bigger than normal, pounding so hard it threatened to burst out of my chest cavity. But I concentrated on my shrink's breathing exercises and fought for control. I was stronger than my panic attacks, stronger than my fear.

McGurn's beady eyes fell upon me and he rose from his chair, fists leaning against the desk. His face was beet red and I could see the veins in his neck pulsating.

"Louise," he said in a tight voice.

"Hi baby," I cooed. "What's going on? I heard you were looking for me."

"Louise, don't play coy with me. I know what you've been up to. I know you've been carousing with Sam. Sneaking behind my back and sleeping with one of my own men."

To his credit, he actually looked more hurt than angry. But what the hell? The guy had a wife and slept with prostitutes on the side. Who was he to lecture on the evils of infidelity?

"I don't know what you're talking about," I pouted, walking over to his desk and plopping my butt down on it. I knew the key was to be as casual as possible. "Who's Sam? That guy that works for you? The one who does all your dirty work? Why would I want to hang out with him? When you got the big cheese, you don't go after the crumbs, baby."

"Don't you lie to me, Louise," McGurn said, his voice

rising with anger. "I had Tommy find you. He saw you with Sam, drinkin' and dancin' at some club down the road."

I shrugged. "I wouldn't doubt that I was dancin' at some club. You know me, baby. I love to dance. But I don't remember any of your guys at this supposed club. And I think I woulda remembered somethin' like that, don't you?" I reached over to chuck his chin, smiling sweetly. "You know my heart belongs to you, Jackie boy."

He frowned and pushed my hand away. "Tommy says he saw you. Do you know how embarrassin' it is for me to have one of my men say my girl is making a fool out of me? Carousing with some other guy just two days before the big plan? Two days before I need her to be my alibi?" He raised a fist and slammed it against his desk, causing me to nearly jump out of my skin.

This was not going as well as I'd hoped.

"Where is this Sam?" I asked, deciding to just go for it. "Maybe you can round him up and ask him if he was with me."

"I already did," McGurn said, looking pleased with himself. "Sent Jimmy and Tony over to get him. He's sitting down in the gin cellar right now. Waiting to be . . . *questioned*." He said the word with such poison that I was pretty convinced this questioning wouldn't be of the verbal kind.

But still, that meant Nick was alive! I wanted to dance. To sing. To cheer out loud and hug someone. Sam wasn't dead! Nick wasn't dead! There was still a chance we could all get out of this alive, go back to the twenty-first century and somehow fall in love with one another again. Live happily ever after.

But this wasn't over yet. Not by a long shot. I restrained my joy. After all, first I had to convince this gangster that I was as innocent as O.J.

"So what did he say when you questioned him?" I asked. "He didn't say he was with me, did he?"

"No. He denied it."

"And when your boys went to collect him, I wasn't there, was I?"

"Uh, no. They said you weren't."

I smiled. Thank God for stupid gangsters who preferred to blow up the joint before they could find out for sure if the boss's girl was actually present.

"So then, besides Tommy saying he saw me dancing with some fella at a bar, what evidence do you have to support the fact that I was cheating on you?" I asked. "It's all total conjecture." Wow. I was damn convincing if I did say so myself. If I got out of all of this mess and back to the twenty-first century, I should so take up law.

"What the hell does conjecture mean?" McGurn asked.

Then again, the guy I was working wasn't exactly a rocket scientist. . . .

"The point is, baby, who you gonna believe?" I asked. "Your dumb-ass bouncer Tommy or your best girl?"

McGurn frowned, and again I could practically see the brain cells trying to fire up in the big doofus's head. My logic was confusing the poor guy.

"But Tommy saw you. He saw you, Louise. And he

ain't got no reason to lie about it. And you, my sweet," the gangster said, "have every reason in the world. Including your life."

I gulped. Could we ixnay on the ife-threatening-lay, perhaps?

"I—"

McGurn reached into his desk and pulled out a pistol. I jumped back. Suddenly the game was being played for much higher stakes.

"Jackie, you don't want to—"

"Louise, I loved you. I loved you!" he cried, his face awash with rage. "And you go and cheat on me with some other fella. Did you suck on his toes, Louise? Did you suck on another guy's toes?"

I stared at him, too petrified to move. All the blood drained from my face. I knew all too well what a bullet felt like when it slammed into your thigh. I didn't want to know—couldn't even imagine—what the pain was like when it hit the heart.

"I—"

This was it. I was going to die. And if Ratty was right, if I died as Louise, there was no way to pop back to the twenty-first century as Dora. This was it. Finito. Sayonara. End of story.

My life flashed before my eyes. Two lives, actually. Me as me and me as Louise. Soon to be vaporized. I'd failed in my mission. I'd failed Nick. I'd failed saving the world. I'd even failed myself.

Could all of this really end right at this moment?

McGurn raised the pistol, staring at me with squinty

eyes. "I loved you, Louise," he repeated. "But you decided it would be better to go and love Sam instead."

"She wasn't with Sam."

I whirled around at the voice from the back of the room, my eyes widening into saucers as I saw Daisy standing there, arms crossed against her chest, an angry frown on her face.

I turned back to Jack. He still had the gun trained on me, but he was looking past me at our five-foot-one interruption.

"Daisy, this is between me and Louise. I suggest you go home," he said in a tight voice. "You're a good kid. You don't want to get mixed up in none of this."

"I'm already mixed up in it," Daisy said, taking big strides across the room and ending at my side. "You've got the wrong girl."

"Tommy said—"

"You know, if you look up dumb in the dictionary, Tommy's ugly mug's gonna be starin' right back at yah," Daisy said, her voice hard and steely. "I know for a fact that Sam was not with Louise."

"Oh, yeah? And how do you know this fact?"

" 'Cause Sam was with me."

Machine Gun stared at her. I stared at her. What did she just say?

"Are you telling me the truth, Daisy?" McGurn asked, switching the pistol from me to her. "You ain't just sayin' that to protect your friend, now are you?"

"Jackie, this ain't friendship. It's business. And you're going to mess it all up if you don't stop letting your emotions rule your job. You got an important thing goin' down tomorrow morning, right? Something you worked out with Al? Well, don't you think you'd be better off worrying about that than who your girlfriend is sleeping with?"

McGurn stood silent for a moment, as if considering her words, then lowered his gun. He sank down into his seat, laid the weapon on the table and rubbed his eyes with his fists.

"You're right. Of course, you're right," he said. My shoulders dropped in relief and I let out the breath I hadn't realized I was holding. I glanced over at Daisy. She shot me a small, quick smile from the corner of her mouth. "I don't know what I was thinkin'. It's just . . ." McGurn looked up at me and I was shocked to see tears in the corners of his eyes. Was the big, bad gangster actually crying? "I've just been under a lot of stress lately," he said, his voice cracking. "This thing we're doin', if it don't work, it could be a big problem."

"Awh, baby, I understand," I said, walking around the desk and putting a comforting hand on his shoulder. "It's perfectly natural to feel all stressed out when you're under this much pressure. But I'm here for you. As you said, I'm your best girl. And I love you. You're going to pull this off. I have perfect faith in you."

"Thanks," he mumbled. I could tell he was very close to bawling like a baby—reminded me suddenly of the mob boss in that *Analyze This* movie with Robert De Niro. He looked up. "God, this is embarrassin'," he said. "Do you girls mind waiting outside for a bit? Gotta get myself together."

I smiled. "Of course, sweetie," I said, rubbing his shoulder one more time for good measure. "You take all the time you need. And then tonight we'll head to our hotel, right? And we'll have a delish Valentine's Day together."

"I'd like that," he said, sniffling.

I rubbed his head soothingly, then headed back around the desk. I motioned for Daisy to follow me and we exited the office.

"Thank—," I started to say as she closed the door behind us.

She put a finger to my lips and shook her head. Right. No talking until we were out of earshot.

She motioned for me to follow, leading me down the stairs and along a corridor. We cut through the kitchen, dodging chefs who waved their ladles at us, suggesting in a not so eloquent fashion that we were unwelcome guests. But Daisy was Girl on a Mission, pausing only to make one rude gesture at the most angry-looking chef. We exited at the far side, entering another corridor. I remembered this was the way Nick and I had escaped the raid on my first night in 1929. That seemed a million years ago.

Daisy pushed open one of the doors and we stepped inside the room. She pulled it closed behind her and switched on the light. It was a small dressing room lined with vanity tables and mirrors. Painted with a crimson and gold motif, it was a little gaudy for my taste. Must be where the showgirls came to get dolled up before performances.

"We should be safe here," she said, fishing in her purse.

She pulled out a cigarette and lit it. It was then that I noticed that her hands were shaking.

"Daisy, thank you so much," I said. I pulled her into a hug, careful not to burn myself on her cig. "You saved my life."

Daisy shrugged out of my hug. "No big deal," she said, eyes to the floor.

"Are you kidding me? He was going to shoot me. He was ready to shoot me dead. And you waltzed in there like some superheroine and got me out. I owe you everything."

Daisy blushed. She slumped down on one of the vanity table benches and took another drag off her cigarette. "You woulda done the same for me," she said.

I could feel the awkward tension in the room. "Daisy," I started, knowing I needed to clear the air, but not quite sure what I was supposed to say. "About before . . ."

"Forget it, Louise," Daisy said, waving her hand. "It's okay. I've been thinking about what you said, and you're right."

"I was?"

"Yeah. I'm wasting my life here in this one-horse town. If I got such big Hollywood dreams, I gotta start pursuing 'em or I'm just gonna rot away. Become a loser like my old man."

"I was actually talking about the other thing."

"Oh. You mean how I'm in love with you?" Daisy asked. Her words were matter-of-fact, but I could hear a hint of hysteria in her voice. "Yeah, I can't say I'm not disappointed. I mean, I had this dream, Louise. You and I goin' to Hollywood. Starting a life together. It woulda been terrif. But you know what? You can't force people to love you. Just like I couldn't force myself to fall in love with a fella. If it ain't in you, you're not going to fall in love with a girl. You ain't gonna fall in love with me."

Her voice cracked on the last sentence and she angrily swiped at her eyes. My heart broke for her and I crossed the room to pull her into a warm hug. This time, she hugged me back, tightly. As if she never wanted to let go. Probably, she didn't.

"I do love you, Daisy," I said, stroking her back. "Just not in that way."

"I know, Louise. It stinks, but I know. I've always known. I've just never been able to give up the hope of it."

"But just because I don't feel that way, doesn't mean another girl won't," I added. "I just know there's a person out there, waiting for someone as special and wonderful as you are."

Daisy pulled away from the hug, smiling through her tears. "You think so, Louise? You really think so?" She sniffed. "'Cause I've been awfully lonely."

"I know so," I said in my most determined voice. I ruffled her little curly black head.

Daisy jumped to her feet. "Oh, I've been so selfish. Here we are discussing my problems when we should be going to rescue Sam!"

"You're right." I'd almost forgotten that we were only out of the frying pan. I may not have had a gun pointed at my face, but Sam was still locked up. "How are we going to get him out?"

Daisy grinned, reaching into her pocket and pulling out a set of keys. "With these!" she cried.

I stared at the keys, then up at her. "They give you keys to the place?"

Daisy laughed. "Nah, I pinched spares from Machine Gun last time I sucked on his toes. You know how gooey he is after a good suck. Figured they might come in handy some day."

"I think you figured right," I agreed excitedly. The day was suddenly looking up. Maybe, just maybe, there would be a happy ending to this story after all. "Let's go rescue Sam."

CHAPTER FIFTEEN

At first I wondered if perhaps Machine Gun had assigned some gangster types to guard Nick in his makeshift gin-soaked prison, but when we got to the door, we found it unguarded. Finally, a win for the good guys. All the baddies were probably busy preparing for tomorrow's massacre.

Daisy unlocked and opened the door. "I'll stand guard," she declared. "Take care of any interruptions."

I smiled. She was such a good friend. Some woman would be lucky to have her someday. "Thanks, girl," I said, reaching over to give her a squeeze.

I made my way down the steps, feeling all Rescue Hero Girl. It was funny, really, me in the position of rescuing Nick. Back when I was in jail I would fantasize daily about the reverse scenario: his bursting through the door, all Indiana Jones or Luke Skywalker on the Death Star, guns ablaze, demanding my freedom in the name of love.

Of course that never happened. But it would be better

to forget that now. The past was in the past. Well, technically it was in the future at the moment, but it was still equally unchangeable if my mission succeeded. Just because he hadn't managed to rescue me didn't mean I could just allow Nick to languish in a 1929 jail nearly eighty years earlier.

"Sam?" I called, wrinkling my nose as I descended the steps. The place reeked of a weird combo of rot and alcohol. "Are you down there?"

"You're back again?" Nick cried from the bottom of the stairs. His voice sounded weary and hoarse. "I've already told you everything I know. Which is nothing. Please . . . leave me alone."

Ugh. They had interrogated him after all. My mind flashed back to Iraq. Darkness. Screams from the next cell. Screams from my own mouth. The endless questions about the U.S. Government that I didn't know the answers to. My inquisitors couldn't grasp the fact that I was only a civilian. A reporter. A simple girl who was definitely not a member of Dubya's inner circle.

I shook my head. This was not the time to be thinking of that. I had a rescue to perform.

"Sam, it's me, Louise. I've come to rescue you."

I could hear his sigh of relief before I found him with my eyes. He was sitting in the corner of the room, knees pulled up to his chest. His hair was caked with grime and he had a nasty cut above his left eye. I wondered how much of his dishevelment was due to the grenade and how much had been at the hands of the gangsters.

He rose to his feet, unsteady, his legs buckling under

him, and took a step forward. He swayed a little and I ran to his side to help him.

"What are you doing here, Louise?" he asked

"Were you not listening?" I teased, hoping to brighten the mood. Seeing him in this state was causing tears to prick at the corners of my eyes. "I've come to rescue you, silly."

"But why? And for that matter how? And where did you—?"

God, he couldn't stop playing reporter for one second, could he? No wonder he got all the good gigs at the network.

"The hows and whys can come later," I interrupted. "Right now we just need to get you out of here."

"I don't want to put you in any more danger," he protested, laying a hand on my arm, channeling Noble but Stupid Hero Guy. "What if the guards come back?"

"Don't worry. Daisy's guarding the door."

"Daisy?" He stared at me. "But she's like five-foot-nothing. How is she going to . . . ?"

"Hey. I wouldn't underestimate Daisy if I were you," I said with a small laugh. "And didn't I ask you to stop with the questions? Jeez, you'd think you wanted to stay down here in this dark, musty old basement."

"Well, I do have a lifetime supply of gin down here," Nick remarked wryly, glancing over at the bottle-filled shelves.

"Yeah, yeah. Well, I'll buy the next round at the speakeasy if you move your ass. Now let's go." He allowed me to lead him over to the stairs. "Can you climb up?" I asked.

"Yeah, I think so."

We took the steps one by one until we reached the top. My eyes widened as they fell upon Daisy, against the wall, making out with Tommy. What the—?

Daisy's eyes flew open and she gestured for us to get out of there. Evidently this was how she'd decided to "take care of" any complications. And here I'd thought perhaps she knew some form of kung fu or had a gun. But hey, her way was probably much more effective, if not more unpleasant for her. I definitely owed her big time.

I led Nick down the hall and out a side door, breathing a sigh of relief when we hit the cold outside air. We had made it. Well, at least for the moment. I had to get him away from the speakeasy.

He shivered against me. I wrapped my arm around the small of his back and gave him a squeeze. "Hang in there, stud," I said, trying to keep my voice light. "We're going to get you somewhere safe."

We walked down the block and came across a sleazy-looking hotel around the corner. A ramshackle building with a saggy front porch in desperate need of paint. The type of place that probably charged by the hour. Just what we needed. Somewhere McGurn would never look. Not to mention someplace I could actually afford. The Rat had showed me where Louise kept her cash, but in a gesture of good faith I'd already sent most of it to Daisy to pay back what she'd fronted to the Madame. (I didn't want the girl to postpone her dream trip to Hollywood on my account.)

"Here we go," I said. "We can get you cleaned up here."

We checked in as Mr. and Mrs. Trump. (Hey, hotels made me think of the entrepreneur, what can I say?) Then we told the clerk that we didn't want to be disturbed under any circumstances. He gave Nick a once-over, evidently taking in his blood and dirt-stained clothing, winked slyly, and said he'd keep the Pope himself away if we gave him an extra twenty. I reached for my wallet.

The room smelled of bleach, and the gray grungy carpet was stained with something unpleasant looking. There was a creaky metal-frame bed in one corner with a threadbare once-blue blanket thrown over it. Nothing else. But then, the normal clientele probably only required that particular piece of furniture.

I locked the door behind us, then walked over to the window and drew the curtains, my paranoia not content to lie back and admit we were safe. Then I turned back to Nick.

"Go ahead and get cleaned up," I suggested, gesturing to the adjoining bathroom. "Take your time."

He nodded appreciatively and planted a small kiss on the top of my head. Then he limped over to the bathroom, shutting the door behind him.

I glanced around the room. No place to sit but the bed. After pulling off my coat and hat and hanging it on a hook, I hopped on, the springs squeaking their protest against the added weight. Not exactly the Ritz, that was for sure. But I guessed it would do. Still, when I got back to the twenty-first century, the first thing I was going to do was book myself on a luxury cruise or something. I *so* needed pampering right about now.

I drummed my fingers against the bed frame. I should have snagged a book somewhere. Of course, I'd probably be too tense to read. Soon the sounds of running bathwater came from the other room and I contented myself in imagining Nick, naked and soapy. That definitely helped to pass the time.

About a half-hour later, Nick emerged from the bathroom, still dripping wet. He had wrapped a towel around his waist, giving me a good glimpse at his perfectly sculptured chest. Not that I was trying to look, mind you. But there it was. Hard to avoid. A few black and blue marks marred his skin, but they just served to make him look more dashing and dangerous.

"Sorry about the near naked look," he said as he walked over to the bed. "There's no way I can put those disgusting, bloody clothes back on right now." He climbed up onto the mattress, careful not to let the towel gape. He let out a sigh and lay back in bed, resting his head on the flat pillow. "I think I washed off fifty pounds of grime."

"Feel better?" I asked from my sitting position on the other side of the bed. A good portion of my willpower was contemplating going over to the dark side and jumping him right then and there. But after what he'd been through, I guessed he might not appreciate the grope-age.

"Much." He turned and looked up at me. "I guess I haven't properly thanked you," he said with a shy grin. "Kind of wimpy, huh? To be saved by a girl?"

I playfully swatted at him, then lay down on my side so I was facing him. I propped my head up with my elbow. "Better to be emasculated than dead, I suppose."

"Of course a girl would say that. I'm not sure most males would agree with you."

I laughed. "Testosterone is a scary thing."

"Anyway, they can't kill me that easily," Nick said with mock bravado. He patted his chest for emphasis. "In fact, I'm darn near indestructible. Kidnappable, sure," he added with a rueful smile. "But evidently not killable."

"Right. Well, luckily you're also rescueable."

He laughed, reaching out to brush a lock of hair that had fallen into my face. I closed my eyes, rejoicing at the feel of his fingers running through my hair. After he brushed the initial piece away, he kept fingering the strands. It felt nice. Real nice.

"Sorry," he said, as if remembering himself. He pulled his hand away and I opened my eyes. "I shouldn't do that."

"It's okay," I said, lowering my eyes, "I like it." He groaned and rolled over onto his side, staring at the wall instead of me. "God, this is so hard," he said.

I cocked my head. "What is?"

He rolled back over to face me. "You're so beautiful and so sweet," he said. "I really like you a lot."

"But . . . ?"

He sighed. "I told you. I'm still in love with my ex-girlfriend. With Dora. She and I were so close. She was my best friend. And I miss her like crazy. Not a day goes by when I don't have her in my thoughts. And half my nights are spent with her tempting me in my dreams." He shot me a sheepish smile.

"It's been a year. I'm verging on pathetic, now. I don't know why I'm having such a hard time letting go. After all, she doesn't miss me one bit. She's totally moved on. Has some new fancy job and has made it very clear she doesn't want anything to do with me. Not that I blame her."

I shook my head, my heart aching. If only he knew how wrong he was about me. As wrong as I'd been about him, I guess. Here I'd thought this whole year that he'd been the one that had moved on. Moving to LA to take on that high profile network anchor job. Rocking the red carpets at Hollywood premieres. Being named one of *People Magazine*'s "50 Most Beautiful People." The glamour, the starlets, the fan clubs. Had it all really been some halfhearted attempt to escape the fog of war? Of losing me? It seemed so unlikely, but here he was. Spilling his guts to a stranger in a strange land. Why would he bother to lie to Louise?

I tried to focus on his words.

"Anyway, I know at some point I have to allow myself to grieve and move on. I can't hold out hope forever. She's made it very clear that she hates me. That she's never coming back. She's got a whole new life in a whole new town and seems to be doing fine. I've got to accept that, be happy that she's happy without me."

"But she's not happy without you," I blurted before I could stop myself. A lump formed in my throat and tears pricked the corners of my eyes. Great. Evidently some of Dora was impossible to hide.

Nick stared at me. "How would you know?" he asked.

Good question. But one I was finally ready to answer. After that confession, he deserved to know the truth. He deserved to know that I was Dora. And that I wasn't over him. That I hadn't moved on. And I was still just as in love.

"How do I know?" I echoed, gathering up my courage. What would he do when he found out? Would he be angry? Horrified? Relieved? Or just really, really confused?

"Uh, yeah," he said. "I mean, you don't know Dora, obviously."

"Actually . . ." What if he totally freaked out? I mean, this was going to come as such a shock.

I swallowed hard, firming my resolve. After all, this was no time for doubts and fears. And besides, what was I afraid of? He'd just admitted that he loved me.

"Actually, I do know her," I said softly. My whole body was trembling like crazy, was wound up as tight as a top.

"No. Trust me, you don't." Nick laughed.

"I do. Because . . . I am Dora."

He chuckled. "Yeah, right," he said. "Funny. You had me for a moment." He ruffled my head. "Nice try, kiddo."

Of course he wasn't going to believe me at first. But I had lots of ammunition.

I sat up in bed. "I'm serious," I said. I paused for a moment, then added, "Nick."

That did it. He jolted up in bed, his eyes wide and unbelieving. His mouth hung open like some cartoon character. He stared at me. "What did you just call me?" he asked in a hoarse whisper.

I took a deep breath. Here went nothing. "Nick, I'm Dora. Your Dora. From the twenty-first century. They sent me back in time to find you."

He leaped off the bed, all blood drained from his face. He looked as if he'd seen a ghost. Perhaps in a way there were some similarities to that situation. After all, I'd just admitted I was someone who wasn't even born yet.

"Dora?" he whispered, his voice seemingly caught in his throat. "But how . . . ? No!" He held out a hand, as if to ward off a blow to the head. The other clung to the towel around his waist. "It can't be!"

I jumped off the bed, approaching him cautiously. He backed away, like a wild animal caught in a trap. I'd never seen him so freaked out. "Nick, calm down," I tried. "I know this comes as a shock. . . ." I reached out to touch his arm, but he dodged me.

"A shock? You're a full-on heart attack!"

I sighed and retreated, sitting back down on the bed. "If you would just sit down. Relax. Listen. I could explain."

He approached the bed cautiously, his eyes boring into me, as if he expected to be able to use X-ray vision to view my true self under my Louise mask.

Then he shook his head. "This is crazy. Or some kind of trick. There's no way you're Dora."

"Why not?" I asked. "Why couldn't I be? After all, you've time-traveled, too. You know it's possible."

"It's just . . . no. I don't accept this."

"What would make you believe me?" I asked. "You want me to tell you what happened in the season finale of *Lost*?"

"Even if you're from the twenty-first century, that still doesn't make you Dora."

"Your name is Nick Fitzgerald. You're thirty-six. You served as a foreign correspondent over in Iraq until last year. Now you work as a network news anchor in Los Angeles. You love lobster, but are allergic. Your favorite singer is David Bowie, but you don't like his new stuff. You enjoy long walks on the beach, but hate sand between your toes." Wow. This was beginning to sound like a Match.com profile. "Oh, and you hate Broadway musicals, which is why I knew you'd never catch on when I sang 'All that Jazz' at the movie producer's party."

"Please," Nick scoffed. "Anyone with access to Google could know that about me."

"Okay, fine," I said, switching tactics. He wanted personal? I'd give him personal. "You consider yourself a caretaker, but secretly love to be cared for. You're a bear when you're sick and refuse to take it easy. You act tough, arrogant, and suave, but you're a total softie at heart. You're a very professional reporter with impartial journalistic ethics, and so your personal feelings about the justification of the Iraqi war have been tough for you to reconcile."

I paused, then smiled and added, "You have a stuffed black bear named Melvin that your grandmother bought you in Tahoe. You brought it to Iraq and when you're stressed out, you sleep with him tucked under your arm."

Nick's ears turned bright red. Ha! That certainly wasn't something Google-able. I giggled. This was kind of fun in a very strange way.

"God," he breathed. He moved in closer, until his face

was mere inches from mine. He lifted his hand and brushed his fingertips down my cheek. I closed my eyes and savored the feathery sensation. "You're really Dora?" he whispered, his voice full of awe. "You're really and truly her?"

"Mm-hm." I smiled.

"And you came back to find me?"

"Yes."

He pulled his hand away and I opened my eyes to better read his expression. His beautiful kaleidoscope eyes met mine, our mouths inches from one another. What was he thinking? Was he happy I was here? Freaked out? Angry? A little of everything mixed together?

"I have a billion and one questions," he murmured. "Who, what, where, why—all the journalistic biggies. But I'm sorry, Dora. At this very second, not one of them seems to be as important as holding you in my arms and kissing you." He paused, then added, "If that's okay with you."

"I think I could be all right with that," I whispered, suddenly shy.

I wanted answers, too. More than anything. Except, perhaps, this. I'd waited too long for this moment. Spent too many cold nights tossing and turning in my bed. Now we were here. Together. Two people against the universe.

The Q&A could wait. At least for the moment.

He closed his eyes and leaned forward, covering my face with soft, tender kisses. My forehead, my cheeks, my eyelids, my nose. I could feel his long eyelashes fluttering against my skin, as tender as a butterfly's caress. My heart felt like it was going to explode. It was almost too much.

That connection between us. The magnetism that had never gone away.

I wanted to laugh and cry and shout and sob—all at the same time. How could I feel so much for one person? It seemed impossible. And to have the feeling returned—well, I couldn't think of anything better in any time.

We had to talk. That much was obvious. I had to know what had really happened in Iraq. And I had to convince him to not change the future by waking up Bugs Moran. But words and explanations were too much and I was content to communicate with my body. My heart. There'd be time to talk afterwards.

"I've missed this," I admitted, almost against my will. I felt open, vulnerable, admitting this to him. But this was not the time to be Self-Protective Girl. I had to trust him. To trust that he wouldn't hurt me again.

"Me too." He smiled against my cheek and then lowered his lips to meet mine. Our mouths caressed, moved against one another, feeling, finding, discovering. These weren't Nick's natural lips and he wasn't kissing mine. But in some weird way that made it all the more fun, the familiarity mixed with the strange.

The intensity of our kisses grew, pressure on my mouth from his lips mounted. I pressed back, parting my lips to allow for a deeper kiss. He responded instantly, delving into my mouth. His hands left my face, traveling down my neck to cup my shoulders. Then he dragged further down my arms, gripping me tightly. He lowered me onto my back and shifted on top of me, his leg pressing between mine. I parted my thighs to allow him room, appreciating the tingly sensation the intimate contact evoked.

God, it'd been so long. Too long. I was more than ready. And this time there was nothing to stop us.

He continued to kiss me as his left hand explored, tracing my hipbone, brushing against my stomach, along my ribcage, to my breast. He cupped it in his hand, his fingertips coming together to gently squeeze the tip. My body responded and I involuntarily pressed myself against his leg, already aching for relief.

But he evidently wanted to take things slow. To enjoy re-experiencing the ecstasy that we'd once shared. He pulled my shirt over my head and lowered his kisses to dust my neck, my shoulder blade, all the while rubbing his thumb in a circular motion against my breast. Skin so sensitive I could feel each ridge of his fingertip.

"It's so strange," he murmured, raising his head a moment to meet my eyes. "To caress a complete stranger's body, but know that it's really yours."

"She has a better body than I do," I couldn't help but crack. "And she's lacking in the ugly facial scars department."

Nick shook his head, his eyes clear and bright. "Even with that tiny flaw, Dora, you're the most beautiful woman I have ever laid eyes on. It makes the rest of you even more special."

I started to laugh bitterly at that, but he pressed a finger to my mouth.

"I'm serious," he said. And he looked it, too. "I wouldn't trade you for anyone." He paused, then added, "This past year, I could have had my pick of women. My job inspires a lot of wanton fans, for some reason." He laughed bitterly. "But I wasn't interested in any of them. I only wanted you."

He lowered his head to kiss me again. This time the sensation of his lips on mine was different. Now there was love in the kiss, a kind of worshipful caress. From it, I could tell without a shadow of a doubt that he meant every word he said.

After what seemed hours of just kissing, he pulled away and smiled at me. "I know this isn't your real body," he murmured, smiling slyly. "But do you think I can still make you scream?"

"Well . . . ," I grinned back, "I guess there's only one way to find out."

"Guess so," he said with a chuckle. He rolled off me, onto his side, and propped himself up with his elbow. Then he reached over to touch me between my legs, reaching down my underwear and dragging a lazy finger along my sex. I couldn't help but let out a small moan at the sensation.

"Hm," he said teasingly, not pulling his hand away. He stroked me gently and I closed my eyes to rejoice in the fire he was stoking.

"So far, so good," I said, looking over at him and smiling.

He leaned forward and took my breast in his mouth, sucking, licking, nibbling gently. It was like liquid lightning shot straight to my core.

"Ah!" I managed to squeak. "I think it's working."

He grinned against my breast. "You're not screaming, though," he said.

He pulled down my skirt and removed my underwear, leaving the thigh-high stockings on. I tried to modestly close my legs, but he pushed them open again, as if he liked me being so exposed, so open to him. Then his fingers went back to work on me. Rubbing, stroking, caressing, pressing, and squeezing. I squirmed under his touch, soaking wet in my desire. Even in this strange body, even with his strange fingertips, he could effortlessly make me reach the point of ecstasy.

And soon, as he rhythmically circled my sex with relentless fingers, he brought me there. To the place where stars explode and fireworks sing. I gasped as the sensation rocked me to my core. Hardly conscious as I grabbed fistfuls of sheets, fistfuls of his hair—something, anything to hold on to as I went over the waterfall with not so much as a barrel to protect me.

"Feel okay?" he asked, moments later, as I lay gasping for breath, moaning in relieved delight.

"Gah," I answered, not at my most articulate.

"Heh." He laughed. "And to think, I've only gotten started."

My turn to play, I rolled over and ran my hands down his chest. His host body really did have amazing abs. But knowing Nick was underneath was what made them all the more delicious. I traced the line of black hair that trailed down to where he was still covered.

I tugged on the towel and tossed it aside, revealing the part of Sam I hadn't yet seen. I wasn't disappointed. Not that Nick as Nick had ever disappointed me, either.

I reached out to stroke him and he groaned in response, his beautiful eyes glazing over as he succumbed to my touch. "It's, uh, been a while," he confessed. I smiled, enjoying his response. There was a power to touching a man in a way that made him weak before you.

A few minutes later, he grabbed my hand and forced it above my head. "You've got to stop," he said in a raspy voice. "You're too good at that. And I'm not so used to controlling this new body of mine."

He grinned wickedly and I smiled back at him, giggling a little. Then, his smile dropped and he adopted a tense, smoldering gaze. I shivered. This was it.

"I want you inside of me," I murmured.

"I think that can be arranged," he agreed. "Though take it easy on me. I'm still a little weak from the whole grenade and torture thing."

He lowered himself on top of me and I widened my legs, allowing him entrance. He pressed into me, entering me, filling me, and I gasped at the sensation of our bodies becoming one flesh. He paused for a moment, his face a mask of concentration; then he smiled, regaining control, and leaned forward to kiss me. He went slowly, pressing deep into me with fluid thrusts.

If he was in pain, he didn't let on. His mouth moved against mine, tenderly exploring and tasting me as if he'd never get his fill. It was so strange. To make love to a complete stranger's body. To squirm under an unfamiliar touch. And yet to know, at the same time, that all of these stranger's actions were puppeteered by the guy I loved more than anyone in the world.

As we moved together, as one strange flesh and one

common mind, his thrusts gradually upped their intensity. I rocked my own hips against him, finding and keeping the rhythm. His mouth moved to my ear, his breath becoming erratic as he whispered my name over and over.

"Dora," he rasped. "Dora, Dora, my love."

That was all it took for me to reach the stars again. To feel the universe come together, as if just for the two of us. I cried out as the elation I felt wracked my very core. I'd waited too long for this. Been too stubborn. Too stupid. Too—

He found it as well, seconds later letting loose a moan of exultation as he came inside of me. I loved the sound of his pleasure. His sharp cries as he pressed against me in those final thrusts. To know I made him feel such ecstasy.

He collapsed atop me, his breathing heavy in my ear. I wrapped my arms around him, squeezing him in a hug, rejoicing in the weight of his body on top of mine. The sheen of sweat. His heavy breath struggling for control. I wanted the moment to last forever.

I'd been so full of hate. And now that hate had gone. And it'd been replaced with an overflowing fountain of love. I felt like belting out a song from *Moulin Rouge*. The one about how wonderful life was, now that Nick was in the world.

"I'm so happy, Dora," Nick whispered in my ear. "To have you back. Even in someone else's body. I can't even explain what it feels like."

"You don't have to," I said, giving him a small squeeze. "I already know."

He lifted his head to look at me. To look at me with those amazing eyes. But the love I saw in them wasn't from the eyes' owner. It was one hundred percent Nick.

He rolled off me and for a moment I felt a pang of emptiness as our bodies separated. But that was silly. He wasn't going anywhere. He was right next to me. I turned on my side and wrapped my arm around his chest, snuggling my head in his shoulder.

He let out a chuckle. "I don't want to ruin the moment, but I'm dying of curiosity here. You gotta tell me how you got here. And why."

I nodded against his chest. I felt so snuggly and warm I just wanted to drift into sleep. But he was right. We had things to discuss. Like, history-changing things.

"Look, Nick," I said, hoping my explanation didn't change anything between us, didn't wrench apart the closeness we shared. "I know about the Time Warriors. I know what you came back in time to do. And so does the FBI. And they sent me back to find you and stop you."

Nick was quiet for a moment. Too quiet. I lifted my head to look at him. He stared back at me with puzzled eyes.

"Stop me?" he repeated. "Stop me from what?"

CHAPTER SIXTEEN

"Stop you from committing yet another St. Valentine's Day massacre, of course," I said, instantly regretting the word choice of *another* the second it came out of my lips. There was no reason to bring up Iraq just yet.

He squinted his eyes. "Committing a what—?"

I snuggled against him, kicking at the tangled sheets to better wrap my feet around his ankles. With my head resting on his chest, I could hear his heartbeat thump against my ear. "Look Nick, you don't have to play all coy. I know all about it."

"Know all about what?" he asked, reaching over to smooth my hair. He kissed the top of my head. "What are you talking about, Dora? I need more to go on here."

I sighed. "Fine. Here's the scoop. I was recruited by the FBI. They told me all about it. How you joined a group called the Time Warriors and you were going back to 1929 to mess with the St. Valentine's Day Massacre. I mean, time travel—who knew?" I snorted. "But anyway, I know all about your mission. To wake up Bugs Moran so he won't sleep through the massacre and he'd get whacked, too. But since something like that would totally change history, they said I had to stop you."

"But Dora," Nick said, his voice laced with confusion. "I don't know anything about the—what did you call them? The Time Fighters?"

Oh, so he was going to play hard to get, eh? I sat up in bed, pulling the sheets up to cover my breasts.

"Come on, Nick, give me a break," I cajoled. "I mean, I know it's all supposed to be so über secret and stuff. Against the Time Warrriors' code of ethics to tell or whatever. But at least give me some credit here."

"I'll give you all the credit in the world, baby," he replied, reaching for my hand. "But I can't admit to something I don't know about."

I stared at him, confusion knotting my insides. He looked back at me, all innocent, meeting my eyes without difficulty. Was he really telling the truth? Did he really not know what the Time Warriors were? If that were true then what . . . ?

"If you aren't with the Time Warriors, then what the hell are you doing back in time?" I asked. Might as well throw all the cards on the table.

He shrugged. "The FBI sent me," he said simply. "To seduce you."

"Seduce me?" I pulled my hand away and inched to the opposite side of the bed, suddenly very afraid.

"Well, not you, exactly. I mean, they said I had to seduce Louise Rolfe. They never told me you were inside, obviously."

"So, wait." My head was spinning. "You're telling me that the FBI recruited you to go back to 1929 and seduce Louise? Why the hell would they ask you to do that? And why did you go along with it?"

"It's an experimental new program they're running," Nick explained. "Operation Past Reconstruction. The idea is to send people to the past to help with court cases that failed, to prevent criminals from running free and causing more havoc."

"Huh?"

"You know, like they sent someone back to talk to the Untouchables to suggest they charge Al Capone for tax evasion."

"But they already got Al Capone for tax evasion."

"Maybe in the version of history we're living. How do you know it turned out that way originally? Maybe old Scarface originally didn't get caught. Maybe he ran for president. Maybe the United States became one corrupt nation under the mob."

I rubbed the back of my neck, trying to sort it all through. I couldn't even begin to grasp the complex quantum physics—or however time travel happens—that he was suggesting.

"It doesn't always work. They gave the O.J. lawyers the bloody glove, but they still managed to screw that one up."

"So, let me get this straight," I said, drawing in a breath. "The FBI sends men back to the past to help with the prosecution of criminals using information they know from the present day."

"Basically, yeah."

"And so, why did you get sent back to seduce Louise?"

"Easy. She's supposed to be Machine Gun's alibi. If I could get Louise to fall in love with Sam and decide not to testify in defense of McGurn, he wouldn't get away with the St. Valentine's Day Massacre. It'd be a big win against organized crime in this country and could really stop a lot of lawlessness. A lot of killings. Break up the Gambino family before it's even born."

"But why do it that way? Why not prevent the massacre from happening in the first place?"

"The FBI doesn't have that jurisdiction. They have only been given permission to aid in the prosecution, not intervene with the crimes themselves."

It was strange, but for some reason, I was almost buying it. This all made sense in a very weird way. But still, I had a lot of unanswered questions. "So why did they send you—a TV news reporter?"

"Actually, I've helped out the government in the past. Over in Iraq. I can't give you details, it's all classified stuff, but let's just say they saw an advantage to using a private citizen journalist for certain missions."

I raised an eyebrow, reassessing. Wow. Nick was a real spy. Who knew? I should have been angry that he'd never told me, but of course spies aren't supposed to tell. In any case, it was kind of cool. My boyfriend, James Bond. I pictured him back in his own skin. In a tux. Sipping martinis that were perfectly shaken, but never stirred. (Unfortunately, in real life he was more of a MGD type and hated tuxes with a passion, but I was not about to let that technicality ruin my fantasy.)

"Okay, fine," I said, pushing the sexy image from my

mind to better concentrate on the real situation that had just presented itself. "You're, like, a spy or something? Well, let me ask you this. If the FBI set up this whole thing, if it was their idea to send you back to the past, why the heck did they send me back to stop you? It doesn't make any sense."

Nick shook his head. "I don't know," he admitted. "That's what I can't figure out."

"They told me you were a part of some rich white man's club, sick of the golf circuit, they said, who bought a machine off the KGB and traveled back in time on a lark. To sleep with Marilyn Monroe and stuff."

Nick frowned, sitting up in bed. "Does that sound like me, Dora?" he asked. "Does it sound like something I'd be into?"

"Well, no, not really. . . ."

"Who told you this? How did they approach you? Did you get their credentials? Are you sure they were the FBI?"

Worry gnawed at my insides. I couldn't answer any of these questions. Well, not in ways that would assure Nick that I wasn't a complete idiot.

"This guy, Agent Fredricks, approached me on the street and asked me to come with him. He brought me to some underground room and there were three men, dressed in black. They had some slide projection with your photo . . ." I trailed off, realizing how lame and naïve I sounded.

"And you believed them?" Nick asked incredulously.

"They said it was a matter of saving the world!"

"Oh, my little Dora," he said. "You're still the same, aren't you? Charging into things without thinking them through."

I frowned, not liking his patronizing tone. "I didn't charge. I thought about it. It seemed legit at the time."

Nick raised an eyebrow. "It seemed legit that some random guy on the street suggested you go back in time to stop me from changing history?"

"Hey, they had badges and stuff. And they knew things. I'm not a complete moron. And besides, they got the 'you' part right. You're here, aren't you?"

Nick ran a hand through his hair. "Yes. True. There's got to be some reason this group sent you. . . ."

Grr. Now I was getting annoyed. Angry, even. Why did he so quickly assume I was the one who had been duped? It could just as easily have been his side that was lying. Or—a troubling thought suddenly dawned— maybe this was part of his plan all along. He'd realized he'd been caught, and now he was trying to throw me off the scent by making me feel as if I were an idiot.

"You know, now that I think about it, how do I even know you're telling me the truth?" I demanded. "What if this is all part of your Time Warriors game? To throw me off the scent? To make me think you aren't going to wake up Moran?"

"Give me a break, Dora."

"No. *You* give *me* a break," I retorted, not appreciating his tone. So arrogant. So typical Nick. "You just expect me to believe your side of the story without question. What, just because we had sex, now I'm supposed to trust you again? Look at what you did to me in Iraq. Was that part of an FBI mission, too? Did they want me to be captured for some reason? Did you sell me out for them?"

"Dora!" Nick cried in an anguished tone. "Will you calm down for a minute? This isn't helping!"

Anger burned in my gut and my hands were shaking. What had I been thinking? Why had I slept with him? Allowed myself to trust him?

"I've got to go," I said in a tight voice. "Louise is supposed to meet McGurn at the hotel, give him his alibi. And I'm not going to let you destroy the world, Nick. It's bad enough I let you destroy my life."

I jumped out of bed and grabbed my clothes. I shoved my hands through the sleeves.

"Dora, don't do this," Nick said. "You need to stay here. You can't be the alibi. By being the alibi, McGurn will go free. And others will die."

"But that what's supposed to happen," I said, pulling my shirt over my head and then stepping into my skirt. "That's how history is supposed to play out."

Nick shook his head. "Screw history. We can make the world better this way. We can make the bad guys pay for all they've done." He rose from the bed and approached me, taking my hands in his. "Imagine, Dora," he said, his earnest eyes boring into mine. "What if by changing this event, by making McGurn pay for his actions, it shuts down organized crime in the U.S.? This could lead to different governments being voted in. Maybe even ones that wouldn't have started a war in Iraq. When you go back to the twenty-first century, you may find a world of peace. A world where there is no Gulf War."

I stopped for a moment. I had to admit, the idea was somewhat appealing. Could he be telling the truth? Was it really possible to change history for the better?

I imagined this world of his. The one where there was no Iraqi war. The one where I didn't get caught. Captured, hurt, humiliated. A world where I didn't have ugly scars, both inside and out. Where I didn't live each day with pain, fear, anger.

What would it be like? I pictured Nick and I as husband and wife. Maybe even as an anchor team at some Los Angeles station. We'd go to Hollywood premieres and Joan Rivers would want to know where I got my dress. I'd smile demurely, of course, and tell her it was a present from my very wonderful husband Nick.

It sounded like heaven. But it also sounded wrong.

"It's too dangerous, Nick," I argued, dropping my hands from his. His touch was making me too vulnerable, and I needed all the strength I had. "Sure, by manipulating the past, the future may become better for some. But for others it could be much worse. Are you willing to do that? Are you willing to take the risk?

"The new governments you see filling in after you supposedly 'vanquish' so-called organized crime—what if they're worse than the ones we know about? What if they let Hitler get away with it? Or start a nuclear war in the fifties?"

"You're looking at this wrong," Nick argued. "Focusing on the negative. What if this leads to the cure for cancer? For AIDS?"

"Nick, it doesn't matter. I truly believe things are supposed to happen for a reason," I said angrily, realizing at that moment, he'd been so brainwashed I'd never be able to convince him. "Even bad things."

I reached up to touch my scar, knowing, of course, it wasn't actually cut into Louise's face. Suddenly I realized that, in my efforts to convince him, I was also doing a damn good job of convincing myself.

I'd been so angry, so bitter, about what had happened in Iraq. How my life had taken such a down turn. But, truth be told, every event in my life, even the emotionally and physically scarring ones, had shaped me into the person I was today.

Sure, I wasn't so beautiful anymore. I wasn't glamorous or famous. But I was me. And I didn't want to change that, go back to the old Dora, who now seemed sorely underdeveloped as a character. I'd learned things about life. About loss. About love. I'd learned what was important at the end of the day. And now that I had, I didn't want to give all that up just to rid myself of some pain.

"Nick, you know what I went through in Iraq. But even that, that painful time that I endured, it made me the me you see before you. And I wouldn't change that. At least not at the risk of destroying the rest of the world."

He shook his head, looking weary. "Maybe you can be that noble, Dora. But I can't."

Anger welled up in my gut. Of course he couldn't. I didn't know why I'd even bothered to open my mouth. Once Nick got something in his head, even God himself couldn't change his mind.

"You know, Nick, you're a selfish bastard," I retorted, my face burning with fury. "You only care about yourself.

Just like in Iraq. You abandoned me on our mission. You went out and found a new girlfriend while I was being tortured in prison."

"What? Dora, that's not—"

"You know what?" I interrupted, my voice cold as ice. "The only history I wish I could change, Nick Fitzgerald, is the one where I ever fell for you."

I charged toward the door, ready to make my escape. He grabbed me by the shoulder.

"I can't let you go," he said. "I'm sorry."

I turned around and kicked him in the groin. He doubled over in pain. "No, *I'm* sorry," I said, my voice oddly calm. "But you can't stop me."

CHAPTER SEVENTEEN

You know, if I wasn't so hurt and angry and bitter and hating life, being a blonde alibi for McGurn would have been a pretty good gig. He presented me a beautiful red silk gown, then took me out on the town to a fancy restaurant and then out to the theatre. He wined me, he dined me, but I couldn't muster any appetite or enjoyment. All I could think of was Nick and what a bastard he'd turned out to be.

At least I could say I was right all along. I'd been fooling myself by thinking that I'd made a mistake hating him, not trusting him. It turned out that my initial instincts had been right on the money. The guy was a selfish jerk, willing to do anything—even change history—to get his own way.

I couldn't believe he'd actually been able to justify in his mind that what he was doing was honorable. Noble, even. Anyone who's seen any kind of sci-fi movie knows that you just don't change history. There was too much risk. Things played out for a reason. I had to believe that.

The possibilities of an alternate future were frightening. I mean, let's say McGurn did go down for the Massacre. He then doesn't whack some guy—let's say he's named Charlie. Charlie, instead of dying, ends up marrying his childhood sweetheart and they have a kid. That kid ends up falling in love with my mother and so she marries him instead of my dad. Then I'm never born! That doesn't seem very good, now does it? And that's just based on one tiny sperm. Imagine what implications McGurn going to jail would have on the rest of the world. Crashing dominoes. Everywhere.

I firmed my resolve. I wasn't going to let that happen. At least not on my watch. I was going to be McGurn's alibi tonight. Then I was going to sneak out of the hotel, head to Bugs's house, and make sure no one woke him up, that he'd miss the Massacre, just as history had him do. Everything was going to play out exactly how it should.

And then I would go back to my unchanged twenty-first century world and forget Nick Fitzgerald ever existed.

I watched as Jack downed his fourth cocktail at dinner, his nose getting redder and redder. He babbled on about nothing, his speech starting to slur. Hopefully he'd be so intoxicated he'd pass out as soon as we got back to the hotel. If not, I had a contingency plan I'd purchased at the local drugstore.

After dinner we headed back to our hotel, where Jack continued to down shots of whiskey. He spent a good deal of time on the phone, firming up the plans for the Massacre. I plopped myself down on the bed, watching, waiting. Bored out of my mind.

When he hit the bathroom, I saw my opportunity. I emptied the packet of sleeping powder into his drink. I needed him to pass out hardcore so I could sneak off to Moran's house. Also, this would help me avoid any toe-related sexual escapades he might have planned for a romantic V-Day evening.

The drugs kicked in around two A.M. and the mobster passed out in his chair, sawing logs like a lumberjack. I rose silently from the bed and walked over to him, wanting to make sure he was out for the count before I made my move. Didn't want him waking up a half hour later and learning I was gone.

I waved a hand in front of his face—no reaction. Good.

Slipping on my shoes and coat, I headed silently for the hotel door, praying it wasn't in need of WD-40. I wrapped my hand around the knob and pulled it open slowly. . . .

It did let out a small squeak, and I glanced over at Jack to see if the sound had woken him. He snorted in his sleep, snuffled a bit, then went back to snoring. I let out a breath. Phew. Good drugs.

I slipped out of the room and closed the door behind me. Then I headed away from the hotel and hailed a late night cab to Bugs's house.

As we drove down the silent, dark Chicago streets, I tried to focus on my mission. But all I could think about was Nick. My heart ached and my stomach churned as my mind replayed that afternoon's conversation. He'd seemed so genuine. So sweet. And I had to admit, making love to him had been incredible. And yet it was all just more lies and double-crossing. He was never going to be a guy I could count on. And I could never let myself trust him again. I shouldn't have indulged in that moment of weakness. Allowed myself to care. Because, like in Iraq, he had once again let me down.

The cab pulled up a block away from Bugs's house. I paid the driver with money I'd fished from McGurn's wallet and hopped out. I watched as it sped off into the night, then walked down the street until I came to the right address. It was a small blue house with one upstairs gable window, crammed between two houses that looked just like it. Definitely not as glamorous a place as I'd imagined a notorious gangster to live, but perhaps he had to keep his lifestyle low-key to fool the IRS.

I walked around the back of the house, looking for a place to hide while I waited 'til dawn. Unfortunately, I lacked Nancy Drew luck, and there were no convenient bushes to hide in. Not to mention it was about twelve degrees and I was still wearing an evening gown.

I caught sight of a low window in the neighbor's house and decided to try it. I was in luck; it slid open easily and I slipped inside. The basement was damp, dark, and cold, but at least it was more secure than hanging around outside. I regretted not waiting in the hotel room longer, enjoying the warmth from the fireplace. But no, if Jack had woken up then I might have never gotten out. And that would ruin everything. It wasn't going to be a comfortable couple of hours, for sure, but saving the world and stopping Nick would be well worth the minor discomfort.

I sat down in a corner and pulled my knees to my chest. Well, here I was, with hours to kill and nothing to think about. Okay, so I actually had a lot to think about, but none of it was pleasant.

Could I really pull this off? Would Nick try to stop me? What if I failed and Nick won? Would the future be greatly changed or would there just be, like, a new New Coke or something?

Nick. The name made me sigh. What would have happened if I'd just gone along with his plan? Would he have wanted to date me again when we got back to the twenty-first century? Had he been serious about all he'd said before I told him I was Dora? Did he really love me? Miss me? Was he really unable to go on with life without me?

Or had that all been part of the act? If I had agreed to do my part in his history-changing plan, would he have used me and dumped me after he got what he wanted?

I guess I'd never find out. It was probably better that way, anyway.

Time passed slowly, but eventually the sky pinkened with pre-dawn light. I glanced at my watch and climbed out the basement window. It was almost time. I rose to my feet, trying to muster up some "save the world" energy.

If only Nick had believed me; had stood by my side for once. We could have been doing this together. I would have felt a hell of a lot more confident with him by my side.

You don't need him, Dora. You don't need anyone. You can do this. You are woman. Time to roar.

I walked around the side of Bug's house and found a low window. I pulled on it, praying the guy wasn't a lock-everything-up-tight kind of guy. But luck again was with me, and the window easily slid open. I climbed inside.

I entered a dark kitchen and waited a moment for my eyes to adjust to the darkness. Then I tiptoed into the living room, careful not to trip on any furniture. For once my clumsiness would not just be embarrassing; it could be the difference between life and death.

I came to a narrow staircase, leading up—most likely to the bedrooms, where Bugs would be asleep. I tiptoed up the stairs, my heart beating wildly, hoping Bugs kept it in good repair and there were no creaky steps to give me away. Fortuitously, it seemed he was on top of the maintenance, and I made it to the landing without so much as a squeak.

I glanced around. There were several doors, all closed. One of which I assumed led to Bugs's bedroom.

But which one?

I shrugged. Only one way to find out. I tried opening the first. A bathroom. The second door led into an empty guest bedroom. The third was locked. I hadn't thought about the possibility that Bugs might keep his door locked.

Feeling less confident, I sneaked to the fourth door. But just as I was wrapping my hands around the knob, a voice stopped me in my tracks.

"Don't move."

I gulped. *Fuck.* I'd been caught.

Turn around and he may shoot. The long ago warning from my Iraqi contact echoed through my brain. *Then again, he might shoot anyway.*

"Uh, is that you, Bugs?" I tried, swallowing down my rising panic.

If only Nick had come. He could have kept guard while I tried the doors. Now, once again, I'd been caught. Just like in Iraq. Once again, Nick had let me down. And this time, I was pretty sure I wouldn't end up in a prison cell. I'd end up dead.

"Who are you?" the man demanded.

I turned around slowly, hands in the air. Sure enough, there stood a squat Irishman with a big nose and a cleft chin, wearing a pinstriped nightshirt and pointing a shiny black pistol at my head.

Bugs Moran.

Think fast, think fast, think fast!

"Uh, heya Mr. Moran, I'm a friend of Daisy's. Is she around?" I asked, my mouth hardly able to form the words my teeth were chattering so badly. Would this work?

I'd heard Daisy say the guy had earned his nickname "Bugs" because he was "Buggy." As in crazy. Fucked up. Off his rocker. There was no way this psycho was going to let me off easy. I was as good as dead. The only question was how many minutes did I have left?

Well, I would stall him as long as possible. Sure, I didn't have much of a prayer of getting out alive, but if I managed to make him late for the Massacre, late enough that he missed getting shot, at least I'd still be saving the world.

Was this how it had originally played out? Were we in some sort of weird time loop thing? The history books never explained why Bugs was late. Just that he'd overslept. Maybe I was always supposed to be here, keeping him from his demise. But then again, if Louise died, then she couldn't be the blonde alibi. Bugs would survive, but McGurn would go down. That couldn't be right either. . . .

The time travel intricacies were too much to wrap my head around. Best to just focus on the man with the gun.

Bugs stared at me, recognition dawning on his face. Maybe turning around hadn't been such a good idea. "Why, you're Louise Rolfe!" he cried incredulously. "You're Machine Gun's moll."

"Well, not really," I corrected, making it up as I went along. "You see, we broke up, actually. And he's planning this big attack on you. The whole Clark Street thing? That's a setup. He wants to kill you."

Bugs raised a skeptical eyebrow, keeping his gun trained on me. "So you came to warn me," he said. "You think I'm gonna believe that Machine Gun's dame shows up in my house at the crack of dawn to warn me that her boyfriend's gonna blow my head off?" He cocked the trigger of the gun. "Seems a little far-fetched to me."

I squeezed my eyes closed. This was not working. I needed more time. If he shot me now, he could still get down to the Massacre on schedule. And then I'd not only be dead, but I'd have failed my mission. Bugs would be killed and McGurn wouldn't have his blonde alibi to get him off. Nick and his Time Warriors would have won.

"I know, but—," I cried, trying one last time.

"She's telling the truth."

Speak of the devil! My eyes flew open at the voice behind me. I whirled around, not caring anymore about Bugs's *don't move* command.

Nick! And he had his gun pointed directly at Bugs.

My heart caught in my throat, my brain hardly believing what my eyes told it to be true. Nick was here! He'd come! He'd actually come! I was saved. And maybe, just maybe, so was the rest of the world.

"Who the hell are you?" Bugs cried. "Jeez Louise, my house is Grand Central Station this morning. Can't a guy even get any sleep around here?"

"Here's the deal," Nick said, his voice steady and calm. "You're going to take that gun off of Louise there and head back to bed. In a half hour, you can leave your bedroom and head down to Clark Street. Then you'll see that Louise is telling the truth."

"And if I don't?" Bugs snarled. "If I just go ahead and shoot the dame?"

"Then I'll shoot you," Nick said in a calm voice. "And you'll be dead, too. Machine Gun will have won."

Bugs trained the gun back on me. I winced. Was he going to take his chances, shoot me anyway, hope that Nick wasn't a great shot?

He didn't. Instead, he lowered the gun and sighed. "So what you're saying is the whole Canadian gin deal was a setup? By McGurn?"

"And Capone," I added.

"And so right now, as we speak, my men are heading to their deaths? But you're not going to let me stop them?"

He shook his head. "Those are family men, you know. They got wives and kids. You want their blood on your hands?"

I bit my lower lip. This was like one of those ethical questions they always threw at you during job interviews. Was it better to shoot down a plane or let it crash into a building?

"I am sorry for your men," Nick said. "But this is how the scenario is supposed to play out. Someone very wise once taught me that things—even bad things—happen for a reason." He spared a glance at me. "And it'd be selfish to try to change them."

"Then why come here to me?" Bugs asked, raking a hand through his greasy hair. "I don't get it. Why do you care if I live, when you're perfectly willing to let the other guys go down? After all, I'm the one they want."

"It's a long story," Nick replied. "Just be thankful we got here on time."

"Well, technically Sam here was a little late," I interjected, not able to resist. "He has a habit of being late on Valentine's Day." I grinned at him, letting him know I was teasing.

"Yeah, well I'm a little slow and stupid," he said with a small smile. "But eventually I catch on."

"I'm glad you do," I murmured, my heart swelling with love. I wanted to cross the room and throw myself in his arms. "Very glad."

"Uh, as touching as this scene may be, can I go back to my room now?" Bugs asked, nodding his head in the direction of his bed. "If I'm supposed to oversleep, I might as well get to it."

"Sure," Nick agreed. "But I'm coming in with you. There will be no jumping out the window to run and warn your men heroics on my watch."

Bugs sighed. Obviously this had been his plan. "Fine."

"And I have to get back to the hotel," I said, looking at my watch. "Before Machine Gun wakes up."

A sudden thought tickled my brain. Should I really leave Nick with Bugs? Was he really on my side? What if the second I took off he freed the gangster and sent him down to Clark Street in a hurry? He'd accomplish his original mission, history would change, and I'd have been suckered once again.

I shook my head. I had to trust him. Trust that if he wanted Bugs to go down, he'd make it happen and he wouldn't be sneaky about it. Anyway, it wasn't like I could stop him. He was the one holding the gun. And if I didn't get back soon and McGurn woke up and found me missing, all bets were off.

"So, we'll meet up this afternoon?" I asked, peering into his face, looking for some reassurance. His clear blue-green eyes met mine and he smiled. Suddenly I didn't have a single doubt. I trusted him. Really trusted him. With the past, the present . . . and even our future.

"Definitely," he said. "Meet you at seven at the—" He glanced over at Bugs, who was listening a little too intently for my liking. "At the place we went to the other day," he amended, not willing to give our whereabouts to a mob boss whom we had just informed was going to lose all his gang in a massacre. Even if we did save his life, it was up in the air how grateful he was actually going to be.

"Sounds like a plan," I said, squeezing Nick's hand. "Thanks for cooperating, Bugs. Really appreciate it."

Bugs scowled. "As if I had a choice, sweetheart."

"Hey!" Nick said, waving the gun. "That's my girl you're talking to there. You be respectful."

His girl. I beamed. I liked the sound of that.

CHAPTER EIGHTEEN

I went back to the hotel (which was definitely five-star—
a hell of a lot nicer than the one I'd stayed in with Nick),
changed into my nightgown, and slipped into bed.
McGurn was still snoring in his chair, right where I'd left
him. He'd probably never even woke up. I was going to
have to write a big thank-you note to the sleeping pill
company.

It would have been nice if I could be so restful, but
there was no way I was going to be able to shut my eyes
and drift out of consciousness until I was assured everything had gone off without a hitch. Until I knew for certain that history was playing out exactly as it was
supposed to play out. That Bugs arrived fashionably late
and didn't join his men in that inner circle of Hell re-
served for mobster types.

Not to mention, I wasn't that keen on letting my
guard down while sharing a room with a guy who'd
threatened to kill me less than twenty-four hours ago.

So I lay in bed, wearily staring at the ceiling. My thoughts unsurprisingly wandered to Nick. How he'd showed up just in time. Saved the day. Didn't let me down again.

Insert dreamy sigh here.

I wondered what had made him change his mind. Was it something I'd said or did? Was it out of his love for me? Would he get in trouble with the FBI? And what was the deal with the two FBI groups, anyway? I felt myself frowning as I went over the two stories in my mind. They just didn't make any sense. It was as if we'd been played somehow. And somewhere someone was looking down and laughing. But who? And why? None of it made any sense.

Too many unanswered questions. But what I really needed to know was what would happen next. Whoever the group was that had sent me here, they certainly couldn't deny that I'd accomplished my mission. Okay, with Nick's help, but so what? History was safe for the moment. Yay for me. So, when would I be going back to the twenty-first century? And how?

Also, when I did get back, would I see Nick? Would he be nearby? Or was he still in LA? Should I fly up to see him or have him come down to San Diego? Would he want to? Would everything be the same once we switched our bodies back? Or would it be awkward, different? I'd assume reentry to our own lives would be pretty hard. Had time passed? Or was it like in Narnia, where a thousand years was like a day?

Ugh. That would mean I'd still have to throw together that "Too Stressed for Sex" story for the 11 P.M. newscast.

There was too much to worry about. I should be thankful that we'd accomplished my mission; concentrate on the present before worrying about the future. Hashing wouldn't help in this case. It was up to the FBI—or whoever they were—to get me back. I just had to enjoy the final moments of the ride.

McGurn snorted a few times then sat up in his chair. I closed my eyes and pretended to be fast asleep. I heard him shuffle around the hotel room for a few moments and then open and close the front door. I laid in wait, wondering where he'd gone and what I should do. But a moment later the door squeaked open again. I peeked with one eye and saw he'd brought in the morning papers. He flipped the first one open with a crack.

"Massacre!" he cried gleefully. "Louise! Wake up! They're calling it the St. Valentine's Day Massacre! That's great!"

"Congrats, honey," I said, sitting up in bed, projecting Supportive Girlfriend role. Because in a moment I knew he wasn't going to be so happy.

"'Firing Squad Kills Seven in Big Gangland Massacre,'" he read. "'Seven of Moran's men...'" He paused, his eyebrows knitting together in confusion. "Hang on one goddamn second," he said, staring down at the paper as if it couldn't possibly be right. Then he looked up at me, his eyes ablaze.

"What's wrong, sweetheart?" I asked, wide-eyed and innocent.

"They missed Moran. Those bozos missed Moran!" Machine Gun raged. "He wasn't there!"

"He wasn't?"

"Fucking Daisy. This is all her fault. I'm going to kill that bitch if I ever see her again."

I cocked my head, worried for my friend. "Daisy's fault?"

"God, you'll never believe this," McGurn said, shaking his head. "I told Daisy to go spend the night with Bugs, like we planned, right? But, according to Tommy, she went and broke Sam out of my club instead! And here I stupidly thought it was you and him havin' the affair." He snorted. "Tommy says she's been flapping her gums about going to Hollywood for weeks. He thinks they went together. If that's where they went, well, they'd better never come back, that's for sure." He stared at the headlines again, then wadded up the paper in his fist and threw it across the room.

Now it was my turn to stare in disbelief. It was all I could do to not start laughing. After everything I'd gone through to make sure Daisy didn't wake Bugs up, the flapper hadn't even been there to begin with. She'd listened to me. She'd headed out west to follow her dream. I hid a small smile, imagining her getting off the train in warm, sunshiny LA, ready to make something of herself. If anyone had a chance it was Daisy.

"I've got to go," Machine Gun said, rising to his feet. He slipped on his boots. "Al's gonna kill me when he finds out. I gotta go meet with some guys. Figure out what happened." He shook his head. "Fucking Moran. I can't believe he flew the coop. No man is that lucky."

"That's too bad, baby," I cooed.

"You, you stay here. You're still my alibi. If any cops show up, you tell 'em I've been here the whole time with you, okay?"

"Sure, baby. I'll be your blonde alibi."

He grinned. "Yeah. I like that. Blonde alibi." He ruffled my head. "Now, if you'll excuse me, I gotta go figure out what the fuck happened."

He left the hotel room and I smooshed out the newspaper he left behind, scanning the article. Sounded like everything went off exactly as it was supposed to. Mission accomplished. Twenty-first Century Girl had made it happen.

So, how come I was still back in time?

That night I headed down to the bar, the same one where we had learned to Charleston. It was nearly empty at this early hour, just the bartender reading the papers. I found a corner table with a red-checkered cloth. This time, remembering my last experience in the joint, I ordered water.

Nick entered the bar a few minutes later, red-faced from the cold. He pulled off his jacket and scarf and hung them on a hook. I fluttered a wave from my corner and caught his eye. A big grin spread across his handsome face. He headed over and sat down across the table. He was wearing a gray flannel suit with a navy blue tie and a snap-brim fedora. Gangster hip was a good look for him, but I couldn't wait to once again get a glimpse of his butt in Levi's.

"You did it!" he whispered, reaching across the table to take my hand and bring it to his lips.

"We did it," I corrected with a shy smile.

He grinned back, a bit ruefully. "Of course I wasn't *supposed* to do it. This is definitely the last time this reporter will be asked to moonlight as a secret spy by the FBI, that's for sure."

The thought sobered me for a moment. As much of a triumph as this was for me, for Nick it was a failure. "I'm sorry," I said, picking up the salt shaker and toying with it.

Nick shook his head. "Don't be. I gave what you said in that motel room a lot of thought, and you were right. Just because we *can* manipulate the past to change the future doesn't mean we *should*."

"Right."

"I'd been so wrapped up in the idea that changing history would make things better. But you—who were hurt more than anyone by the way things played out—were the most determined that things should stay as they are. Everything happens for a reason, you said." He shrugged. "I realized you were right. Even though life can be unbearably painful, even though horrible things happen . . . Who are we to try to change them for our own selfish interests?" He paused, then added, "It just struck me as wrong somehow. Like, if we want to achieve a better tomorrow, we shouldn't focus on yesterday."

I nodded, so happy that he'd come to this conclusion. Not to mention that he'd come to it because of something I had said. Maybe I was more convincing than I gave myself credit for.

"Won't you get in trouble?"

He shrugged. "Probably. But it'll be worth it. We saved

the world, right?" He grinned at me and I grinned back. "Can't argue with that."

"Right," I said, offering up a high five. He smacked my hand with his. "We're practically superheroes."

We laughed for a moment, then grew silent. The tinny sounds of cheerful jazz floated through the bar as we lost ourselves in our separate thoughts. I stared down at my hands, wondering what would come next.

Nick broke the silence. "Dora, will you forgive me," he asked, "for all that happened in Iraq?"

I looked up. This wasn't the first time he'd asked me that, of course. But this was the first time I actually contemplated saying yes. Still, as much as I loved Nick, I couldn't just let him back in my life without hearing the whole story. There were so many unanswered questions.

"What happened there, Nick? I need to know the truth."

"I know," he said, his tone ultra-serious. "And I want to tell you. Badly. I want to set the record straight, if you're ready to listen."

I nodded. I was ready to listen. Finally. I felt a strength inside now that I hadn't known before. Something that would hold me fast, no matter what words came out of his mouth. I could take it. I wasn't afraid anymore.

"Uh, you have to promise not to kick me anywhere remotely near my nether region, even if you don't like my explanation."

I made a face. "Sorry about that."

"Twice in one week, Dora. There's only so much of that a man can take!"

"I know," I said, abashed. Poor Nick. I really was a

beast. "I promise. Cross my heart, hope to die, all that jazz."

"Okay," he said. "I believe you." He cleared his throat. "Anyway, the reason I'd been bringing you along on the Colonel Devens negotiations was that I really wanted you to get the story. I felt like the network had been underestimating your skill as a reporter and was always passing you by when it came to the important assignments. I figured if you were able to secure the interview yourself, they'd see what a great reporter you are."

"That's so sweet," I said. "Though it still doesn't explain why you were late."

He shrugged. "Actually, I was right on time. I walked in and spotted you and the Colonel sitting at a small table across the bar. Devens seemed really relaxed. You even had him laughing. I was worried if I came over I'd disrupt your flow. So I decided to let you handle it and I ran out to try to find you some flowers." He blushed. "It was Valentine's Day, if you remember."

"I remember." There was nothing about that day I'd ever forget.

"It took me a while to find a bouquet, but I was determined. You were always teasing me about not being romantic enough and I wanted to prove you wrong." He laughed bitterly. "When I finally got back to the bar you and Colonel Devens were nowhere to be found. The barmaid said you'd left five minutes before. I figured you just went back to the hotel. Not once did it cross my mind that you had taken off with him."

He stared down at his hands. "I know it's no excuse, but I never thought in a million years there was even the remotest possibility that Devens would take you along on a raid that day. He'd been told, time and time again, that once we agreed on a date, the network would assign a specially trained war photographer for the assignment. It was never ever supposed to be you, and he knew that."

"Well, he told me now or never. And I didn't want to let the network down."

Nick smiled. "My Dora. So dedicated. So determined." He reached out across the table and took my hand in his, stroking my thumb with his own. "I went back to the hotel to find you and give you your roses. But you weren't there. I waited for hours, but you never showed. By the end of the day I started to panic. I called Devens and that's when I found out what had happened." He scowled. "I wanted to go down there and punch his lights out. For putting you in danger. For getting you captured. But he was in trouble himself, and as mad as I was at him, I was also furious at myself. I should have never left you alone, put you in that position. I felt it was my fault you were captured." He swallowed hard. "I'm sorry."

"That's all well and good," I said, fighting back the lump in my throat, the tears in my eyes. "But why didn't you . . . rescue me? Why didn't you try to help? I was in that prison for weeks. And when I spoke to our friends, they told me you were boozing it up with some Iraqi chick. Do you know how that made me feel?" I asked, the tears now streaming down my cheeks. "To be afraid for my life and hear that the guy I thought loved me had totally moved on?"

"God, was that what they told you?" Nick asked, looking incredulous. "No wonder you hated me so much." He slammed a fist against the table, then took a deep breath.

"Her name was Ina," he said slowly. "She was the daughter of a low-ranking government official that had jurisdiction over the prison you were in. I'd met her on another assignment, before I'd ever met you, and I knew she liked me. And more importantly, I knew she was daddy's little girl. I figured that if I wined and dined her, I might be able to convince her father to let you go. I wasn't seeing a lot of our friends, because I didn't want to explain." He sighed. "I know that sounds terrible, but I didn't know what else to do. I would have done anything to save you, and my U.S. Government contacts had already refused to pull any strings. Lousy bastards said your case was too high profile, what with Devens and all." He balled his hands into fists and banged one against the table. "I would have killed men, if I thought it would have helped—stormed that prison like some kind of Rambo." He laughed bitterly, then joked, "But I'm a lover, not a fighter. And so I did what I do best." He cast his eyes down and stared at his hands. "But I didn't sleep with her. I was just trying to get you out."

I couldn't believe all that I was hearing. It was like some crazy dream. Could it all be true? Could he have really only been with that girl for my sake?

"Anyway, it took longer than I anticipated, but it finally worked," he said. "She convinced her dad to let you go." He shrugged. "But as soon as you got out of prison they sent you straight home. I didn't get a chance to come find you. I figured I'd get in touch. I called your cell phone a bunch of times, but you never called back. It wasn't until later that I realized you'd probably lost it in the raid and it was never returned." He looked sheepish. "Pretty stupid.

"As you know, the network kept me on assignment for a few months. I tried calling you in the States, but you moved. Your parents, your friends—no one would give me your number. They all called me a monster and nothing I could do would persuade them otherwise. I even hired a private investigator to flush you out. That's when I learned you went to San Diego. I'll never forget how my hands shook as I dialed that phone number he got. But you wouldn't let me make that apology. You called me a monster. Accused me of betraying you. And then you hung up and never answered again. The phone just rang and rang."

"No voicemail," I mumbled, feeling like an idiot. Why had I been so stubborn? Why hadn't I at least let him explain? Things could have been so different. So, so different. And I'd been punished for my stupidity.

"And so I decided there was nothing I could do but leave you alone. As they always say, if you love someone you should let them go. If they love you, they'll come back." He sighed deeply, then looked up, meeting my eyes for the first time. "Until now, you didn't come back."

My insides felt like they were melting away. God, I'd been such a fool. Such a total fool. I should have trusted him. I should have known there was some explanation for his behavior. After all, this was Nick. My Nick. A man who loved me. A man who would never in a billion years consciously betray me.

I stood and walked around the table, throwing myself into his arms, collapsing and surrendering completely. I held on as tight as I could, burying my head in his shoulder.

The tears came then, as if a dam had burst. A year's worth of pent up frustration and pain swallowed me and I clung to him, seeking strength in his warm body.

"I love you, Dora," he whispered in my ear. "I never stopped loving you."

"I love you too, Nick," I sobbed. "More than anything in the world. I'm so sorry. I'm so, so sorry. I was such an idiot."

He wrapped his arms around me and stroked my back with his hands. "Shh. Stop apologizing. You have nothing to apologize for."

"But I was so stupid. I should have listened to you. I should have never doubted you."

"It's okay, Dora. As long as you believe me now, that's all I care about. That's all that matters."

We held each other for a long time, neither wanting to let go. But eventually we parted and sat back down in our speakeasy seats, still holding hands.

"So, uh, now what?" I asked. "I mean, I thought maybe once the Massacre happened we'd be catapulted back to the twenty-first century or something. I mean, why are we still here?"

"I don't know." Nick raked a hand through his hair. "I'm not sure."

I suddenly remembered the one person/rodent who would know.

"I have a contact. We could ask him," I said.

"Really?" Nick raised his eyebrows. "Actually, I have a contact, too."

"What's yours?" I couldn't resist asking. "The Easter Bunny?"

"Actually, this is going to sound bizarre, but it's a talking rat." Nick laughed. "Like, literally. Can you believe that?"

Oh. My. God. I stared at him, wide-eyed in disbelief. "What? Ratty? Ratty's your contact, too?"

"Ratty?" Nick cocked his head. "Well, he's a rat all right. Claims that back in the twenty-first century he's an FBI agent called Rogers or something. Sarcastic little fellow. Not always that supportive."

For a moment, I thought I might fall off my chair, I was in such shock. "He's my contact, too," I cried. "So he's been, what, double-teaming us this whole time? What a lousy rat!"

"But why would he?" Nick asked. "I mean, to what purpose?"

"I have no idea." I took a sip of my water, trying to steady my nerves. Something was really off here, and it was starting to scare me. "Let's think for a moment." I set down the cup. "So The Rat told me my mission was to stop you from waking Bugs up and changing history."

"And The Rat told me *my* job was to seduce you so you wouldn't be with Machine Gun and thus couldn't testify as McGurn's alibi."

"Huh." O-kay. None of this was making any sense.

"So the only thing in common is that both our missions required we get in contact with one another."

I nodded slowly. "Almost as if someone planned it. To get us back together."

"But that's ridiculous. Who would do that? And why?"

"There's only one way to find out."

"Oh?"

"Go see Ratty."

"Right." Nick rose from his seat. "Time to talk to The Rat."

On the way to my rooming house we stopped at a grocer and bought the most expensive cheese in the case. As Nick said, the Geneva Convention prohibited torturing, so we might try extortion. Bribery.

Luckily, the landlady wasn't around and we were able to go up to my apartment without me getting lectured on the evils of bringing boys to the house. I unlocked the door and we stepped inside.

"Hi, honey, I'm home!" I called.

"About time. I've been waiting all day," The Rat growled, his typical pleasant greeting. "So, did you screw it up? Is Moran dead? Massacred, 'cause you fell down on the job?"

"Thanks for the vote of confidence, but no. Moran's healthy as a horse. Everything worked out exactly as it was supposed to. Mission accomplished."

"And I seduced the girl," Nick interjected. "Just like you asked me to."

The Rat let out a squeak of surprise, scattling around. "Nick?" he cried. "What are you doing here?" He turned to me. "You told him, didn't you? You went and told him you were Dora."

"Yes, she told me," Nick said, approaching The Rat.

He reached down and grabbed the rodent by its tail. "Now how's about you tell me what's been going on here. What game are you playing?"

"I demand you to put me down!" The Rat squealed. "Assault of an FBI officer is a federal offense."

Nick plunked The Rat down on the bed and sat beside him. The Rat ruffled his fur and started licking his paws in an overacted state of righteous indignation.

I reached into the bag and pulled out the cheese. "If you tell us what's going on, you can have some of this."

The Rat's nose twitched. "What is that?"

"Le fromage. Trés expensive."

"Oh," The Rat sniffed. "Not interested." But another twitch of his nose gave his game away.

"No?" I asked, sitting down on the other side of him. "I guess Nick and I will just eat it then." I peeled open the block, in what I hoped was a rat-provocative manner, and broke off a chunk. I slowly handed it over the Rat's head to Nick. "Here, Nick, try some."

"You're not tempting me at all. La, la, la," The Rat said.

"Good. I'm not trying to. I'm just enjoying some lovely cheese."

"It is really delicious," Nick agreed. "I just love port salut. Just the right nutty little bite."

"Argh! Okay, okay! I'll tell you everything. I'm hankering for that hunk of cheese!" The Rat cried, rolling onto his back and kicking up his little legs in frustration.

I smiled down at him. "Tell first. Then you can eat."

"Okay, fine." The Rat rolled back onto his paws. "But

for the record, you guys totally suck." He looked up at us with his beady black eyes. "Here's the deal. You've heard about the Time Warriors, right?"

"That's the group Nick supposedly joined," I said. "The one where the members go back and relive historical events just for the fun of it. Bought a time machine from the KGB."

The Rat laughed. "Was that the story they fed you? Wow, they get more inventive every time." He shook his head. "Someday, someone's going to call them on their believability factor." He paused. "Then again, you bought it, hook, line, and sinker!"

I pressed my lips together. "Uh, can we get on with the story, please? I mean, if you really want that cheese."

"Right. Sorry. Well, the Time Warriors don't actually have a time machine. Neither does the FBI. Probably nobody does, come to think of it. Plus, the FBI has nothing to do with any of this. Those men you met with? They work for the Time Warriors."

"What?" I cried. "But that doesn't make any sense. Of course they have a time machine. We're back in time, aren't we?"

"Nah, you only think you are." The Rat shrugged. "Actually, you're participating in the latest in virtual reality simulation. Our computers create a living, breathing version of a time capsule of the past. Then we can send in players to interact with that world. It's beautiful technology, perfectly seamless. And by using a special drug we developed ourselves, we can trick people's brains into thinking everything they see is real."

I stared at The Rat, barely able to comprehend what he was saying. I wasn't in the 1920s? I hadn't been transported back in time? This was all some kind of game?

"Virtual reality?" Nick mouthed at me, looking almost as freaked out as I felt.

I tried to answer, but realized I couldn't find any appropriate words. I was Alice down the rabbit hole and suddenly I wasn't sure which end was up. I was Arnold in *Total Recall*. Michael Douglas in *The Game*. Jennifer Jason Leigh in *eXistenZ*.

"So we're not really here? This is some computer simulation?" I finally managed to spit out.

I poked the bed. It seemed real. I looked out the window. Real-looking snow fell from the sky. I pinched myself hard. The pain definitely didn't seem to be coming from my imagination.

It seemed impossible. Crazy, even. But then, what was really more likely: a complex computer program or a real trip through the space-time continuum? Scarily enough, the virtual reality thing was actually a more realistic scenario.

But still! All the people we'd met? All the places we'd gone? All the things that we'd seen? They were all . . . what? Faked? Imaginary?

"Right."

"But . . . why?" I asked. "Why give us missions to save the world when the world was completely made up? All that stuff about history and destiny and changing the future—it was all just a game? None of this makes any sense."

The Rat licked his paw, as if bored. "If you didn't have some kind of quest or mission, you'd just sit around eating bon-bons and drinking gin. What kind of game would that be?" He gestured to the chunk of cheese. Still dazed, I broke him off a chunk. He nibbled. "Good stuff," he said. "In real life, I'm lactose intolerant. Gotta get my fix when I can."

"So you're not an FBI agent?"

"Nope. I'm an actor. You might have seen me on *Law & Order?*"

"And the others?"

"Well, the extras are what we call NPCs. Non-player characters. Computer programs, basically. But your main people—Bugs, Daisy, McGurn, Tommy—those are all real people, playing their parts."

It was weird, but part of me was relieved that at least the people I'd been interacting with weren't just binary code. Especially Daisy. In many ways, she'd become a friend. Someone I cared about. A twinge of sadness tugged at me. I wondered if I'd get to meet the real person behind the character. Or would that make things even harder?

"And you have no idea why we were put into this . . . game," I asked slowly. "It's not for some bizarre new reality show, is it?" That would be just my luck.

"No, this stuff is top secret. We'd never put it on TV," The Rat said, much to my relief. "But I'll tell you what. These games aren't cheap. Someone paid good money to set this up for you."

"Tom! I bet it was Tom."

Surprised, I glanced at Nick, my eyes widening at the recognition dawning on his face. Had he figured out who had set us up? Was it someone he knew?

"Do you know a guy named Tom Fitzgerald?" Nick asked The Rat.

"Yeah, sure," The Rat said, mouth full of cheese. "That's the CEO."

Nick's face grew red. "Oh my god. I'm going to kill that bastard."

"Tom? You mean your brother Tom?" Realization was coming on like a tidal wave, though a bit late. "Your dot-com billionaire brother Tom? The one who's always trying to get me to take you back?"

"Of course," Nick said. "It makes perfect sense now. Tom's been working on some top secret video game thing for the last few years. I was always asking him about it, but he refused to spill the beans. Claimed he didn't want to see his life's work showing up on the six o'clock news. I figured he was developing a new Pac-Man or something. Shows how much I know."

"So your brother is behind this? Has he been watching the whole time?" I imagined some multi-monitored control room with lots of flashing lights. And Nick's geeky bro chowing down Chee-tohs as he watched us make love. Sharing in that personal moment that should have been just the two of us. "How horrible!"

The Rat shook his head. "Don't worry, Princess," he assured me. "We have privacy standards in place. Peep shows are strictly forbidden. You start to look like you're about to get it on, we cue the roaring-fire shot. Just like on the soaps."

314

"So this whole thing is recorded, then?" Nick asked, looking more than a little worried.

"Sure. Not like we're about to broadcast it on Must See TV or anything," The Rat said. "But we figure our clients would probably enjoy the replay."

I shook my head, trying to take it all in. "So, our missions. All that changing history or not. What was that all about? I mean, if it's a game, it has to have a goal. An object. A way to win."

"Haven't you figured that out yet? You two really are a bit dim." He sighed. "The object of the game was to get you two back together, obviously. To admit you were both stubborn idiots and fall back in love."

I stared at the rodent. That was it? That was all I had to do? Here I thought I was trying to save the world. And all I really needed to do was save my own heart.

Nick burst into laughter. For a moment, I wasn't sure I found the scenario quite so funny. But his laughter was infectious and soon I found myself giggling along with him. It was just too bizarre. Too surreal. What else could you do but laugh?

"Leave it to Tom to come up with something so complex," Nick said, still chuckling. "This is like the twenty-first century version of locking two people in a closet to work out their differences." He reached over and squeezed my shoulder. "I guess we won then," he said, looking at me with loving eyes. "We beat the game."

"Hm," The Rat said thoughtfully. "Maybe. Though you might get bonus points for a heavy make out session. . . ." He looked from one of us to the other then sighed as we made no move to comply while he was watching. He scampered off the bed. "I was so hoping for that lesbian thing to have played out . . . ," he muttered as he headed toward the exit.

I watched The Rat scamper under the door, then turned to Nick, catching his blue-green eyes. Soon I'd be looking into his real brown eyes once again. Touching his real body.

"I can't believe this," I murmured. "All of this crazy setup just to get me to fall back in love with you."

"It was worth it," he replied, reaching over to take my hand in his, "to get you back."

I smiled. Even the shock of finding out it was all a game couldn't dampen the love I felt for this man.

"So now we go back to our real lives, I guess," I said. "You won't mind that I'm scarred and ugly in my real skin? I'm not as pretty as Louise, that's for sure."

"Are you kidding?" Nick asked in an incredulous voice that even I couldn't help believing. "You're the most beautiful girl in the world."

He leaned forward, cupping my chin in his hands, and pressed his lips against mine. Then he pulled away. "I love you, Dora."

I grinned. "I love you, Nick."

And suddenly everything went black.

EPILOGUE

Valentine's Day
The present

I'd never seen so many heart-shaped balloons in one place before: rubber, foil, sparkly. Normally a hater of all things saccharine sweet, I'd have groaned at the over-the-top Valentine's Day decorations. But now each and every obnoxious balloon was an indicator that I was home.

Home. In the twenty-first century. In real life.

A half hour ago I'd opened my eyes and found myself in the same titanium room they'd put me to sleep in, with the same gel cap over my head, wearing the same suit I'd had on before. Technicians in white coats welcomed me back, congratulated me for winning the game.

"How long have I been gone?" I asked. Had it been days, weeks? I had no sense of time and it was freaking me out.

A female technician with long blonde hair glanced at her watch. "A little over three hours," she said. "Time runs differently in the game," she added, seeing my shocked expression. "It's sort of like with dreams. You can have ten-minute dreams that seem to go on for days. It's the same with this."

"Wow."

"We have to do it this way," she said. "Otherwise, think of all the contingencies. Food, water, bathroom. Missing work."

I screwed up my face. "Ugh. Does this mean I'm on the air tonight?" Did I still have to find an interviewee who was too stressed for sex? At least now I no longer counted myself in that group.

"No, we took care that," the technician said. "You don't need to go back to work tonight, and you have the rest of the week off as well."

"I do?" I stared at her. These people thought of everything. Which was good, actually, seeing as I could barely form words at the moment, never mind try to report live.

She patted me on the shoulder. "You do," she assured me. "Now, come with me and we'll get you showered."

I climbed out of the chair and followed her out of the room, grateful for the opportunity to clean up. I may have only been out an hour, but I was feeling kind of ripe.

I let the hot water cascade over me, still in a daze. I had so many unanswered questions. I didn't know whether I should be angry or ecstatic—threaten to sue or offer up my most profound thanks. All I knew for certain was I had to find Nick. To see him with my own eyes. To hold him with my own hands. Breathe him in with my own nose. And to feel him with my body.

After showering and changing into a new suit they'd provided (they really did think of everything!) I was led down a hallway and into a large conference room, decorated for a party. There were cheese and fruit and dessert plates. A bartender in one corner poured glass after glass of champagne. Helium balloons blanketed the ceiling. And there were people. Many people. None whom I recognized, but who were all, to my relief, dressed like they belonged in the twenty-first century.

"Congratulations, sweetie!" A petite blonde woman with sparkling purple eyes pushed through the crowd of people and stopped in front of me. She was wearing a lacy corset top and hip low-rise jeans. "You did it! I knew you could. You were awesome, too. Truly awesome."

Awesome. It was amazing how nice twenty-first century slang sounded to my ears. "Um, thanks?"

She laughed. "Sorry," she said. "I'm Daisy. Well, I'm really Joanne. But I played Daisy in your game."

My eyes widened. "Oh!" I cried. She was Daisy? I gave her a once-over. Besides her height, she looked nothing like the vivacious flapper I'd grown to love. "Sorry, I'm a little out of it still, I think."

"No prob." She smiled. "It's a little overwhelming, I know. I remember the first time I played. I was completely freaked out, let me tell you. But then I met Sarah." She turned and motioned for a tall, buxom blonde in the corner to come over. The girl hustled to Joanne/Daisy's side, putting an arm around her waist and smiling down at me. Ah-ha. Guess the lesbian thing wasn't just part of the act. And it made me happy to know that at least in real life, Daisy had found her girl. "Sarah played Machine Gun," Joanne explained.

I raised an eyebrow. Machine Gun? So, wait. That meant . . .

"Huh," I marveled. "Wow. So you don't have to—"

"Nope. You can play a guy or a girl. Your choice. It's kind of fun for Sarah and I. I mean, we're real-life partners. But it's a new experience to try being with each other as the opposite sex." She grinned at her girlfriend. "The morning you caught me sneaking out of the speakeasy, that wasn't in the script. I never thought you'd wake up so early. So we improvised. Daisy was never supposed to be a prostitute in the original version of the game. But that's the cool thing about the Time Warrior system. The world itself is static, but the characters are completely dynamic. So while you were talking to Machine Gun Sarah here, we were busy rebuilding. Injecting a Mrs. Grundy character into the game to play the madame at the last minute. That's why she probably seemed a little out of place, what with the whole shotgun scene and all. We had to steal her program from an Old West VR we did last week and didn't have much time to customize."

"I see," I said, though in reality, I was pretty lost. This all seemed so complex. "So what was with the lesbian stuff then? How did that all tie in?"

"That was all Joanne," Sarah said, digging an elbow into her partner's ribs. "She wasn't supposed to kiss you."

Joanne blushed. "Yeah, yeah. Well, it seemed unfair

that you had a girlfriend in the game and I was stuck as a sidekick."

"Could be worse," a tall, broad-shouldered man with dark hair and eyes said as he walked up behind the girls, putting a hand on each of their shoulders. They looked up at him and giggled in sync. "You could have spent the game as a rat."

"Ratty?" I asked, pretty sure my mouth was gaping at this point. So, he really was good-looking in real life. Go figure.

He laughed. "Ratty. Special Agent Rogers. Trent Buckman. Whatever." He reached out a hand and I shook it. "Good job, kiddo. You were one of the best players we've had in a while."

"This is all so . . . I mean, I . . ." I didn't know what to say. Where to start?

"It's okay," Ratty—er, I mean Trent—said, patting my arm. "It'll take a few days to all sink in. Just remember. You won the game. So go collect your prize." He motioned across the room, past the buffet and bar and silly decorations, under the banner that read TIME WARRIORS.

Nick.

My breath caught in my throat. My heart fluttered.

He was dressed in a black suit with a navy blue tie. Armani, if I could hazard a guess. Dashing Nick. The Colin Farrell of network news. One of *People Magazine's* "50 Most Beautiful."

And the man who loved me more than anyone. Silly, scared, scarred me.

But then, I wasn't anymore, was I? I'd been through

hell and back, even if it had been a game. I'd dared big. I'd risked my life. I'd defied danger. And I'd come out the other side. Okay. I was still physically scarred, to be sure. But mentally, I was feeling pretty damn good about myself.

I quickly said my good-byes to the actors and hustled across the room.

"Nick," I cried, approaching him.

His eyes lit up as he saw me. "Dora!"

"Nice to see you got your skin back."

"Nice to see you got yours," he said with a grin, his eyes dragging up my body in a way that made me tremble. Scarred and all, there was no mistaking that look. He wanted me. The real me.

As much as I wanted him.

"I just met the actors who played Daisy and Machine Gun. And The Rat. I just met the guy who played Ratty!"

He grinned. "It's all crazy, huh? I still feel like I'm dreaming."

"Me, too. It doesn't seem real. Yet . . ."

"Yet you're here," he said shyly. "And you're speaking to me. In the end, I think that's all that matters."

He pulled me into an embrace and I pressed myself against him. Feeling him. Rejoicing in his touch. His real-life touch. We held on to each other, neither seeming to want to let go.

He pulled away first. "I have something for you," he said, reaching into a bag. He pulled out a large box wrapped in ribbon. "I've been wanting to give this to you forever, it seems."

I took the box and pulled at the decorative bow. Then I lifted the cover.

Roses. Dried and pressed into a glass frame.

I looked up. "Are these . . . ?"

"I told you the reason I was late was I had to run all over Baghdad to try to find some roses. I know you love them, and I wanted our Valentine's Day to be special." He shrugged sheepishly. "When you disappeared, I brought them home and put them in a vase. Even though I knew you wouldn't be able to appreciate them, I couldn't bear to throw them out. And every day you were gone, I looked at those roses. And I vowed that someday, somehow I'd be able to give them to you."

I felt tears welling up in my eyes, but there was no reason to brush them away. "And now you have," I murmured, looking down at the frame. Each petal had been carefully preserved, pressed into glass. They were the most beautiful flowers I'd ever seen.

"Now I have," he agreed, pulling me into his warm arms. I rested my face against his chest, sobbing uncontrollably. For all we'd lost. For all we'd gained. For the past. For the future.

A Connecticut Fashionista in King Arthur's Court
MARIANNE MANCUSI

Once upon a time, there lived a fashion editor named Kat, who certainly was not the typical damsel in distress. But when a gypsy curse sent her back in time to the days of King Arthur, she found she'd need every ounce of her 21st-century wits to navigate the legend. After all, just surviving without changing history or scuffing your Manolos takes some doing!

Luckily, she's got her very own knight in shining armor, Lancelot du Lac, on her side…even though she's not quite sure she wants him there. After all, shouldn't he be off romancing Queen Guenevere or something? Will Kat manage to stay out of trouble long enough to get back to her world? And what will Lancelot's forbidden love mean for the kingdom of Camelot?

Talk Gertie To Me

LOIS WINSTON

Nori Stedworth is living the good life. That is, until the dot-com company she works for goes bust, she finds her fiancé cavorting in the Jacuzzi with her best friend, and her mom flies in for a surprise visit....

Now suddenly, from out of nowhere, Nori's alter ego from adolescence, Gertie, is throwing her two cents in about everything in Nori's life. Like, Nori's new job at a radio station might finally be her niche. Like, Nori's droolworthy boss, Mac, just might be the man of her dreams. Like, it's time Nori stopped hiding in the shadows. Move over, Gertie—Nori's stepping up to the mic.

COMPLETELY IRRESISTIBLE

SHERIDON SMYTHE

It all started with three spoiled standard poodles with an uncanny knack for mischief. Kasidy Evans knew she'd have her hands full, but she never imagined she'd find them engaged in a tug of war with a gloriously naked man—over his shorts. Apparently the willful canines took exception to their new owner, and Kasidy had to agree. Wyatt Love was nothing but a gigolo. Kasidy told herself his gorgeous, bronzed body was off limits, and his unexpected sweetness did not touch her heart, but the truth was, she found Wyatt Love…

COMPLETELY IRRESISTIBLE